Also from Ken Vanderpool

WHEN THE MUSIC DIES
FACE THE MUSIC

STOP THE MUSIC

STOP THE MUSIC

Ken Vanderpool

ISBN 978-0-9903655-1-8

Printed in the United States of America

Cover and Interior Design
By Sandra Vanderpool

Saint Michael, the Archangel,
defend us in battle; be our defense against the
wickedness and snares of the devil.
May God rebuke him, we humbly pray;
and do thou, O Prince of the heavenly host,
by the power of God, thrust into Hell Satan
and the other evil spirits who prowl
about the world for the ruin of souls.
Amen

Chapter I

Tony's Cafe
Nashville

The wallet-sized photograph in his hand depicted Tim Slater's precious and private world. He smiled as he remembered his daughter's words from this morning.

"Now you can look at me all day, Daddy."

Four-year-old Sophia smiled and gave the photo a wet waffle syrup kiss. She shoved it deep into the breast pocket of her father's navy blue blazer as he prepared to leave for work. The photo featured the smiling faces of Tim's wife Megan and their bright young daughter.

Veteran Homicide Detective Tim Slater leaned against the dented front fender of the unmarked Chevy Impala he shared with his partner, Dave Thurman. He dragged the back of his index finger across the corner of his eye to catch a tear before gravity could cause anyone to think this tough cop was emotional. He pushed the photo back into place, patted his pocket and took another drag off his smoke.

Tim glanced over his shoulder through the large windows fronting Tony's Cafe. Thurman was in line at the cash register, waiting behind three rotund seventy-something ladies who appeared to be in negotiations on how best to pay their dinner check.

Thurman shrugged his shoulders as if to say, "What can I do?"

Tim shook out another cigarette from his pack and lit it with the remains of the first. As he pulled the mouthful of smoke down into his lungs and enjoyed the calming rush from the nicotine, he heard the shot.

He recognized it at once as the report of a pistol. The sound from the second shot followed, yet it seemed less perceptible. The cigarette fell from his fingers. His disciplined reaction, the result from years of Threat Response Training, failed him. His hand moved to his chest instead of his Glock.

He felt the warmth escaping his body. He coughed. He struggled to capture a half breath. He pushed it back out and begged his lungs for another. He winced, closed his eyes and collapsed.

Chapter 2

The Streets of
South Nashville

Sergeant Mike Neal was on his way home after his first day back at work following a well-deserved week of vacation. His first time away from work in more than a year. He and Carol Spencer had enjoyed a clandestine week on the sun-soaked beaches of Cancun, Mexico.

They both knew if they were to spend their vacation together it would have to be outside the country. This would surely eliminate any risk of being seen together and accused of violating MNPD Captain Alberto Moretti's Law: 'There shall be no fraternization between members of the team. Find your *amore* outside the unit'.

Carol, now 41, was a seasoned police department photographer and Mike was one of Metro Nashville Police Department's top investigators. They'd worked side by side for a dozen years on many of the same cases, but when they did, it was all business. Their private relationship was known by a scant few of their closest friends and discussed openly by none.

Mike's years as an investigator with the U.S. Army's Criminal Investigations Command, better known as CID, accelerated his promotion to Homicide Detective in 2002. At the age of thirty-seven, he'd been one of the youngest officers advanced to the Homicide Unit.

Not long after his promotion, he worked a crime scene in South Nashville where Carol was the assigned photo-criminalist. He was not only impressed by her skills as a meticulous photographer, he was impressed by everything else she had to offer.

Tonight he drove the streets between the Criminal Justice Center and his home with his mind on autopilot. He was focused on how far behind on his work the vacation had put him and how he was going to deal with it when he heard his radio's alternating tone warning of the coming all points bulletin. These things were never good. He rotated the volume knob to be sure to catch the report.

As soon as the channel was clear of all traffic, the dispatcher broadcast her emergency message. "Attention all units. 10-83, officer down. Attention all units in the vicinity of 2nd Avenue South and Chestnut, Tony's Cafe, respond Code 3. Repeat, 10-83, officer down. Respond Code 3. Med-Com is Code 3."

Mike concentrated on the continuous flow of officers responding on the radio, their sirens in the background, confirming their rapid response.

Currently 10-7 and on his way home, there was no need for him to answer the dispatcher. He rubbed his short graying brown hair back and forth rapidly. He knew he was no more than three or four miles from Tony's.

"Shit."

He lit up the car's strobes and turned on his siren. He checked his mirrors and made a tire-screeching U-turn in the middle of Franklin Road.

He turned up the radio's volume again so he could hear it over the siren. The radio chatter about the incident was almost constant. Mike listened for information on the officer who'd been shot. He knew Dispatch wouldn't announce anything sensitive on the radio, and after fourteen years on the force, he had hundreds of friends. He wanted to know who was hurt and how serious it was.

Mike passed Greer Stadium and followed Chestnut Street ninety degrees to his left. The road curved back to his right. Ahead, He could see the entire street was illuminated, pulsing blue and red. Strobes from over twenty police cruisers and a half dozen Nashville Fire Department units lit up the entire length of the street.

He silenced the siren, parked his car on a side street and jogged toward the cafe. He stepped between two cruisers and saw a team of Emergency Medical Technicians at the rear of their ambulance, but they were not working on anyone. He hoped this was a good sign.

Mike spotted Officer Rich Jacobs setting up a folding table at the outer taped perimeter for the crime scene access log. This was the only location through which anyone was allowed to enter or leave the crime scene. The log was used to document all persons accessing the crime scene area. All first responders were familiar with the requirement. Individuals, whose assignments did not place them on the crime scene investigation team, were required to remain outside the yellow tape.

"Any news?"

"Doesn't look good."

"Who was hit?"

"Tim Slater."

"Oh, shit. Are you sure?"

"Yeah. They took him to Vanderbilt. Thurman's over there with the Lieutenant." Jacobs pointed.

"How bad is it?"

"Not sure."

"Did he get the shooter?"

"You'll have to ask them. I heard he never drew his pistol."

"What?"

Jacobs shrugged.

Mike added his personal information to the log, yanked two Tyvek shoe covers from the box on the table and pulled them on. "Thanks, Rich."

Mike snugged up his tie and in response to his surging adrenaline, took large breaths as he crossed the gravel lot to the Lieutenant and Thurman, hoping all the way for better news than Jacobs had shared.

Mike and Tim Slater had spent time together over the last dozen or so years as temporary partners whenever vacations or illness called for it. Mike admired Tim's skills and dedication to the job. Whenever the two got the chance to work together, they always commented they'd each learned something from the other and had an enjoyable time doing it.

Mike stopped and stood next to Lieutenant D. W. Burris without speaking. He listened to Thurman's ongoing explanation of the incident.

"I was inside, waiting to pay our dinner checks. I heard the shots. They had to come from there." He indicated the dark area around the trees to the right of the cafe's parking lot. "Tim was leaning against the front fender of the car and smoking." Thurman looked at Mike. "He always burned one before we got back in the car after a meal. He knew—" Thurman's face wrinkled and he pushed his lips together. "He knew I didn't like to smell his cigarettes." Thurman bowed his head.

Mike and Burris looked at each other.

"Where was he hit?" Burris asked, trying to get Thurman to focus.

"Here." Thurman pointed to his chest. "And here." He lowered his finger to his upper abdomen.

"He didn't have on his vest?" Burris asked.

"We were eating dinner," Thurman said, pleading for understanding.

Burris nodded.

"He was bleeding bad. I covered the wounds and held pressure until the EMTs got here. It was all I could do."

"Was he conscious?" Burris asked.

Thurman shook his head. He rubbed his hands together in response to his nervousness and saw Tim's dried blood on both of them.

"They got here pretty fast. Man, I hope he gets through this okay." Thurman looked up at Mike. "Since when do homicide detectives get shot on dinner break?"

"I don't know." Mike put his hand on Thurman's shoulder and squeezed. "Hang on. We'll find out who did this."

"Can we try to find out before I get shot too?"

"Have you received any threats? Have you seen suspects' friends or family members displaying aggressive behavior while you were making an arrest?"

"No more than usual, families yelling and calling us names when we haul away their kin; it's been the same stuff as always."

"Nothing stands out as particularly threatening?"

"No. Nothing I can recall."

"Think about it. You may remember something later."

Thurman nodded.

"Where is your vest?" Mike asked.

"In the trunk."

"I'll get it." Mike looked at Burris and tossed his head as a signal to walk with him.

"I'll be right back," Burris said.

Mike pulled out the vest and checked inside the collar for Thurman's name. Shielded from Thurman's view by the trunk lid, he turned to the lieutenant. "I want this case."

Burris pushed a long strand of hair from his gray pompadour back into place and looked at him with a wrinkled brow. "He's not dead yet and you've got enough to do trying to get caught up after being out for a week."

"If we lose Tim, I want this case. He's not one of my direct reports. So, there's no conflict."

The two men swapped stares. Burris started back toward Thurman without giving him a response.

Mike trailed Burris and handed Thurman the vest. He pulled it over his head and fastened the velcro straps around his torso. Out of habit, he grabbed the neck of the vest just below his throat and tugged. One of the things that irritated many of the officers about their Kevlar vests was the way they sometimes rode up toward their necks as they got in and out of their cars all day. Several had developed the habit of tugging on the collar of the vest below their neck.

"I'm going over to check on the criminalists. I'll see you in a few minutes." Mike pulled a pair of nitrile gloves from his sport jacket pocket and tugged them on as he walked.

"Hey, Mike." Wendy Egan, one of the MNPD's multi-skilled criminalists, was busy outside the inner perimeter preparing her evidence collection paraphernalia in order to begin her search. Her specialty was fingerprints along with hair and fiber analysis.

The department's noisy gasoline-powered generator started up and in seconds the two banks of portable floodlights turned the darkness of the crime scene into near daylight.

Mike shielded his eyes from the light with his hand as he looked at Wendy.

"I need you guys to get me something I can use—anything. We

have to nail whoever did this and we need to do it fast."

"I understand. Have you heard anything from the hospital?"

Mike shook his head. "Not yet. Sergeant Smith is picking up *his* wife and then Megan Slater. Seems the wives are friends. I'm sure he'll let us know something when they get to the hospital. Hopefully Tim will be conscious and able to tell him what he saw."

"Let me know when you hear, okay? Tim is a great guy. I've always enjoyed working with him on his cases."

"Yes, he's sharp, a real intuitive investigator. I'll call you. What's been completed so far?"

"I have a rough sketch of the scene template. I'll be polishing it up now that we have some light. Carlos will finish up his video and then begin shooting his stills."

"I usually ask the photographers for stills of any rubberneckers they spot watching the scene from outside the outer tape, but Carlos may have trouble tonight since we're holding the outer perimeter farther back than usual. Tell him to keep an eye out for anyone who looks suspicious and let's make sure we get a few photos of them."

"Copy that."

"Carlos," Mike said as he saw the photographer approaching. *"Como estas?"*

Carlos Padilla was one of the department's three primary crime scene photographers. Carol Spencer was the senior photographer. Carol trained Carlos when he came on board. He was next in seniority and time on the job with five years service.

"Me va bien. Que pasa, Sargento?"

"Usted, mi amigo. Cuanto tiempo mas?"

"Diez—quince minutos, mas o menos."

"Gracias, Señor Padilla."

"De nada, mi amigo." Carlos smiled.

Carlos knew Mike was studying Spanish with a set of audio CDs in his limited free time and he was glad to help him practice what he'd learned whenever he could.

The strong and growing presence of Spanish speaking people in Music City had long ago begun to create challenges for many of the officers and especially investigators attempting to collect evidence and communicate with witnesses who spoke limited or no English.

"Give me a call when you're ready to walk the inner perimeter.

I'm going to check out Tony's digital video recorder and hopefully find something of value to give us a direction. I'm glad he took our advice and installed one last year."

"Good luck," Wendy said as she wrestled with her Tyvek coveralls.

Mike was headed toward the cafe when he heard a familiar voice shout his name. He turned to see Sergeant Steve Hill, the crime scene supervisor, approaching.

"One of my officers was canvassing the neighborhood behind the cafe and spoke with an elderly couple who said they've been sitting out on their front porch for a while; they think they saw the shooter go in front of their house."

Mike's eyebrows went up. "Let's go."

Chapter 3

The Jackson Home
Nashville

"I saw him," eighty-year-old Malcolm Jackson insisted to his wife. He refused to look at her.

"You can't see or hear shit," Stella said, as she pushed her calloused bare feet against the aging wooden planks of their front porch and rocked in her chair. The loose boards continued their rhythmic squeaking complaints.

"Woman, you'd be surprised what I can hear. And, I hear a lot more outta you than I want to."

"Kiss my—."

The trio of officers stepped from the street onto the sidewalk in front of the Jackson's paint-starved clapboard home.

"Mr. and Mrs. Jackson," the young patrol officer said as he reached the edge of the wooden porch, "these are the officers I told you about. This is Sergeant Mike Neal, detective in our Homicide Unit and this is Sergeant Steven Hill, my supervisor."

"Welcome gentlemen." Mrs. Jackson stood, holding onto her chair as if unsure whether or not she could stand without falling. "Ya'll come on up here on the porch and make yourselves at home. Can I get you somethin' to drink? I got sweet tea in yonder, in the icebox."

"Thank you ma'am, but we're fine. We'd like to talk with you folks for a few minutes about what you saw earlier."

She nodded. "Alright."

"Sergeant Hill, why don't the two of you take Mr. Jackson inside and talk about what he saw. Mrs. Jackson and I will sit out here on the porch and chat a while."

Hill closed the front door behind them. The screen door, tugged closed by the spring's tension, slapped the door frame making a noise like the shot from a small caliber revolver.

"Have a seat Sergeant." Stella gestured toward her husband's chair as she fell back into her rocker.

"Thank you, ma'am."

The well-dressed detective moved the chair so he was facing her. He sat, pulled a pair of drugstore readers from his jacket's breast pocket and then took out a notepad and a pen.

"Let's start at the beginning, before you heard or saw anything. What were you two doing?"

"Well—after supper, me and Malcolm, we come out here on the porch when the heat ain't so bad and enjoy the night air."

"You said you heard gunshots?"

"Yessir, two of 'em. Pop. Pop. I looked over at Malcolm. He looked at me." She stopped rocking and gazed over the tops of her smudged glasses at the detective. "This ain't the first time we heard gunshots in the neighborhood."

After a moment, she went back to her rocking. "We started to get up and go inside, but before we could manage, a man came fast-walkin' out from those trees over there behind you and took off down the sidewalk goin' that-a-way." She pointed. "I don't think he saw us. We were real still. He crossed the street to a car over there in front of Josephine's house. Hers is the one with the busted up picket fence."

"How long after you heard the gunshots before you saw this person go in front of your house?"

"Oh. Maybe five or six seconds, I'd say, at the most."

"What kind of car did he get into?"

"It was a red one, sorta dark red."

"Do you know what make of car it was?"

"What?"

"Was it American made or a foreign make?"

"I'm not sure, honey. My eyes ain't bad, but from here, it was hard to tell. If the street light wasn't lit up, I couldn't tell you that much. They just replaced the bulb in that thing a few weeks ago."

"Could you tell if the car was large or small?"

"It wasn't what I'd call a small car, and it wasn't large like a Cadillac or a Lincoln either." She hesitated. "I'd say it was a medium-sized car."

"Okay. That's good." He continued to take notes.

"Tell me about the man. What did he look like?"

"He wasn't as tall as you. He was smaller built, too. He wasn't near as good-lookin' as you are either." She smiled, exposing all eight of her randomly placed teeth.

"You could see his face?"

"Oh yeah. Not straight on like you are facin' me now, but sorta at an angle. I saw him good. I was tryin' to figure out if he was one of them boys from around here. The hoody covered the back half of his head, like from his ear back," she held her hand along side her head, "but I could see his skin and tell, he wasn't black. He was light skinned. White, maybe Mexican or somethin', but I don't think so. I'm pretty sure he was a white boy."

"Could you see his hair?"

"Not real good, but I'm pretty sure his hair was dark. It looked like he had dark eyebrows. He needed a shave. His beard was dark, too."

"What about his clothes? What was he wearing?"

"Blue jeans and the hoody thing, a dark one, black or blue or green, maybe. It was dark. I can't be sure 'bout the color, but it was definitely dark."

"Shoes?"

"They looked like tennis shoes or basketball shoes, or whatever they call 'em nowadays. He had his hands in the big pocket in the front of his jacket. And, he was walkin' like a black man."

"What do you mean he was walking like a black man? With a swagger?"

"No, sugar. The boys 'round the neighborhood, they walk with both their hands inside their hoody pocket so their gun don't fall out. He was walkin' like that, like he had a gun in the big pocket he didn't want to fall out."

She turned her head when she heard her husband's voice getting loud inside the house as he told the officers what he saw.

She turned in her rocker and shouted to the window, "They don't want to hear all your bullshit, Jackson. Just tell 'em what you think you saw."

After a few minutes, the front door opened and the three men came out on the porch.

"Mrs. Jackson," the detective said, "is there anything else you can think of about what you saw or heard that might be important?"

"Well, I'm pretty sure the car he drove off in was missin' the bumper."

"The rear bumper?"

"Yessir."

"This could be valuable information, Mrs. Jackson. Thank you for being so observant."

"Glad I could help." She looked at Malcolm to check his response. There was none. He moved his chair back into position, facing the street.

"Thank you both for talking with us. We may need to talk with you again, if it would be okay?"

"That's fine, sugar." She offered her tooth-challenged smile again.

"Good evening." The good-looking detective waved.

The officers stepped off the porch and made their way back down the street in the direction of the cafe.

Stella looked at Malcolm. He sat in his chair, as if frozen there, still staring out into the night.

"Did you tell those officers the car was missin' the rear bumper?"

Malcolm Jackson turned away from his wife without saying a word.

"I didn't think so." She folded her arthritic hands across her ample apron-covered belly. She pushed down on the floor with her curled -up toes, and went back to her rocking. "I didn't think so," she said again, only louder and with a contented smile.

Chapter 4

Tony's Cafe
Nashville

As Mike stepped into the bright light radiating from the criminalists' banks of flood lights, Wendy saw him. "Mike. You got a minute?"

"Sure, what do you have?"

"I wanted you to know. We waited for you, but the Lieutenant told us to get started and walk the scene."

"That's okay, as long as we do it right. Keep looking. Get with Sergeant Hill and expand the inner perimeter to include the Jackson's yard and sidewalk. He'll explain. I'm headed to the DVR, again."

Mike moved through the open emergency exit door of the cafe. Tony had opened the cafe's emergency exit at the far end of the restaurant away from the main entrance and the crime scene. This allowed the officers working the scene to come in, grab a snack and get back to work.

"Tony? Are you in here?" Mike shouted as he scanned the restaurant's ceiling refreshing his memory of the camera locations.

"Coming." Tony pushed open the swinging stainless steel covered door separating the kitchen and dining areas. The large pepperoni held above his head was steaming. "Here you are gentlemen. Enjoy. It's on the house."

The officers of the MNPD had frequented Tony's Cafe for years. The food was always hot and tasted good. Whenever an officer came to the register to pay his bill, Tony always cut the amount in half and gave them their change. With a location not far from one of the city's more active crime areas, he appreciated all the police presence he could get.

"Tony, where is your DVR for these cameras?"

"Come with me." He retraced his steps through the door into the kitchen with Mike close behind. "It's back here, above my desk."

Tony pulled a small ring of keys which had been hooked to his belt loop and shoved one into the white door's lock.

"Here," he pointed to the DVR unit on the second shelf. "If you need to make a copy, the blanks are in here." He pulled open a drawer for Mike to see the plastic spindle with a dozen or more unused discs.

"Do you need me to show you how to use it."

Mike smiled. "No, thanks. I think I've got it."

"Gimme a shout if you need anything. You want some pizza?"

"No, but I do need one thing."

"What's that?"

"Your permission to search any part of your premises we need to in order to investigate this crime."

"No problem, Sergeant. You got it. You sure you don't want one of my double-meat calzones?"

"I'm good. Thanks."

"Okay. Good luck."

Mike nodded and urged Tony out of the cramped space by pushing the door to the tiny room closed behind him. Mike sat in the uncomfortable straight back chair and scanned the right side panel of the split-screen image on the fifteen inch monitor for the digital recorder's options. The unit was not cutting edge, but looked to be getting the job done since it was accepting feeds from only two cameras.

The camera facing the dining area was of limited value to Mike. Over time, the mounting screw must have loosened and the view was now drooped to about half what it had once shown on the screen.

The camera mounted above the kitchen window, through which the food was delivered to the wait staff, showed the high value image of the cash register, front counter and the cafe's front entry. A portion of the parking lot close to the cafe was also partially visible through the large window.

Mike located the playback button and after selecting it, entered the date and the approximate time Thurman said they'd arrived. The screen went blank for almost a minute while the hard drive groaned out its search. A still image of the cafe's front counter and cash register came up on the screen. Mike clicked the Play icon.

He slowed the playback speed as soon as he saw the detectives' unmarked Chevy pull off the street into the parking lot. As Slater and Thurman exited their car and approached the entrance on foot, Mike spotted the headlights from a second car coming from the same direction and crossing in front of the cafe. The car slowed as it reached the front of the cafe. The driver turned his head toward the two detectives and continued to stare until he was past the cafe. The car was too far away for Mike to be sure, and the color quality of the monitor was less than optimal. It looked to be a dark red Toyota Camry with no rear bumper. The driver looked to be light-skinned as Mrs. Jackson indicated.

Mike knew better than to think this type of inexpensive digital recorder would have a zoom feature. He would have to rely on Dean McMurray to work some digital magic in the Audio/Visual lab and try to bring forward the face of this driver. He also knew Dean's chances of success were not good.

Mike paused the playback and made notes on the time of the detectives' arrival and the drive-by of the Camry. He pulled out his cell phone and called Sergeant Hill.

"Steve, the old lady was right. I saw it on the DVR recording. A dark red Camry was following Slater and Thurman when they pulled in Tony's parking lot. The car slowed out on the street when the guys got out of their car and the driver watched them enter Tony's. It was hard to see, but I'm pretty sure it was missing the rear bumper. It has to be our shooter."

"I'm on it," Hill said. "We'll tighten the search."

Mike restarted the video and continued to watch at a reduced speed.

As Slater and Thurman entered the cafe, they waved and spoke in the direction of the kitchen window. No doubt, they were in greeting Tony through the food window.

When Mike saw Tim smile, he stopped the video and stared, recalling the times they'd worked as partners. Tim always dressed well. Like Mike, slacks and a sport jacket were his uniform of choice.

He remembered Tim's logical and methodical approach to their investigations. He would always ask Mike, "What do you see?" The weeks they spent together were productive.

As the detectives exited the camera's field of view and moved into the dining area, Mike increased the playback speed. He was convinced there was little to see while they were eating their calzones.

Slater finished first and walked back toward the entrance. Mike slowed the video again as Tim passed into the camera's view and waved to the kitchen. He stepped to the front door as he removed a cigarette from his shirt pocket.

He cleared the entrance and as the door closed behind him, he lit the cigarette before walking to their car. At the car, it looked as though he pulled something from his jacket pocket and examined it as he smoked. He looked at it for several minutes. Mike thought it looked like a small photograph.

In the foreground of the recorded image three large women came into view from the right. They approached the cash register clawing through their purses as they went. Dave Thurman walked up immediately behind them. The flowery reflections of their dresses in the large front window diminished Mike's view of Tim, still out by the car. Thurman looked out at Tim and shrugged, no doubt frustrated at having to wait.

Just after Tim lit a new smoke and tossed the old butt to the ground, he abruptly bent forward and put his hand to his chest. At the same moment, Thurman jerked his head toward the window. He pushed back the right jacket panel of his cheap plaid suit and pulled his service pistol. He looked back toward the kitchen with an emotional frown and yelled something, most likely for Tony or someone else to call 911.

The three ladies, in unison, attempted to squat as Thurman charged the door. He must have told them to get down as he passed by.

He dropped to a crouch as soon as he was through the door. He ran low to Slater and knelt by him. Over his pistol's sights, Thurman scanned the area to the left of the camera's view where he'd told Burris the shots must have originated.

Mike couldn't see into the area where Thurman was looking.

In seconds, Tony rushed across the image dodging the old ladies, their mouths agape and their hands in the air. He moved out the door and over to Thurman and Slater. The trunk to the car came open and Tony moved to the back and returned with the unit's first aid kit. Thurman, as he'd told Mike and Burris, must have been preparing dressings and applying pressure to the wounds in an attempt to stop the bleeding. The view through the window was not completely clear.

In no more than four or five minutes the red strobes from the first emergency vehicle arrived. The crew was in a large Nashville Fire Department truck. By the time the firefighters got to Slater, the NFD ambulance pulled in and the EMTs moved in rapidly to try and stabilize Slater. Blue lights from more than a dozen cruisers arrived almost bumper to bumper within the next minute.

Mike let the video play until he saw the EMTs place Tim onto their gurney and move him to the rear of the ambulance. After they sped away, bound for the hospital, he watched Lieutenant Burris approach Thurman. Shortly afterward, he saw himself enter the frame. He stopped the video.

He stared at the frozen image filled with bright red and blue lights and uniformed emergency responders. He wondered what could have prompted the ambush and what, if anything, could have been done to prevent it.

They were all exposed to danger anytime they were on the job, but no one expected something like this. There had to be some unusual motivation driving someone to do this.

Chapter 5

Tony's Cafe
Nashville

After making two DVD copies of the entire traumatic episode, Mike thanked Tony on his way back through the cafe's kitchen and out to the emergency exit. He stood outside the door and scanned the parking lot, searching for Lieutenant Burris. He wanted to let him know what he'd seen on the video and also check on Tim's condition.

The repetitive thumping overhead from a helicopter's rotors caused Mike to look up. At first, he couldn't tell if it was an MNPD air support unit assisting with the search for the red car or a local media helicopter positioning itself for video of the crime scene. When the fifteen million candle power search light dropped its blinding cone of daylight on the ground, he knew it was one of the department's units.

He finally spotted both Burris and Thurman at the rear of an NFD firetruck. Thurman was sitting on the chrome diamond plate steel bumper with his head in his hands.

Burris caught Mike's attention. He began to move his head from side to side.

Mike knew they'd lost Tim. He stood, temporarily numbed

inside by the news. His neck muscles tightened. He closed his eyes for a moment.

He watched Thurman, who looked to be sobbing. The entire scene felt surreal. He witnessed death and its repercussions daily. This was different. This was family. The pain and heartache Mike was used to seeing in the faces of his victim's families was now on his face and the faces of his fellow officers. He felt nauseous.

Tim Slater was the first detective from the Homicide Unit to be killed in the line of duty in over twenty-two years. The detectives in the unit frequently joked about the action being over by the time they were called in. They felt relatively safe doing their investigative work, after the fact. This presumption of security would now require more scrutiny.

Mike thought about Tim's wife Megan and their daughter, so very young. He said a prayer for them, and one for Tim.

Mike saw Wendy examining something in a bag. He stepped closer. "What have you found?"

"These." She held up a clear evidence bag with two brass cartridge casings. "Nine mil, Luger."

"Great. Anything else?"

"I've gathered some bark warts from the ground around this Hackberry tree. Based upon the interior surface of the warts and these light-colored spots here," she indicated, "along the tree in this area, they look to be recently broken away from the trunk. The irregular shapes and rough edges on the tree's jagged bark provide good collection points for hair and fiber evidence. In fact, I was able to find these." She handed him another bag with a dozen or more coarse-looking hairs at a length of between one and a half and two inches. "They were stuck to the bark on the same tree, here on this side, opposite the cafe."

"They don't look to be human," Mike said.

"They're not. I don't think they're from a dog or a cat either. They're too coarse."

He looked up at Wendy. "That doesn't leave a lot of other logical sources." Mike looked inside the paper bag again for a closer inspection. "What makes you think they're not from a dog?"

"I found them at a height of fifty-one inches from the ground.

"Hmm."

"We'll know for sure where they came from when we get them in the lab."

"Good job. Anything else?"

"I have a few relatively coarse black hairs, about three to four inches, that appear to be human. I found them around the base of the Hackberry."

"You don't sound very optimistic."

"Well, I've seen Tony's crew." She gestured toward the cafe.

Mike turned to look through the windows into the cafe. All Tony's kitchen employees were Latino with thick black hair. Mike looked back at Wendy and smiled.

"I see your point."

"We'll do buccal swabs on all the folks working here to be sure, but unless some of these hairs were pulled out with the follicle remaining, we can't match DNA anyway," Wendy said. "I ran my vacuum over all sides of this tree, but especially back here where I believe the suspect would have stood had he been using this large tree as his vantage point. I vacuumed down here at the base of the tree, in case anything fell. I'm also vacuuming these other smaller trees. Hopefully, I'll pick up some more trace evidence."

"Good." He waited a moment. "By the way, I don't know if you've heard."

Wendy put a winced look on her face. She could tell from Mike's tone, bad news was coming.

"Tim didn't make it."

"Oh, no." Wendy bowed her head.

Mike waited. "So, we really need whatever you can find to help us. Double check everything. No stone unturned. Let's do this right for Tim."

"For sure. Let me get back to work. I'll tell Carlos."

"Thanks."

With an outdoor crime scene at night, Mike knew they faced numerous challenges. Trace evidence could be contaminated or blown away by the wind. It could be destroyed, carried away, or added to, by animals. Evidence in the dark of night could simply be missed or inadvertently destroyed by one of the criminalists. Waiting until daylight could mean further loss or contamination of evidence by the elements. It was a gamble any way you went.

The shortness of time between this crime and the Crime Scene Unit's response should help to minimize most of those factors. Expeditious collection of evidence was always called for, but the apparent short length of time the shooter was at the scene could limit the mere existence of evidence.

This wasn't the first time Mike felt the deck was stacked against him.

Chapter 6

Tony's Cafe
Nashville

When Mike completed his status update with Steve Hill, he asked the Sergeant if he knew where Thurman was.

"Last time I saw him, he was inside the cafe with the lieutenant."

Mike didn't want to interrupt his boss, but he felt compelled to get as much moving forward on this case as possible. He needed to talk with Thurman.

He stepped inside the cafe and saw the two men in a booth talking over coffee. Mike walked up beside Thurman and waited to be acknowledged by Burris.

"Have they found your red Camry yet?" Burris asked.

"Not yet, but we'll find it."

Burris looked back at Thurman. "I want you to take it easy for the next twenty-four and try to come up with anything you can to help Mike find whoever did this. We can't fail Tim. We owe him."

"Yes sir, we do. I learned a lot from him."

Mike had no doubts, and the lieutenant's comment made it clear, the case was now his.

Burris glanced at his wristwatch as he stood. "I've got to get a couple hours of sleep. Maybe I'll be able to stay awake for the Captain's briefing at eleven." He patted Thurman on the shoulder and gave Mike a nod and a conservative smile. "See you men later."

Mike took Burris's seat and looked toward the kitchen. "Tony."

"Yeah."

"Do you have any fresh coffee?"

"I just made a pot. Coming up. Cream only."

Mike was impressed with Tony's memory of how he took his coffee.

"So. It's tough. I've never lost a partner on the force, but I lost my partner and best friend in CID when he and I were investigating a case in Iraq. I think I understand how you feel. How long had you guys been together?"

"Almost two and a half years."

"Yeah? That's a long time to be with someone day in and day out."

Thurman nodded. "We were good together. I'm pretty sure Tim felt that way too. We cleared a bunch of cases and put several assholes behind bars."

"Good. It's what keeps us coming back, huh?" Mike nodded, hoping the small talk was loosening Thurman up.

"Are you sure you don't have any ideas on who may have had a motive for this? Any family or friends who displayed aggressive talk or actions during an arrest? Anyone Tim may have had a confrontation with?"

Thurman looked up at Mike and shrugged. "I've been trying to think of something we may have done or said to stir anything up. I don't recall anything that could be considered threatening. It's been fairly normal stuff."

"Here you are, gentlemen. Fresh coffee for both of you."

"Thanks, Tony."

"Enjoy."

"Hey, Tony. Did the Lieutenant or Sergeant Hill talk to you about the crime scene?"

"No. What about it?"

"We're going to have to ask you to close the cafe for a day or so."

"What? Close?" Tony stood with his mouth open and his brow wrinkled.

"We have to continue to work the case and we can't do what we need to do for Detective Slater with customers coming and going through the middle of the crime scene out there. A good portion of your parking lot is included in the crime scene. You understand don't you?"

"I—I guess."

"I'm sorry Tony. I wished we didn't have to do it this way, but we have to control the area until we've exhausted our investigation."

Tony dropped his gaze and slow-nodded. He turned and went back to the kitchen.

"I hate it for him," Mike said.

"Tim always liked him and his food. We ate here at least once a week, sometimes more."

"Okay. Give me a brief run down on your most recent cases. Maybe talking about them will jog your memory and something will pop."

"Our most recent case was the murder of a young Chinese girl. We got the call a few hours before we came here."

"Where was this?"

"It was in the parking lot of a factory down by the river, on Visco. The company makes caskets."

"Burial caskets?"

"Yeah. Weird, huh?"

"A little ironic, I'd say. What happened?"

"This young Chinese girl was strangled and left behind a trash dumpster. No apparent sexual assault. She was found by another employee who was tossing her trash after she came back from lunch."

"How far along did you two get with the investigation?"

"We talked with the General Manager, the operations guy and a couple of employees who knew her and spoke some broken English. Several of the employees were either Latino or Asian. Most had a language barrier we had trouble breaking."

"Did you get the impression any were illegals?"

"We discussed it, but Tim wanted to back burner the issue until we made some progress with the homicide. He said we'd call ICE (U.S. Immigration and Customs Enforcement) once we felt we had everything we needed from these folks."

"I would have made the same call. But, it's something to be considered. We've had cases of trafficking to staff places like this.

We need to make sure this isn't the case here."

"That's what Tim said."

"Good. What else did you discover?"

"One of her coworkers said she was twenty years old. She worked second shift in the sewing department. That's where most of the women worked, day or night. The GM said she'd been there almost a year."

"Did you find out where she lived?"

"One of the other young girls said she was her roommate at an apartment in the Woodbine area. I asked how many roommates she had and she hesitated. She talked with another girl there who spoke pretty good English. She told me there were eight of them who lived in a two bedroom apartment."

"I'll assume their landlord was not aware of this?"

"I doubt it."

"Was there anyone you talked to at this place who you or Tim thought might look good for the girl's murder?"

"We only spoke to one person who acted as though they weren't too happy about talking with us."

"Oh?"

"Yeah. The operations guy, Ross. Victor Ross was his name."

"What was his issue?"

"Not sure. Tim's the one who talked with him. I talked with the GM, Paul Elliott. Tim said Ross had one of those standoffish personalities. He acted like the homicide was our problem in our city and we got paid to deal with it. He had better things to worry about."

"One of those jerks. I've dealt with several."

"I'll bet you have."

"Why did you two leave the investigation when you did?"

"Tim came to me and told me he had to get some food in him soon or he was going to fall out. We'd been busy and hadn't eaten since breakfast. He was feeling weak. He'd been sick lately. I was worried about him, but he said it was a chest cold and it would pass. I didn't want him falling out on me, so we agreed to take a thirty minute break and run over here. He called Tony before we left and ordered the food so it would be ready when we got here and save us time."

"Nothing odd happened on the way over? Any indication you were being followed?"

"No. Not that I recall."

"Did you see a red Camry on the drive over or maybe back at the factory?"

"I don't think so. Why do you ask?"

"Just curious. I saw one on the video drive by when you guys pulled into Tony's parking lot."

Thurman shrugged.

"Any other cases in the last few days with suspicious folks?"

Thurman thought a moment. "We caught a case last Friday with a skinny old guy who got pretty pissed off when we hauled off his son."

"Yeah?"

"He said he lived with his thirty-something son who worked for a local freight company. The son got in a fight with one of their neighbors, things got out of hand and the neighbor fell, hit his head and died."

"What was the name?"

"The old man and his son's last name was Whittle. The neighbor was Dempsey, I think. The murder book is back at the CJC (Criminal Justice Center) in Tim's cubicle."

"Okay."

"The old guy kept cussing us saying his son was his sole support and he had no income other than a small Social Security check. He said he couldn't pay for rent or his meds or doctor on what he got from the government. He was pretty pissed. He said this was just one more way the government was screwing him and his family."

"Always somebody else's fault."

"Yeah. I kinda felt sorry for the old dude, though. None of this was his fault."

"Were there any of your recently cleared cases that still had baggage?"

Thurman thought for a moment, and then shook his head. "None I know of."

"What have you two talked about lately other than work?"

"Mostly Tim talked about his little girl, Sophia, and the funny stuff she did. It was the only times I remember seeing him laugh in the last few months. You know she was really his granddaughter, right?"

"Yes, I heard he and his wife adopted her when Tim's daughter was killed in the car wreck."

"Yeah. They didn't know who the father was. Tim said it was for the best. It was a sad time. Tim loved Sophia so much and bragged about how smart she was all the time, but that's what parents and especially grandparents do, right?"

"That's right. How old is she now?"

"She's four. You know he and Megan had recently found out Sophia has diabetes."

"Oh, no. I didn't know."

"Yeah. He was devastated by it. He was depressed for days."

"I can imagine. Bad news like that is always a kick in the gut."

"When the doctor discovered it, he asked Tim about her birth parents' medical history. He said his daughter Becky didn't have any health issues he knew of. They hadn't thought about it, but now he and Megan were worried what other issues could be lurking in Sophia's paternal heredity. He talked about it for days. I listened. I didn't know what to say."

Mike nodded.

"What about his and Megan's relationship? Was it still good?"

"Oh, yeah. Even with the news about Sophia, Tim said she was his rock."

"As far as you know, was Tim having any issues outside the job which might bring about anything like this? Anything at all in his personal life?"

Thurman took a sip from his coffee. "There's always his ex-wife Judy."

"What about her?"

"She worried the piss out of him most of the time."

"Over what?"

"You name it. She felt like he should still be taking care of her, I guess. Tim said she'd had a number of failed short-term relationships since theirs and she always wanted to come back to him for whatever she could get. Seems she was coming around a lot.

"Tim told me she received ownership of his life insurance policy in the divorce settlement—a hundred thousand dollar policy.

"He said Megan tried her best to tolerate her, but she was beginning to get fed up with her. Tim was too nice for his own good. I told him I'd get a restraining order if it was me. He said,

'Sophia is still Judy's granddaughter.' Man, what a convoluted mess."

"Yeah, and the little girl will be the real loser, especially now. She doesn't have Tim to get between them."

Both men sat quietly for a minute and sipped their coffee.

"Anything else?"

"I'm trying to think, but I'm exhausted. I need to get some sleep soon and maybe my mind will start working again afterward."

"I understand. Why don't you go home. Call me on my cell in about," Mike checked his watch, "six or seven hours. That should get your batteries recharged. When you get back to work, you need to focus on your open cases prior to the casket factory. I'll take that one and I'll work Tim's murder."

"Okay. If that's what you want. Will you let me know if I can help with Tim's case?"

"Sure. I'll be calling you to ask questions, but you're too involved. Burris would never let you work Tim's case. We'll stay in touch on the Asian girl's murder, and since it's fresh, I can take that one off of you. I may also visit Mr. Whittle, to be sure."

Both detectives turned when they saw a uniformed officer walk up outside the cafe window. He pointed to Mike and then toward Sergeant Steve Hill back near the inner perimeter tape. Hill motioned for Mike to come see him.

Chapter 7

Criminal Justice Center
Downtown Nashville

Too many of Mike's days were dominated by the selfish, violent acts of thoughtless people. He needed only one hour each day to grab some cardio and push up a few weights in order for him to fight off the stress of the job. This also worked to keep his metabolism up and his weight down, where they belonged. It was a rare week when he was able to work out more than three or four times. This morning, like most, did not allow the indulgence. His two and a half hour nap was the top priority.

He was in the break room, pouring his third cup of coffee since arriving at the CJC, when he heard movement in the area near his office. He grabbed up his cup and started back toward his desk. As he came to the Lieutenant's door, he stopped.

"Good morning."

"Hey, Mike. Did you get some shut-eye?"

"A little. I supported it with a large energy drink and several of these." He held up his coffee.

"Don't rely too heavily on those things. They won't keep you vertical for long."

"Copy that."

"What's the latest on Tim's case?"

"Sergeant Hill told me this morning, two of our patrol officers in Joelton got a call on a car fire back on one of the remote roads near the county's fringes."

"And?"

"It was a red Camry."

"I was afraid of that."

"By the time they arrived, the fire was approaching the fuel tank. They decided it was best to film it with their dash cam and stay back."

"No bumper?"

"No bumper. They ran the tag and the VIN and discovered it was reported stolen yesterday. A lady called it in and said she was sure it was her boyfriend who took it. They were at odds at the time, and he had the extra key to the car. Once the NFD had the car fire out, the officers saw there was no key in the ignition and the steering column had been popped open. They picked up the boyfriend for questioning; he had a strong alibi and still had the key on his key ring."

"What about physical evidence from the cafe crime scene?"

"CSU is entering the two cartridge casings into the BrassTRAX System this morning. Hopefully, we'll get a hit on the breech and extractor markings from NIBIN (National Integrated Ballistic Information Network) in the next twenty-four to forty-eight hours."

"Is this our best physical evidence so far?"

"Possibly. Wendy also collected pieces of tree bark which had been freshly broken away from one of the trees. She's testing it for hair, fiber and GSR (gunshot residue). We're hoping it may have been the shooter's vantage point and maybe he left us something to work with.

"She also located some strange looking hairs on the largest tree. She's got them in the lab so she can find out the source. It looked like dog hair to me, but she says it isn't."

"She has good instincts. We've done well trusting her skills in the past."

"She's good. No doubt about it."

"What about shoe impressions?"

"Turns out the area beneath the trees is where Tony's employees take their breaks and smoke. The ground is so trampled down and thick with butts and fall leaves, Wendy said impressions were virtually impossible. She did pull soil samples from several places around the scene, so we'll have those as the investigation moves forward.

"We're still talking to folks in the neighborhood and the people related to the team's recent cases. I'm going through their murder books this morning and making a list of folks I want to follow up with."

"Good. Give me a call later, so I can update Captain Moretti."

"Will do."

Before Mike turned toward his desk, something, he wasn't sure what, made him glance up at the sign that hung over the Lieutenant's door. Burris hung the sign the day he was promoted and moved into the office. Mike had been walking by the sign for years and not given it much thought. He presumed Tim's case caused him to notice it today.

"The assignment to investigate the death of another human being is an awesome responsibility. Do not underestimate your duty to the citizens of Nashville or your role in the survivor family's search for understanding and peace."　　　Lt. D.W. Burris

Mike took a sip from his cup and turned a corner in the cubicle farm on his way back to his desk. He almost tripped over Dean McMurray's wheelchair coming down the aisle at full speed.

"Whoa."

"Sorry, Deano. I didn't see you."

"I'm glad you missed me with your cup of heat. I'll try and stand up next time so you can see me coming down the aisle."

Mike smiled at Dean's ever-present sarcasm.

Dean was known for his upbeat attitude and self-deprecating sense of humor. Rather than seek out sympathy, this former MNPD patrol officer always tried to help the people around him to be more comfortable with his physical limitations.

The drunken motorist who put him in his wheelchair took away his ability to ever walk again or serve his home city as a uniformed patrol officer, but Dean did not allow him to take away his optimism or his appetite for life. He found a way to contribute to the department. His attitude and his self-taught IT and Audio/Visual skills sold the chief on it. He was now the enthusiastic Supervisor in the A/V Lab.

"So, where have you been?" Mike asked. "Your office has been dark for over a week."

"You didn't hear? The chief sent me to Atlanta. I represented the MNPD at the LEO (Law Enforcement Officer) EXPO. It's a technology show for all the cool stuff available or being developed for use by law enforcement. It's like an IT EXPO, but for law enforcement geeks like me."

"Sounds like fun."

"For me, yes. Most of you guys would probably be bored to sleep."

"Maybe not. What did you get to see?"

"The most fascinating technology was the work being done with Ion Beam Forensic Analysis. It can determine an object's physical makeup with non-destructive light analysis, it's highly discriminating, ultra sensitive and great for trace evidence of all kinds including gunshot residue and even fingerprint comparison. These Ion Beams can even be used to determine whether or not a piece of art is a forgery. The potential forensic benefits from this cutting edge process seem limitless."

"That's pretty impressive."

"Yeah. The Chief asked me to conduct a meeting next week with the Crime Scene Unit folks to share what I learned about all the new toys coming down the road for them."

"They'll enjoy that."

"I thought so. Oh, yeah. There was a guy there from the National Institute of Justice who talked about some of the projects being funded in the area of biometrics. He spoke on facial recognition algorithms, iris recognition software, nanotechnology and what I found fascinating, forensic acoustics. He called it Sound DNA for voice recognition, reliable to one person in twenty-eight million. Unbelievable, huh?"

"Truly. Was there anything I can relate to?"

"The one thing generally considered as major cool by everyone there was the proliferation of UAVs. There must have been twenty or thirty purveyors of these things. They were flying all over the conference hall air space. Two of them even collided, crashed and burned. Well, they didn't burn, but they did crash."

"I give up. UAV?"

"Unmanned Aerial Vehicles. Drones."

"Oh."

"The possibilities for a tool like this are endless. We're gonna start seeing a lot more of these babies in the air. FAA recently approved private daytime flights to five hundred feet as long as they're kept within the operator's line of sight. The chief hasn't approved us for one, but I bought one of my own."

"I'm not surprised."

"I couldn't resist. I love it."

"These babies could help with so many of our day to day tasks: Crowd control, traffic management, searching for lost kids and high-speed chases could be virtually eliminated. The drone could follow the suspect until he reached his destination and, unlike with a helicopter, he'd never know it was up there."

"I'll bet we hear from the ACLU on those things. Those folks are all about the Fourth Amendment and the public's right to privacy."

"There's always someone out there ready to spoil all the fun."

"It's good to see you. I'm glad you're back. I need to get back to work myself."

Dean gave Mike a solemn look. "Hey, man. I heard about Tim."

Mike nodded.

"Your case?"

"Yeah."

"Good luck." Dean bumped fists with Mike. "Tim was a great investigator."

"For sure. Thanks, buddy. I'll see you later."

Dean rolled himself through the unit, spun his chair around and backed out the door with the smile still on his face. "Have a great day, Sarge. Call me if there's anything at all I can do to help you."

"Thanks, Deano."

Every time Mike encountered Dean, he felt a resurgence in his own attitude. If this man could maintain such a positive outlook on life after what had been done to him by a thoughtless drunk, Mike knew he had no excuse to ever feel any way but blessed.

Chapter 8

Peaceful Solace, LLC
Nashville

Mike was familiar with the street and the approximate location of what was surely the city's only casket factory. He'd driven Visco Drive often while investigating a domestic homicide a few years before the 2010 Nashville flood. The suspect-husband of the victim had worked as a driver for a local beverage distributor located down by the Cumberland River.

As he rolled up on the casket factory parking lot, he decided to check out some of the facility's exterior before going inside. He drove by the trash dumpster to see where the girl's body had been found. The dumpster was located at the far end of the parking lot, away from the building.

Most of the cars on the east end of the building, were ten to fifteen year old Honda Civics, Preludes, or Acura Integras customized with loud drift spec exhaust systems, lowered bodies and painted in bright, sometimes neon, colors. This style of vehicle conversion told Mike, most of the people who worked here were likely either Latino or Asian. He had to wonder, how many were green card carrying permanent residents of the United States? But, that was a question for ICE. He was not here to investigate immigration issues. He was focused on a homicide, possibly two.

He drove to the parking area in front of the main entrance where he found three available parking spaces marked *Visitors*. The vehicles parked in this front parking area were all more conservative. Most were American made. He parked in one of the open spots and approached the front door.

Inside the lobby, Mike found two low-cost club chairs on either side of a table on his right and nothing but a small sliding window in the wall to his left. He leaned close to the window and looked around with his eyes only an inch from the glass. One of the ladies saw him and came to his rescue.

She pushed open half the sliding window. "May I help you?"

"Yes ma'am. I hope so. I'm Sergeant Mike Neal with the Nashville Police Department. I'm here to see your General Manager, Mr. Elliott."

"I'll let him know you're here." She pushed the window closed and picked up the handset to a desk phone.

Mike turned and walked toward the chairs and table where he saw a half dozen well-worn magazines. His curiosity made him check the dates. The magazines were from 2013. These were even older than the ones at his barbershop. He rubbed the stubble on his head and thought it was almost time for another haircut. He paced up and down the narrow hallway, waiting.

"Sir?"

"Yes." Mike turned toward the voice and the open door.

"Mr. Elliott can see you now."

"Thank you."

As he followed the lady through the door and down the hallway of the open office concept, Mike fished a business card from his jacket pocket. Ahead he could see a fifty-something man in his shirt sleeves working at the desk in a private office. His escort looked to be aiming for the man's door.

"Mr. Elliott? This is Sergeant Mike Neal with the Nashville Police Department."

"Thank you, Doris." Elliott gestured toward one of the chairs in front of his desk. "Sergeant, please have a seat."

Mike offered his card and sat. "You folks weren't here when we had the flood, were you?"

"No. We moved in a couple of years later after the building sat empty. The owner was anxious to negotiate and we were able to get an attractive lease. We're a bit cautious and still don't utilize the basement, only the two upper floors. You never know when it might rain again." Elliott smiled. "I'm told we still have a snake problem down there from time to time, so I stay out."

Mike nodded.

"Mr. Elliott, you need to know, I will be taking over the investigation into the murder of your employee, Lian Xiong."

"Oh, okay."

"I've read your statement from last night, and the one from Victor Ross. I understand you were both here at the time." Mike knew from Thurman's brief report neither Elliott nor Ross were at the factory when the young woman was killed. He'd learned a lot over the years, asking questions to which he already knew the answers.

"I came in when I was called, and based upon what the detective told me last evening, I was not here at the time she was killed."

"Where were you?"

"I got home from work around 5:30 and was there all evening with my wife. We had dinner and watched some television. I received the call and I came back."

"Was Ross here when the girl was killed?"

"I don't think so. He works days. Like me, he came in last night when he was called about the ... . I heard Dwayne Puckett was the one who called him."

"Who is Puckett?"

"He's the night supervisor in the sewing department."

"So, he was Lian Xiong's supervisor?"

"Yes."

"I didn't see a statement from him in the file. Any idea why?"

"I—don't know about that, but he was here when I arrived."

Mike suspected Tim Slater's intention was to interview Puckett when they returned from Tony's, since the man worked nights and would not be leaving the facility until much later."

"I'll need to talk with him. Do you have a room where we can have a private discussion?"

"Yes. But, he won't be here until five o'clock. He works nights."

"I see. Do you know who the last person was to see or speak with the girl?

"No. I'm sorry. I don't."

"Who else here knew her and might be able to tell me anything about her that could help our investigation?"

"I—I don't know of anyone on days who might know her. Human Resources said she had only worked with us less than a year; all her time has been on nights. If you could come back after five, maybe you could find out about her friends then and also talk with Puckett."

"Okay." Mike stood.

"Can you let your people know I'll be back to speak with them?"

"Yes. Is there anything else I can help you with?"

"I'm sure there will be more questions." Mike stood. "Thank you for seeing me."

Elliott escorted Mike back to the lobby.

Mike backed his car from the visitors spot. He turned to leave, and instead circled the facility so he could see what the rear of the building looked like. He turned left at the corner and drove slowly down the lane used by the large trucks coming to pick up the company's shipments.

On his left, at the rear of the red brick building, he saw three Latino men in colorful welders caps and large brown leather aprons with multiple dark burn marks across the front. They were talking and smoking, no doubt taking their break. As he drove by, the men stared at him with lowered brows and looks that said, *quien eres?* or 'who are you?'.

Between the dock doors and the concrete steps leading inside the building, Mike saw a bright yellow rectangle painted on the pavement next to the wall. Parked inside the rectangle was a large red motorcycle, a Ducati. Mike was no cycle nut, but he knew enough to know this shiny Italian bike cost as much as a new car and more than some.

Only one of the dock doors was open. As he drove past it, he looked inside and saw a man, a large man, standing back away from the opening at the edge of the darkness with his muscular arms folded across his thick chest.

He wondered if this was Victor Ross.

Chapter 9

Peaceful Solace, LLC
Nashville

Victor Ross sat focused at his desk, staring at the twenty-seven inch multi-image monitor cycling through eight simultaneous live camera feeds from the thirty-two cameras he had personally located throughout the facility. Ross was not only in charge of shipping, receiving and warehousing for the company; he was responsible for facility maintenance and security as well. He had volunteered for those additional assignments as soon as he was hired.

On the monitor, he spotted the new detective Elliott had warned him was coming. As the cop left the lobby, Ross clicked on the camera image outside the entrance. The detective started out of the parking lot, but at the last minute turned left and drove toward the back of the building.

"What the—?"

Ross squinted and cycled the video's split-screen display. He watched the unmarked Impala move toward the rear of the building. He stood, cursed and bolted from his office.

Ross stood back from the open dock and waited. He assumed the cop must be driving slow, checking out anything he could see which might grab his interest. This intruder's mere presence was enough to irritate Ross. He didn't need this heightened level of scrutiny.

As the cop drove by the door and the two men made eye contact, Ross convinced himself. *This prick is going to be trouble.*

"He's going to be even worse than the two last night," Elliott said as he walked up behind Ross. "He's a sergeant in Homicide. He's coming back at five to talk with Puckett and any others on the night crew who knew the girl or saw her last night before she was killed."

Ross turned to look at Elliott. "Why?"

"He said the detectives last night didn't talk to Puckett."

"By design—Paul."

Elliott looked at Ross and forced himself to remain silent. He had a list of questions for Ross, but he didn't dare ask them. He thought it was best he didn't know the answers. Plausible deniability was what the politicians called it. The more he thought about it, the better it sounded.

Ross wrinkled his brow and said, "Why don't you go back up front, pull on your fuzzy slippers and do whatever it is you do all day." Ross waved his muscular arm in the air. "I'll take care of all this shit back here."

He stomped toward his office, leaving Elliott standing in the middle of the shipping floor and looking, once again, like something other than the General Manager of the company.

Ross slammed the door to his office and fell back in his chair. He grabbed his cell phone, scrolled the contacts list, tapped Dwayne Puckett's name and waited.

"Hello."

"Are you at home?"

"Yeah, I was trying to get some sleep so I'd be ready for work tonight, why?"

"Don't bother."

"What do you mean?"

"You're not coming to work tonight."

"Yes, I am."

"No—you're not."

"I'm not?"

"You're sick. You're taking a sick day. It's been approved by your supervisor."

"Why am I taking a sick day?"

"Do you not remember last night?"

Puckett was quiet.

"I asked you a question. I'd like an answer."

"I remember, okay?"

"Today, we had a visit from a new cop. This one is a Sergeant in Homicide."

"What happened to the ones from last night?"

"What the hell difference does it make?"

Puckett hesitated. "None, I guess."

"This one is coming back in here at five. He expects to interview you and whoever else on the night shift knew the girl. Who else knew you were acting like a dog in heat whenever you were around her?"

Puckett exhaled audibly. "Nobody."

"I wouldn't be so sure about that. People notice things. Even people who can't speak the language know lust when they see it. Listen. After we finish talking, if you get a call, don't answer it, unless it's me. You do have my cell number in your phone?"

"Yeah."

"So, if your phone rings, what are you going to do?"

"Look to see if it's you."

"If it's not?"

"I won't answer it."

"Good. If somebody comes to your door, anybody, you don't answer it."

"Anybody?"

"Nobody."

"If I'm sick, wouldn't I be home in the bed?"

Ross took in a deep breath. "You've never called in sick when you weren't?"

After some thought, Puckett answered, "Okay, I get it."

"Your poor judgment and lack of self-control has brought us an unacceptable amount of attention from the police. This cannot continue. Do you understand?"

"I suppose nothing you're doing downstairs brings us any risk?"

Ross began to stew. He held back his initial response. "What I'm doing downstairs is of no concern to you. It's none of your damn business. I thought we'd covered this already?"

"It's my business if it's exposing my ass along with everyone else's."

Ross paused. "Okay. Get this straight." He cleared his throat. "I'm not going to tell you again. Do not think you are in a position to barter with me on any level. You—will—lose."

Puckett was quiet.

"Can I assume you're clear on this?"

He hesitated. "I'm clear."

"If anything here changes, I will call you on your cell. Otherwise, do exactly as I told you, assuming you want to stay out of jail."

"What about tomorrow? Will I still be sick tomorrow?"

"We'll worry about tomorrow, tomorrow. You just do what I tell you today."

"Fine."

Chapter 10

Starwood Apartments
Nashville

Mike reached across the Impala's front seat and pulled the murder book open. He was searching for the apartment number for George Whittle.

"26-D," Mike said out loud.

He'd reviewed the book this morning for the facts of the case, but did not commit the address to memory. The huge low cost apartment complex had thirty buildings with eight units per building.

Mike parked among the elder autos, some of which must be out of commission. He pushed the doorbell button precariously mounted on the narrow door facing. There was no answer. He rang again and knocked afterward. Still no answer.

"Mr. Whittle, this is Detective Neal with The Nashville Police Department. I need to speak with you for a few minutes, please."

Through the door, after a minute or two of silence, he heard a response. "The police have already been here and hauled my boy off. Haven't you done enough damage to me? Go away."

"I'm not here to hurt you Mr. Whittle. I'd like to try and help you. Please let me in so we can talk and I can find out how I can help."

"You can help by leaving."

"Mr. Whittle, I'm not going to leave. I have to speak with you about what happened if I'm going to be able to help you find a way to pay your bills."

Mike listened. He was confident the last statement would get Whittle's attention. He hoped to hear the pop of the deadbolt as it was unlocked. After a minute, he did. The old man pulled the door open enough to see Mike and for Mike to see him squinting at the brightness from the outdoors. The foul smell of the air escaping the apartment convinced Mike, Whittle had not opened his windows or doors and enjoyed any fresh air in quite a long time.

"Hello, Mr. Whittle. I'm Sergeant Mike Neal." Mike offered the gaunt old man his business card through the opening. "Mr. Whittle, can I come in so we can talk?" Mike waited for a positive response, but got none. "I know your son's arrest may have had a detrimental effect on your livelihood, but I may be able to help you get through this. Won't you let me try? I know some folks who help people in situations like you have."

Gradually the door came open more and finally Mike saw Whittle standing behind the door waiting for him to enter.

"Thank you, Mr. Whittle." Mike stepped inside.

The stagnant sweaty odor of the apartment was at first a bit overwhelming, but he managed to deal with it, as he frequently did, by popping a peppermint in his mouth. This funk was not a new olfactory experience. One of the idiosyncrasies involved in working the Homicide Unit was the never-ending conglomeration of unpleasant odors.

"You can leave the door open if you'd like," Mike said, hoping the old man would take the hint.

George Whittle offered no comment, but continued to push the door slowly until it met the casing. He leaned his lanky frame against it until it latched. He threw the deadbolt, then turned and began a slow penguin-like shuffle toward the middle of the room.

Mike waited until Whittle made it to the furniture before choosing his seat. Whittle took the chair. Mike sat on the sofa.

It took a couple of minutes for Whittle to get situated in his chair, pull his afghan around him and arrange all his favorite things on the table next to him the way he liked it. He finally stopped shifting things around and looked up at Mike.

He had the old man's attention. "Mr. Whittle, I've read the book on the case against your son Bobby, but I'd like for you to tell me what you know about what happened. Can you do that for me?"

"I guess so."

"Can you start by telling me about what led up to the confrontation with your neighbor, Mr. Dempsey."

Whittle sat looking at Mike. "I rode the bus that morning to my Doctor's appointment. Bobby was at work so he couldn't take me. When I got back, I walked back here from the bus stop. My legs were killing me. I was worn out. I was about to start up those damned metal steps out there when I heard the loud muffler. I knew it was Dempsey. He has the loudest car in the complex. I hurried, trying to get inside before the jerk could get to the steps. I was starting to make the turn at the landing and go up the second set of steps when Dempsey came running up the stairs. I tried to move out of his way, but he made a point of running into me and knocking my cane out of my hand. It almost fell between the steps, but I stepped on it when I fell and stopped it. I injured my knee on the steel steps when I fell."

Whittle inched his pants leg up in order to show Mike his scar.

"That had to hurt. Why do you think Dempsey knocked you down?"

"The guy's a bully, plain and simple. He doesn't pick on anyone who can fight back."

"How did your son get involved?"

"When Bobby got home, I had an ice bag on my knee trying to hold down the swelling. He pulled the ice bag off to take a look. I was trying to keep it covered so he wouldn't get upset. I take blood thinners, so it was bruised pretty bad. He asked me what happened. I told him. He didn't like Dempsey anyway. When I told him what happened, he got pissed off and left. I asked him where he was going. He said to the beer store. He was gone almost an hour. When he came back he had a twelve pack.

"About a half hour after he got back and started drinking the beer, there was a knock on the door. It was two cops. They came in and asked him a bunch of questions. When they were through, they put handcuffs on him, arrested him and took him away. I tried to get them to stop, but they wouldn't. They said they couldn't. I told them how sick I am and I have no way to pay the bills. Bobby is my support. I can't buy meds or pay the rent. They took him and left anyway. They didn't care.

"A little later two detectives came here and asked me a lot of questions. I didn't know everything they wanted me to tell them, but I told them about my situation. I guess I got mad and said a few things I shouldn't have. They didn't act like they wanted to help me either. I don't know what I'm going to do."

Whittle started crying.

"Okay. Like I said a while ago at the door, I think I might be able to help you. I know a lady in the Department of Human Services. This is the kind of thing she's good at. She helps folks like you."

"Can she help me pay my bills?"

"I can't be sure what all she can do until she visits with you, but I'm sure she will do everything she can. She is a very nice lady." Mike pulled out one of his business cards and wrote his friend's name and number on the back. "I will call her and ask her to contact you for a visit and an interview real soon. Okay?"

"Okay."

Mike stood. "Mr. Whittle, I'm sorry about your troubles. I hope your luck changes soon."

This old man didn't seem capable of loading a semi-automatic pistol, much less firing it accurately—twice.

However, Mike had witnessed through his career a number of sorrowful events where unpredictable turmoil had been produced by a brief bout of passion.

Chapter II

Mike Neal's Home
Green Hills Area

Mike collected the makings for his favorite club sandwich from the refrigerator and positioned them on the counter around his plate. He was assembling the meat and cheese masterpiece when he heard a knock on the kitchen door. He turned to look through the door's nine pane window. It was Jennifer Holliman from upstairs.

Jennifer and her teenage son Mason were not only the renters of Mike's upstairs two bedroom apartment, but after twelve years, they were also his good friends. Mike enjoyed their company and he enjoyed watching Mason grow up. Mike was the closest thing to a father Mason had known.

"Good afternoon."

"Hello there, would you like a club sandwich?"

"I'd love one, but I've already eaten. Thanks anyway." As she did each month, Jennifer placed her rent check on Mike's kitchen table, between the salt and the pepper shakers.

"Soda?" Mike asked as he collected the sandwich ingredients into his arms and returned them to the fridge.

"I'd like one. Thanks." Mike brought his sandwich and two colas to the table.

"So, how's Mason?" He took a bite of his sandwich and looked at Jennifer as he chewed.

"He's okay." She opened her drink.

"Just okay?" Mike mumbled.

Jennifer smiled. "It's—well, it's time for one of those father-son talks and his father, as you know, is nowhere around."

"Thank goodness."

Jennifer's ex-husband, Rick Carson, was convicted in 2002, when Mason was not yet two, for conspiracy to traffic cocaine across the Mexican border into Texas. He and his associates south of the border were using unwitting Mexicans, seeking a better life in America, as their drug mules.

Carson might have gotten away with his crimes had Jennifer not overheard one of his late night cell phone conversations. Her decision to take her young son out of her husband's influence and testify about what she'd heard earned them positions on the U.S. Marshal's Witness Protection List, new names and a discreet home in Nashville with an experienced cop as their landlord.

Jennifer gave Mike an uncomfortable looking smile.

"What?" Mike asked.

"He's having some issues."

"He is a teenager. It's what they do."

"He has questions he's uncomfortable discussing with me." She sipped her drink.

"Oh. Those questions." Mike grunted.

"I asked him if he'd be more at ease talking with someone else. He said he thought he might. I suggested he talk with his doctor. He didn't care for the idea."

"Hmm." Mike took a big bite of his sandwich.

"He wants to talk with you."

Mike almost choked. He grabbed his cola, chewed fast and washed down the sandwich. "Talk to me? About what?"

"About things a teenager wants to know, but doesn't want anyone to know he wants to know."

"That's clear as mud."

"Mike, you were a teenage boy once weren't you?"

"I don't remember. I don't think so. Maybe. If so, it was a long time ago."

"You're not only Mason's friend, you are his father figure, he looks up to you. He doesn't have anyone else he can count on." Jennifer looked at Mike. "Would you be willing to talk with Mason for a while to help him deal with his questions and his teenage years?"

Mike finished chewing his last bite, and took a mouthful of cola to wash it down. He wiped his mouth with a napkin, sat back in his chair and exhaled. He caught a large burp as it attempted to escape. He managed to control its exit and its volume. "Excuse me. Of course I'll talk with him."

Jennifer's facial expression displayed her relief. "Thank you, Mike. You are so good for us."

"It's mutual." He stood and took his plate to the sink. "I'll have to check my schedule and let you know when I can find some time. I'm full right now with the investigation into the murder of one of our detectives, Tim Slater."

"I saw it on the news and I meant to ask you about it."

"It's quite sad. He was a really good person."

"I'm sure. I won't keep you." Jennifer stood. "Thanks again for your help. Mason will be glad to hear."

"I'll try to get free as soon as I can. I'll let you know."

"That's fine." She stepped forward, wrapped her arms around Mike's thick chest, laid her head against it and squeezed. She looked up and kissed him on his left cheek. "Please be careful out there. I don't know what we'd do without you."

"I will. See ya later."

Jennifer pulled the door closed behind her.

Whenever Mike looked at Jennifer, he saw Mason's mom and his friend of over ten years. Granted, she was quite attractive with her long blond hair and her firm body. She never left her apartment if she wasn't dressed well and with the perfect makeup.

But, Mike looked at Jennifer much like he remembered his little sister, Connie. If Connie was still alive, they would be about the same age.

Occasionally, when they were together, he felt like Jennifer viewed him with a different tilt. He'd caught her looking at his butt and smiling when she realized he'd seen her. Then again, maybe he was only being suspicious.

Chapter 12

Mike Neal's Home
Green Hills Area

When Jennifer left, Mike placed a call to his friend at DHS and told her about Mr. George Whittle. She agreed to call the old man and stop by the apartment for a visit in the next few days to see if she could help him. She confirmed for Mike there were various programs in place designed to assist folks like Mr. Whittle.

He pulled his laptop across the kitchen table and parked it in front of him. He brought up his access portal to the MNPD database and saw there was no arrest history for Paul Elliott. As expected, his search on Victor Ross was more productive.

In addition to the two relatively minor motorcycle speeding tickets he'd found in Ross's motor vehicle record at the DMV, Mike saw where seven months ago, outside a local Nashville sports bar, Victor Ross had his name added to a list of people interviewed by one of Mike's former partners who is now one of his direct reports, Homicide Detective Cris Vega. A known drug dealer was beaten to death in the parking lot at the time Ross and several others were inside the bar.

Mike thought he would have to discuss this with Cris soon and get the facts on Ross's involvement, or lack of it, in this murder.

Mike closed out the MNPD site and double-clicked the icon for the FBI's NCIC (National Crime Information Center) database search.

The local database had offered Mike a picture of Ross's relatively clean recent past while in Nashville, but the NCIC search, with over twelve million records reaching back as far as forty-seven years always provided a more comprehensive snapshot of a suspect. The database showed Victor Ross had never owned real estate anywhere in the United States, but he did own a criminal record.

Mike scrolled the screen. The earliest listing was a charge of drunk and disorderly in 1990. At age 18, this was likely not long after he left high school. The next entry reflected a charge of resisting arrest in 1992 along with a charge of assault. Both were ultimately dismissed.

His NCIC record ended with his enlistment in the US Army in 1995. Mike knew he would have to contact his friend Jerry Moses at Fort Campbell, Kentucky in order to get a look at Ross's military records.

Mike left his home and was on his way back to the factory to talk with the Sewing Department supervisor on the night crew. It was 16:45 when he made the call. He was less than six miles away and hoped he would arrive at approximately the same time as Dwayne Puckett.

"Peaceful Solace, may I help you."

"Mr. Paul Elliott, please. This is Sergeant Mike Neal calling."

"I'm sorry, sir. Mr. Elliott has left for the day. Can you hold a moment?"

"Yes."

Mike speculated as to the reason for his being parked on hold. Maybe she had another call.

"Hello."

"Yes. This is Sergeant Mike Neal with the Nashville Police Department. Who am I speaking with?"

"Victor Ross."

"Mr. Elliott was supposed to have arranged for me to speak with Dwayne Puckett today at five. I'm on my way there now. Do you know if Mr. Puckett has arrived yet?"

"Puckett won't be here tonight."

"Why not?"

"He called in sick this afternoon."

"Sick?"

"That's what he said. I think his exact words were, 'I'm shittin' my guts out,' or something to that effect."

This was too convenient. Mike needed to talk with Puckett more than any other person at the factory. He couldn't help but think someone had warned the man.

"Can you give Mr. Elliott a message for me?"

"I guess so," Ross said with an irritated tone.

"Tell Mr. Elliott I will be there tomorrow at five o'clock sharp and I will expect him to have Dwayne Puckett there waiting, sick or otherwise. If he doesn't, and I have to go searching for Puckett, it will not bode well for him. Do you think you could tell him?"

"I don't see why not."

"Good." Mike disconnected the call and tossed his cell phone in the passenger's seat.

Ross came across on the phone the same way Mike expected, based upon his view of the man standing at the rear shipping dock with his arms folded in a closed-off defensive posture.

Chapter 13

Walker-Roche Funeral Home
Nashville

Mike pulled his car into the parking area at the rear of the funeral home. The lot was over-filled with blue and white patrol cars and officers' personal vehicles. Some were parked illegally, likely without concern. He finally spotted an available space and pulled the Impala in.

There were only a few funeral homes in the city Mike hadn't visited in his almost fourteen years in Homicide. He'd worked cases in all the precincts, more in some and only a few in others. On more than one occasion his respectful visit with the family at the funeral home had netted him a fact, a name, or a connection that became a valuable link leading to or supporting the success of his investigation.

The area outside the funeral home's rear entrance was swarming with uniformed officers smoking, talking and avoiding the depressing atmosphere inside. Some were even joking and laughing with each other. This was the way many officers had of dealing with the ever-present depressing side of their work.

Officers in the thick of day-to-day street policing frequently developed a bizarre sense of humor in response to their stressful work, but it normally surfaced only when they were in groups of their fellow officers. Anyone outside the Blue Family might think they were being insensitive or rude. They weren't. These men and women were caring individuals. It's why they were in the job. However, the frequent overexposure to the ugliest acts of humanity and the depressing side of life caused them to become desensitized to the pain in order to deal with it. They understood this coping mechanism and allowed it to help them get through their emotionally demanding work.

Mike knew many of the officers in the gathering outside the rear entrance. He shook hands with, or spoke to, over half the group. Most of the uniformed officers who had known Tim also knew Mike. Both detectives had earned the respect of the uniformed officers by showing respect for *their* work. Mike and Tim had both worn the uniform for years before becoming investigators. They knew the world of the patrol officer and they knew how important their role was to the investigator's success.

He stepped into the long hallway directing mourners to the front lobby. In the distance he could see another throng of dark blue bodies milling about.

"Hello, Mike." Detective Doug Wolfe shook Mike's hand.

"Hey, Doug. Busy place, huh?" Mike waved to Norm Wallace and Jerry Rains.

"Tim had a lot of friends."

"He did, and this turnout speaks to his life as a friend to all these people. It's good to see you. I'm going in to try and talk with Megan."

The reposing room was packed with folks paying their last respects to Tim and to Megan. There was a line of people waiting to speak with her and then view Tim's body. Mike took this time to sign the register and flip through the signed pages to see if there might be any mourners he was not familiar with.

He finished his unproductive register scan and stepped to the line waiting to see Megan. As he waited, he scanned the room and spotted a collection of Tim's photos on a nearby table. Some of the shots were from his years on patrol and at least one had a young Officer Mike Neal in the group photo taken in front of the South Precinct.

An elderly couple was ahead of him and were talking with Megan while he waited. Megan looked up at Mike and smiled as the couple spoke. After a few minutes, the couple finished their offering of sympathy and stepped toward the casket.

Megan held out her arms toward Mike and the two shared a hug.

"Thank you for coming."

He nodded. "I'm so sorry."

"I know."

"He was such a good person and so good at his job. I only worked with him occasionally, but we enjoyed our time together. We had a lot in common."

"He was a great father and husband. I can't believe he's gone." She started to cry.

Mike gave her his shoulder and waited. He glanced behind him to see how many were waiting to speak with her. There was still a line.

"I'd better let you speak with these other folks who are waiting."

"Okay."

"I will need to talk with you as soon as possible, but we can wait until after the funeral."

"Sure. Thank you, Mike. I'm glad you have the case."

"I'll do my best."

"I know you will. Tim thought so highly of you."

"It was mutual. I'll call you, okay. Hang in there for Sophia."

She nodded and dabbed her nose.

Mike stepped toward the open casket and paused. Tim looked good in his dress blues, but he looked as though he may have lost a few pounds since they'd talked last. He was an impressive man, both in appearance and in the quality of his work. His loss would bring a void to the Homicide Unit. His expertise and years of experience could not be replaced.

Mike said a prayer and then turned and walked out into the large lobby where most of the plain clothes detectives and criminalists, who he worked with on a daily basis, had assembled. They were standing, talking in small groups, surrounded by elaborate brocade and paisley patterned furniture from several decades previous.

"Hey, Mike." Norm Wallace, one of his former partners, turned to include Mike in the group of three detectives he was talking with. "It's rough. We're gonna miss him."

"Yes. He'll be missed by a lot of folks." Mike looked around Norm's wide body at Carol Spencer who was across the room talking one-on-one with Jake Archer. Jake was known throughout the department as a womanizer of the first degree. He'd been married and divorced three times in the last fifteen years. He was not the kind of guy Mike wanted Carol exposed to.

"Listen," Mike said to Norm. "Follow me, okay?"

"Sure. Where are we going?"

"Just follow me and play along."

Mike stepped around Norm and strolled toward Carol with Norm on his heels.

"Good evening, Carol. Jake."

"Hi, Mike. Hey, Norm. How are you guys?"

"Okay, under the circumstances," Norm said.

"It's a sad time," Jake said.

"Yes, it is," Carol said. "Mike, have you talked with Megan yet?"

"Yes. I spoke with her a few minutes ago."

"Well, guys. I'm gonna run." With his disingenuous interest interrupted, Jake gave a half-wave and walked toward the front door.

"That's my cue," Norm said. "See you Carol. By the way, as usual, you look great."

"Why, thank you. Tell Cheryl I said hello. We need to get together if Saint Thomas will ever let her escape the OR."

"I'll tell her. The OR nurses work some crazy hours, especially the thoracic group. I call it kidnapping. She calls it job security."

"The way Nashville is growing and folks are moving here, I don't think any of us have anything to worry about concerning job security."

"Amen to that," Norm agreed. "See ya partner."

"Take care, Norm." Mike bumped fists with the big man. Mike and Norm had been partners for going on three years when, after chasing a suspect, Norm succumbed to a heart attack and Mike had to rush him to the ER. The closest was Saint Thomas Hospital and as luck would have it, Cheryl was on duty in the thoracic unit.

Norm lost thirty-five pounds and was down to only two-hundred and eighty. His six foot four inch frame carried it well.

"Norm was right, you know."

"About what?"

"You look delicious." She looked around the room while she

spoke. "Don't start unless you're prepared to finish."

"Oh, I'm prepared. I'm always prepared."

"Mike," she said in a warning tone.

"Hey. What was the business with Jake the Snake?"

"It's called conversation between fellow employees."

"You know his history don't you?"

"I wasn't considering dating him. He walked up and started talking. I didn't want to be rude just because he has a—caddish reputation."

"Okay."

"Why? Are you jealous?"

"Are you kidding? Of him?"

"Whatever."

Mike spotted Detective Cris Vega inside the reposing room talking with Megan. Mike had partnered with Cris briefly following Norm's heart attack and also while the big man worked his way back to a hundred percent.

"What are you looking at?"

"Cris. I need to talk to her about a suspect in one of Tim's cases."

"Talking with me while you're looking at another girl," Carol kidded Mike.

"Hey, it's the price we pay for being in demand."

"Oh, brother. There go my shoes. I forgot to apply the BS repellant."

Mike and Cris made eye contact and he tossed his head toward the rear entrance.

"I have to go now."

"I guess I'll have to look for Jake."

"Do not do that."

"Hey, it's the price we pay for being in demand." She brushed her long dark hair behind her left shoulder.

Mike looked around the room and allowed his hand to rub against hers.

"You do look fantastic."

"Thanks. See you later."

"You bet you will." Mike smiled and then walked toward the rear exit.

Mike motioned for Cris to go to her right and down the hallway to the back.

"Did you get to talk with Megan?"

"Yes," Cris said, "briefly."

"She may need another girl to share her feelings with."

"Girl?"

"You know what I mean."

"You are such a guy."

"It works for me."

"So, where are we going?"

"I thought we'd grab a beer and talk a minute about one of your cases from a few months back. I had a name pop up on a search of our database. Seems you talked with this guy at one of your crime scenes a while back."

"Okay. You buying?"

"Of course."

"Then I'm up for it."

Chapter 14

The Local Bar
Downtown Nashville

"I'm not sure I've ever been here," Cris said. "I love the name."

"I met the guy who manages this place when I was having dinner last month at Ted's. I came here the next week. It's not bad, mainly a young crowd. At least *you'll* fit in."

Cris laughed.

"Let's sit here." Mike pulled out Cris's chair at a high top table and then sat in his own.

Mike and Cris spent three years as partners following Norm Wallace's heart attack in 2003. They developed a mutual respect and a devotion to their work.

The product of a Houston, Texas Latino law enforcement family, her father was a Sergeant in the HPD patrol division.

Cris was small in stature compared to the men in the department, but even at five-foot five, her ability as a detective established a sizable competence that gained her respect throughout the department.

"So, which case are you interested in?"

"You and Rains had a homicide at 100 Proof Bar a few months back."

"Yeah. A drug dealer was beaten to death in the parking lot. It's still not cleared."

"One of your interviews that night was with a guy by the name of Victor Ross. Do you remember him?"

"Yeah, mouthy guy. Tats, muscles, over-confident attitude, another of God's gifts to females. What about him?"

"Earlier, on the night Tim was ambushed, he and Thurman caught the case of a young Chinese girl who was strangled outside her employer's place of business. They worked it for a few hours. Thurman said Tim had been under the weather and he needed to eat, so they left for a quick meal at Tony's. The shipping manager at the factory where the young girl was killed was—."

"Victor Ross," Cris interrupted.

"Yep. So, what can you tell me about Ross and that night at 100 Proof?"

"It was quite an active crime scene. We had dozens of people standing outside the secondary perimeter and eyeballing everything we did. A few were making disparaging comments about the victim and shouting questions at us. We were all on display. Ross was one of the more verbal. So, I took him off to the side and asked him what he knew about the victim and his murder. He told me the man was a dealer who had approached him more than once in the same parking lot. He said he wasn't surprised someone had killed him."

"And your case is still open?"

"Yeah. It's one of those where no one seems to care this guy was killed. He was just another dirty piece of societal trash who won't be missed by anyone."

"No family?"

Cris shook her head. "None we could find."

"Did you do any searches on Ross's background, or was he considered just another spectator?"

"There was really no reason to pursue anything. With so many people there, he was only peripheral activity and there was no valid reason to waste time on him."

Mike nodded. "Did you see what just happened?"

"What?" Cris looked around.

"The bartender. Did you see what he did?"

"I don't think so. Did he pocket some cash?"

"See those three guys at the end of the bar down there?"

Cris leaned forward. "Yeah."

"They're doing Jack Daniel's shots and paying cash. Every other time the bartender serves them, he takes the whiskey from a bottle under the bar, rather than the one behind the bar."

"Why does he do it? Does he have a cheaper brand in the other bottle?"

"No, you can't do that with Jack Daniel's. The oaky charcoal-filtered taste is distinctive. Nothing else tastes like it."

"You would know."

"Correct. No, the deal is the bottle under the bar is also Jack, but one *he* brought in, probably in his backpack when he came to work. Whenever he fills their drinks from *his* bottle, he pockets their cash. They don't know or care. They're getting exactly what they're paying for. Meanwhile, he's turning a thirty dollar bottle into a hundred dollar bottle. And, no one's the wiser. Except us of course."

"Are we going to tell the manager?"

"I'll tell him. When I tell him he'll want to comp my tab as thanks, so I'll wait until this weekend, bring a date, have dinner and wine. Then I'll tell him."

"You are something else, Sergeant."

"It's proper compensation for my investigative work. Besides, he's off tonight. He wouldn't want me telling anyone else here. It might give them ideas, or they could warn the bartender."

"How did you know he was doing it?"

"I have a friend, Nick, who used to manage a few restaurants here in town. He's now the sales manager for a local wine and spirits wholesaler. He told me about some of the tricks restaurant and bar workers pull to pad their pockets at their employer's expense."

"That one's pretty slick."

"Just one more way the crooks are winning."

Chapter 15

Mike Neal's Home
Green Hills Area

Mike's eyes were half closed as he left his car in the driveway and stumbled toward his kitchen door. On the second attempt, he put the correct key in the lock and opened the door. He moved through his house on memory, his eyes opening only occasionally as he plodded toward the bedroom.

He was about ready to fall out, but he knew he had to get his shower in first so he could hit the ground running in the morning. He turned on the hot water and went to his closet to hang up his jacket and put his clothes in the hamper.

His nose caught a whiff of perfume. It was Carol's, his favorite and the one he gave her for her last birthday. He thought the scent must be left over from her last visit.

He hurried through his abbreviated shower and did only a cursory job of drying his body. He brushed his teeth and swore to himself he would shave in the morning. He pulled on a clean pair of boxers, set his alarm and fell into bed.

He was mere seconds from unconsciousness when an arm came over his body and two warm breasts pressed against his back.

"Hi."

"Hi, there."

"Why didn't you say something when I came in."

"I was hoping to surprise you when you got in the bed."

"With the deprived sleep state I'm currently in, you might have gotten away with it. Did you park in the garage?"

"Yes. I knew you wouldn't see my car." She interlaced the fingers of her right hand with his.

"The best way to surprise me is to get one of my suspects to confess to a murder I'm investigating. That almost always surprises me."

"I didn't realize you were short on sleep. You seemed okay at the funeral home."

"I was acting."

"Really?"

"Yeah. I'm trying out for a role on the TV show *Nashville* next week."

She slapped him gently on his butt, then she reached around and stroked his chest. "I wanted to take your mind off the stress. I know Tim's case has to be taxing."

"Thank you. You're always so thoughtful. Any other time, I'd be up for it," he whispered. "Uh—no pun intended of course."

Carol laughed and kissed him on his neck.

"Honey, I've got to be honest with you. What I need most right now is something you can't give me. I need about three or four hours of sleep so I can function in some capacity tomorrow, attend Tim's funeral without passing out and hopefully move forward with his case."

"I understand."

"I know you do. Thank you. Let me get past this and we'll have some time together, I promise. Okay?"

"I love you."

"I love you more," he mumbled. He gave her a quick kiss and rolled over. In less than a minute, he was snoring.

"Impossible." Carol whispered and then kissed his shoulder.

Carol had been divorced for more than a year when they met. She wasn't shopping for a replacement at the time, but Mike's interest and his large smile were welcome. Before long, they were seeing each other outside of work and swapping covert lust-filled glances whenever their assignments put them in proximity.

After twelve years of an on again-off again undercover relationship, they were both currently at a high point. They were a fit for each other. They knew it. However, they shared a stressful work-world where divorce was too often the norm.

She laid there silent, but wide awake, looking at Mike's muscular back and thinking, not about how long they've been together as lovers without making a commitment, but about how blessed she felt having Mike as her friend and her lover.

She loved him now more than ever. She couldn't imagine not being able to talk with him at a moment's notice, or share with him some good or bad news she'd been given. Being with him, even if it was only working the same crime scene and having no personal contact other than an occasional meeting of their eyes, was high value.

Knowing he was there. It was enough. Knowing he loved her. It was enough. Knowing what happened to Tim Slater could, on any day, happen to Mike. It was enough to devastate her. The thought of that possibility brought tears—again.

She touched the corners of her eyes with the sheet as she thought about Megan and what she must be going through, facing her future without Tim. Raising Sophia without Tim. She couldn't imagine being in her shoes.

Carol rarely thought of her ex any more. Their divorce was final over thirteen years ago. It had taken only weeks for her bruises and scars, some physical and others psychological, to heal once she made the decision to leave him and to file suit.

She wasn't sure why his distant memory had entered her thoughts tonight, but she felt confident it could be her unconscious self telling her no matter what happened today, no matter what happens tomorrow, she was much better off having known and loved a man who was more than worthy of her love.

Chapter 16

Saint Edward Church
South Nashville

Mike drove his car into the parking lot on the east end of the church property. This lot had been reserved for MNPD personnel only. There were uniformed officers at both entrances. Marked blue and white cruisers were quickly filling the lot. He parked in one of the more distant spaces from the church. When time allowed, Mike tried to park a good distance from his destinations so he could add the walk to his daily exercise routine. This also gave him time alone to think.

He was checking his tie in the visor mirror before exiting the car, when his phone rang. He'd forgotten to silence his cell phone before leaving home. He was glad the call had reminded him. Mike could see the caller was his friend Captain Terry Moses at Fort Campbell Army Base just over the state line in southern Kentucky.

"Mike Neal."

"Hey, Mike. It's Terry."

"Good morning. Are you calling with good news?"

"Not exactly. I ran the search on your guy Ross."

"Great."

"It came back blocked."

"What? What do you mean blocked?"

"The system wouldn't allow me access to his military history."

"I thought you still had some pull at Campbell."

"That's not the point. Someone of rank has locked out his background."

"That's a bit odd, isn't it? Any idea why?"

"I can't tell yet. I've encountered this before, but it was usually when the individual was still employed by the government in a covert capacity or in some other sensitive area such as a private security contractor. I've requested improved access from my Colonel. He's checking it out, so hopefully I'll be able to get you some usable information within a day or so."

"Great. I knew you were still a player up there."

"Oh, yes. All I've ever wanted is to be a player," Moses said with dripping sarcasm. "I'll call you when I know more."

"Thanks, Terry. You're the man."

Mike had known Moses since 2005 when he investigated a North Nashville homicide with connections at Fort Campbell. The husband of the deceased woman was one of Moses's men. Moses was Mike's contact at Fort Campbell during the investigation and Mike's years in the Middle East with Army CID gave the two men an instant positive connection.

Mike pushed up the sun visor when he'd finished checking his tie in the mirror. He grabbed his dress blue hat, blew a speck of lint from the top and exited the car. Outside, he stood looking into the driver side window at the reflection of his coat. Everything looked to be intact and in position. He placed his hat on his head and measured the distance from the bill to the bridge of his nose, two fingers.

Mike walked to the entrance and climbed the brick steps in silence along with a number of other uniformed officers. He could hear soft piano music coming from inside the church. He stepped through the narthex, accepted the five by seven inch printed program offered by the usher and stood at the entrance to the sanctuary scanning the collection of people and pews looking for his team.

A large hand and long dark blue arm rose high above the seated congregation. Mike recognized it as belonging to Norm Wallace. He walked to the pew where his direct reports were saving him a seat. Norm stepped into the aisle to allow Mike to enter.

"I like to sit on the end. Just in case I have to go out, I won't step on anybody's toes."

Mike looked down at Norm's size 18 EEE's, as if he'd never seen the over-sized boats he wore. "That could be a traumatic experience for someone."

"Hey, Boss." Cris Vega said, not sure what else to say at a time like this.

"Hi." Mike leaned forward and looked down the pew. "Y'all look nice."

Thanks and nods were offered by all.

"Boy. I hate these things," Cris said.

"Me too."

"You don't, uh by chance, have an extra handkerchief do you, just in case?"

"Hey. I was a boy scout, Detective Vega."

"I knew it."

For the most part, the detectives sat in silence while they waited for the service to begin. Mike opened the printed program and read the list of contributors and the tasks each would be performing. The first speaker was to be Captain Alberto Moretti, head of the Homicide and Cold Case Units.

Mike leaned to his left and, without speaking, pointed to the captain's name. He looked at Cris and smiled. She looked up at him and gave him a critical stare. Mike was only one of three people in the department, even in the city, who knew Captain Moretti was Cris's uncle. She'd never used it to her advantage and Mike knew she would never need to. Cris Vega was one of the best detectives Mike had ever worked with. He was grateful to Burris for assigning her to his team.

Mike saw movement to his right and looked up to see the choir taking their places to the right of the piano. Once they were in place, the MNPD Funeral Commander, Lieutenant Russell Whiteside stepped to the center front of the church and raised his white gloved palms to indicate the congregation should stand and face the center aisle.

The music and the choir began a hymn Mike remembered from his youth. Candle and cross bearers entered the church followed by the deacon who was one of the MNPD's reserve chaplains. He was followed by the celebrant priest, who after walking the center aisle, turned and faced the rear of the sanctuary. The choir went silent, and the celebrant welcomed the MNPD Honor Guard delivering the colors and escorting the flag-draped casket.

Mike could feel his emotions swelling as the drummer and bagpiper began their tribute. Once the casket was brought in, the deceased's family and friends were nearing their last chance to see their loved one and offer their goodbyes.

He felt a tap on his back. He reached into his pocket and held a white handkerchief over his shoulder.

"Thanks, Mike."

The speeches were over. The songs were sung. The eulogy was completed. It was time for Tim Slater's friends and fellow law enforcement officers to share their personal prayers, offer their respect and say their goodbyes.

Men from the funeral home came forward, folded back Old Glory and prepared Tim's casket for the final viewing.

Two officers from the honor guard took up positions at either end of the casket.

Lieutenant Whiteside signaled for the MNPD officers on the left side of the sanctuary facing the alter to stand. All stood and tucked their hats beneath their left arms. As Whiteside stepped to the ends of the individual pews, the officers filed out and moved to the front. When finished, each officer was asked to step outside and take up their assigned positions on the church's front concrete walkway.

It was time for Mike's team to stand. They turned to their left and waited to be released for the solemn march toward the altar and Tim's casket. Mike watched his fellow officers at the casket as they paid their last respects. He could tell which were former military by the way they snapped to attention and saluted their fellow officer.

Mike stepped forward each time one of his team completed their goodbye and then exited the church. It was Cris's turn. She stepped to the side of the casket and looked down at Tim. Mike could tell she was about ready to lose it. But, she stood her five feet five inches up straight and saluted. She turned to her right and marched up the aisle toward the back of the church.

As Mike reached the casket, he did something he hadn't

planned. His feelings took over. He put his right hand on the sleeve of Tim's uniform near his friend's white glove. He bent forward and whispered, "Hey, buddy. I am so sorry. I assure you, I will do everything in my power to find out who did this and see he gets what he deserves. We will see Megan and Sophia are taken care of and get everything they need. You rest in peace, brother. We will miss you."

Mike crossed himself and took a step back. He snapped to attention and saluted Tim, bringing his hand down slowly to his side. He did a right face turn and walked to the center aisle, emotions in check. He looked up in time to see Megan Slater looking at him with her tissues at her nose. He tightened his lips in an effort to hold back his emotions. He marched outside, placed his hat on his head and measured two fingers.

The number of uniformed officers outside the church, both from the MNPD and numerous other area agencies, approached a thousand. Mike felt proud to see this tribute. He saw his fellow detectives assembling on the wide sidewalk at the church's main entrance and he moved in their direction.

"Okay officers," Lieutenant Whiteside said. "Line up, equal numbers on each side of the walkway. The pallbearers will be bringing the casket out the front door and through here on their way to the hearse. As soon as the church doors open, you will receive the *Attention* command, followed by the *Present Arms* salute. Everyone got it? When I give the command, you'll go to *Attention*. Then I'll give *Present Arms, and* you'll salute. You'll hold the salute until the hearse doors close and I give the command *Order Arms*. Everyone stand at *Parade Rest* until then. Share this with the officers coming out now. Thanks."

There were so many in line to pay their respects, it was almost a half-hour before the church doors opened and the command was given.

"*Attention—Present Arms.*"

The two rows of officers in their dark blue uniforms were frozen in their salute. The pallbearers escorted the casket between them and along the sidewalk, out to the waiting hearse. Once the casket was secured and the hearse's rear door was closed, Whiteside gave the command, *"Order Arms"*. Officers, *"Stand at— Ease"*.

"Is everyone clear on the procession to the cemetery?" There were head nods and no verbal responses, positive or negative. Unfortunately, for several of the officers in attendance today, this was not their first funeral for a fellow officer.

"*Officers—Dismissed.*"

Mike walked without delay to his car and pulled it forward in line to exit the lot onto Thompson Lane. Traffic officers were in place at the exits to hold normal traffic and allow the MNPD vehicles, their strobes flashing, to join the procession. Mike pulled out and flipped on his blue lights.

As he drove the slow mile from Saint Edwards Church to Woodlawn Memorial Park, Mike thought about all the pomp and circumstance being displayed. He felt it was deserved.

After clearing the railroad overpass, Mike saw up ahead at the entrance to Woodlawn, two of the Nashville Fire Department's largest ladder trucks on either side of the cemetery entrance with their ladders extended fully at 45 degree angles. Between the ladders was a cable supporting a huge American flag, maintained by the NFD for this purpose, hanging vertically with the union toward the east.

As an Iraq war veteran, Mike always noticed Old Glory and was proud when people displayed it properly.

One thing Mike wasn't happy to see was the row of media vans along Thompson Lane past the entrance to the cemetery with their antennas extended skyward to capture and broadcast what they could of the graveside ceremony. He was experienced enough to know there was little he could ever do about the media other than hold them back some distance from the sensationalism they thrived on. The public had a right to know what was going on in their city, but he was thinking more about the privacy for Megan and Sophia, and for the rest of Tim's family.

He followed the car ahead of him and drove to where he was instructed by the officers staged throughout the huge cemetery which occupied both sides of Thompson Lane. Mike pulled his car up close to a marked cruiser and stopped when signaled by a young patrol officer, likely ex-military based on his robotic movements. It was doubtful the young man knew Tim Slater, but he was proudly executing his honored assignment.

Mike exited his car and looked back to the east to see the tent and the grave close to three hundred yards away. In an attempt to distract himself from the present, he mentally added this walk to his daily workout and wondered if he would get to include any cardio or lift any weights later. He decided, today, it didn't matter.

Chapter 17

Peaceful Solace, LLC
Nashville

It was back in the fall of 2012 when U.S. Army Lieutenant Colonel Jonathan Briggs successfully arranged his collaboration with Peaceful Solace, LLC General Manager Paul Elliott. Elliott was the father of Briggs's First Sergeant and right hand man, James Elliott.

Briggs investigated Paul Elliott's past and found he had no prior arrests, no record of any kind. What he did have, was a healthy love of money. This allowed Briggs to draw Elliott into a win-win arrangement allowing them both to pad their pockets with tens of thousands of dollars each month.

With initial terms of $100,000 in cash up front and a conservative estimate of another $25,000 in profits each month, Elliott couldn't resist. This compensation was to be in exchange for the use of his company's facility and its products to distribute Briggs's elicit goods to his buyers. The purchase of Elliott's manufactured caskets as a method for transporting the illicit goods and Briggs's agreement to buy them at market prices, only made the deal much more attractive for Elliott. This arrangement could cause his casket sales to double and Elliott to become even richer than he'd once thought. He was all in.

The cost of the caskets, their packaging and freight were all easily covered for Briggs by the exorbitant prices he was able to charge for his goods. When Elliott began to have trouble keeping up with the casket orders, Briggs told him to hire more people or get his crew to be more productive. He needed the orders filled without delay.

Briggs knew, based upon the production excuses Elliott was giving, in order for his plans to be fulfilled, he needed his own man on site making sure things happened as scheduled.

Victor Ross had been a transplanted resident of Nashville since 2010. Born and raised in eastern Pennsylvania, he had trouble relating to the good ol' boys in the south. He was convinced he was smarter than all of them.

Ross was recommended to Briggs because of his logistics experience by a mutual friend currently stationed at Fort Campbell. He warned Briggs about Ross's stubbornness and his somewhat sordid past while in the Army and afterward working for a security contractor, but somewhere in all the data Briggs saw what he believed he needed. He wanted a strong man who thrived on being able to make some of his own decisions in order to get his job done. Ross's history told Briggs this man hadn't been given a chance to do that.

Ross's past conduct may have been driven by his being micromanaged by his superiors. Briggs believed Ross's behavior to be his way of pushing back against the control imposed on him and the limited options he was given on doing his job. Victor Ross looked to be one who needed to be his own man. Briggs needed someone who could handle the work he needed done and do so without constant supervision.

Briggs interviewed Ross during a forty minute Skype call from Bagram, Afghanistan. He told him to see Paul Elliott at the casket factory and inform him he was hired by Briggs and he would be handling Briggs's business out of Peaceful Solace going forward. Briggs assured Ross, the more of his goods moved through the casket factory and on to Briggs's customers, the more Ross would be paid. Control over his income was not something Ross had ever experienced. He was ready for the assignment.

Ross reported for work on a day when General Manager Paul Elliott's plans were in flux. He had no time to deal with a new man at Ross's level. Production was creating rework and shipping schedules were not being met.

The Guatemala born Operations Supervisor Elliott had hired months ago was not so concerned with meeting Elliott's schedule. His philosophy had migrated down into the troops and bogged down production.

He told Elliott, "They will ship when they are ready." Elliott's concept of 'The dead won't wait' failed to translate for the supervisor and the workers.

When Ross arrived, Elliott met him in his office and soon had him out for a tour of the facility. As they were watching the cutting and stamping of the steel, the operations supervisor approached.

"Victor Ross, this is Francisco Torres," Elliott said.

Torres offered his hand, but Ross looked at Elliott and ignored Torres.

"So, is production on schedule?" Elliott asked, knowing the answer would not be what he wanted to hear.

"Like I told you. The caskets will ship as soon as they are ready."

Ross squinted and looked at Elliott. "Don't you have a production schedule to follow?"

"Yes. But, Francisco has been having some issues lately meeting our commitments."

"What kind of issues?" Ross looked directly at Torres for the first time.

"My people don't do their best work when they are pressured?"

Ross tilted his head and asked, "Since when are we concerned about your peoples' issues that are causing them to fail at meeting the work schedule?"

"You can't pressure your way to success. These people are artists. The work they do requires them to be meticulous."

"The pay they get requires them to get the job done and done on time."

Torres rolled his eyes.

Ross turned his back to Torres and spoke to Elliot. "If you want me and the package you discussed with Briggs, this enchilada's got to go."

Torres looked at Elliott. Elliott looked at Ross.

"You've got my phone number," Ross walked to the exit.

Chapter 18

Woodlawn Memorial Park
South Nashville

In near silence, hundreds of solemn officers left their vehicles and paced the cemetery's asphalt arteries toward the green tent. The small tent, with no sides and with folding wooden chairs positioned beneath it, was traditionally set up to shield the family from the hot sun and, if needed, from the rain. The weather was rarely allowed to affect a police officer's final tribute.

As instructed by the Funeral Commander, the arriving officers were to assume their positions along side their peers at Tim's gravesite. Shoulder to shoulder, they would form lines facing the spot where their friend and fellow LEO would be laid to rest.

As Mike strolled the distance toward the tent, and the artificial turf-covered dirt which paralleled the grave, he scanned the line of incoming cars with their roof, grill and window strobes flashing. He couldn't help but think about the impressive response from law enforcement across the state and even some who came from outside Tennessee. There likely was not a single officer present today who hadn't considered the possibility this could one day be their own tribute. This was not an uncommon thought, only one rarely discussed.

Mike reached the gravesite and took up his position along side Lieutenant D.W. Burris, on the second line facing the grave. The two men nodded to each other. The assembled officers, standing at parade rest, watched in near silence as their peers arrived and assumed their spots in the blue lines.

"Did you pull Tim's phone records?" Burris whispered.

"Yes. Thurman's too. I didn't see anything odd. The calls all matched up with their active cases, other miscellaneous numbers within the department, some personal contacts and Megan's cell phone. What about Sergeant Smith? Did you get to talk with him?"

"Yes," Burris said. "Same story. He didn't have anything to give you a lead. He said Thurman should be your best source within the department."

Mike nodded.

With black mourning bands over their badges and sincere stares, hundreds of MNPD officers formed dozens of long curved blue lines wrapping around the grave and the tent. The family and civilian friends, most dressed in black, had begun to take their positions beneath the tent. The mass of gravesite sympathizers, already well over a thousand, remained quiet and reverent as they waited.

Megan and Sophia's limousine had arrived with the hearse near the gravesite several minutes earlier, but they'd been asked to wait until the honor guard was in place before they exited their car.

The Funeral Commander stepped to the limo and pulled open Megan's door. "Mrs. Slater." He gestured for her to come out.

The honor guard, bagpiper and drummer were in place. Sergeant Smith and his wife came around the limo, met with Megan and Sophia on their side and were all escorted to the tent by one of Whiteside's assistants. They were soon in position beneath the tent and in front of their chairs.

"*Honor Guard,*" the Commander shouted, "*Attention.*" After a pause, Whiteside gave a command and the piper finished filling his bagpipes with air. The drummer began to build his subdued marching beat and the Honor Guard stepped out slowly to the sound of *Amazing Grace* and began their deliberate march to the the grave.

The director from the funeral home assembled the pallbearers at the rear of the hearse. He grasped the handle at the end of the casket and pulled it across the rollers and into their waiting white-gloved hands. The group of six turned the casket so the head and Old Glory's stars, or Union as it is known, led the way. They fell in behind the priest and the deacon and began their march toward the gravesite.

Mike watched Megan as her grieving increased at the sight of the MNPD Honor Guard leading the way for Tim's casket approaching his final resting place.

Lieutenant Burris leaned toward Mike and whispered, "In the last month, we've buried two retired officers, one motorcycle officer who was killed by a thoughtless motorist who pulled in front of him when he was answering a Code 3, and now—this." He paused. "I like the bagpipes and *Amazing Grace* as much as anyone, but we have got to find a way to stop this music."

Mike nodded his head, not sure of what to say in response to Burris's comment.

The Honor Guard took their places. The pallbearers carefully brought the casket to the grave and with all due respect placed it atop the lowering belts. The men stood at attention and, in unison, saluted their fellow officer one last time before stepping to the side of the tent.

The elderly priest stepped forward to the foot of the casket, and raised his arms to symbolically embrace all the mourners. "Let us pray." He paused to allow the mourners to quieten and prepare themselves for prayer. "As we gather to commend our brother Timothy Slater to God our heavenly Father and to commit his body to the earth, let us express in prayer our common faith in the resurrection. As Jesus Christ was raised from the dead, we too are called to follow Him through death to the glory where God will be all in all. We pray this prayer in The Name of The Father, The Son and The Holy Spirit."

"Amen," was spoken by hundreds.

"In the twenty-fifth chapter of Matthew, we read. Come, you who are blessed by my Father, says the Lord, inherit the kingdom prepared for you from the foundation of the world.

"Trusting in God, we have prayed together for Tim and now we come to the last farewell. There is sadness in parting, but we take comfort in the hope that one day we shall see Tim and again enjoy his friendship. Let us console one another in the faith of Jesus Christ."

The deacon stepped forward and held up the brass censer so the priest could add incense to the burner. While everything was quiet, Megan searched her pockets for more tissues. Sophia took this opportunity to step toward the flag-draped casket and put her small hand on the top. She slapped the casket three times and said aloud, "Daddy, you can come out now. Everybody's here."

Gasps came from dozens standing close enough to hear her soft and innocent plea. Tears flowed from those around her. Many, including the men, grabbed for tissues or pushed away the product of their emotions with their hands.

Megan reached out her hand to call her daughter back from the casket. Sophia shrugged her tiny shoulders in response and returned to her mother's hug. "I'll explain later, baby." Megan cried.

Several throughout the crowd were still drying their eyes when incense smoke began floating from the censer. The priest took the long chain and began walking around and blessing Tim while praying over him in Latin.

When the priest had finished, he handed off the censer to the deacon, and once again stood at the foot of the casket and lifted his arms.

"Let us pray." He paused. "Into Your hands, Father of mercies, we commend our brother Tim in the sure and certain hope that, together with all who have died in Christ, he will rise with Him on the last day. We ask this through Christ our Lord. In the name of The Father, The Son and The Holy Spirit. Amen."

The priest stepped to where Megan and Sophia were seated, took both their hands in his left hand, and with his right hand, gave them a blessing.

"Thank you, Father," Megan said.

"You are most welcome, my child." The priest kissed Sophia on her forehead and then stood. He made his way to the rear of the crowd, blessing and thanking mourners for their presence and support for Tim's family as he went.

The Funeral Commander signaled the pallbearers. They lined up on either side of the casket and began folding the flag. When they were finished, the MNPD's Chief of Police stepped forward and accepted the tri-folded flag from the pallbearer. He turned and walked to Megan. He rotated the flag between his hands so the long side of the folded flag faced her and he bent forward.

"On behalf of the mayor and the grateful city of Nashville, I would like to present to you this flag honoring your husband's service. He will be greatly missed by us all."

"Thank you." Megan placed the flag on her lap and wiped away more tears.

Sophia was intrigued by the flag and began to pick at the stars.

From a distance of maybe twenty yards from the tent, there began the ringing of a large brass bell maintained by the MNPD for this purpose. Rather than the traditional 21 Gun Salute, some families whose loved ones were taken from them with the use of a firearm, preferred to have the bell rung 21 times.

When the ringing of the bell was finished, there was a short period of silence. After a moment, the sound of a radio microphone being keyed was broadcast from the speaker mounted in the grill of an MNPD cruiser parked nearby. When the alternating warble of the All Points Announcement came across the speaker, all law enforcement officers present knew what this represented. It was the saddest part of the ceremony, the Final Roll Call.

"Attention all units, all sectors—clear the air except for emergency traffic."

Everyone throughout the cemetery was silent.

"39D."

The speaker paused.

"39 Delta."

He paused again.

"Headquarters to 39 Delta, Detective Timothy Slater."

Mike looked at Megan. She was sobbing into her tissues and Sergeant Smith's wife, also crying, had her arm around her shoulders.

"Attention all cars, 39 Delta, Detective Timothy Slater is 10-7 for the remainder."

There was another pause.

"End of Watch—Monday, May 12, 2014, 20:36.

"Detective Slater, we honor you for the ultimate sacrifice and we thank you for your service to the Metropolitan Government and to the citizens of Nashville and Davidson County.

"Gracious Heavenly Father, please wrap Your loving arms around him, keeping him safe. And, place Your hands of protection over our brothers and sisters remaining here. We pray humbly in in Your name. Amen."

Few eyes were dry. Nothing drove home the loss of a fellow officer like the Last Roll Call and End of Watch announcement.

The department's bugler, standing in the distance, began playing Taps.

As the bugler finished, the Funeral Commander stepped to a place near Megan and invited the family, seated behind her, to pay their last respects.

Megan, Sergeant Smith and his wife remained seated and allowed all the others to pass by the casket before leaving. Several shared their sympathies with Megan as they left.

Mike was glad to see Tim's fellow officers, especially his colleague detectives remained in place out of respect for Meagan. As the family and friends from the tent moved away, Megan stood with Sergeant Smith who helped her over to the casket.

She placed a hand on the shining bronze surface, bent and kissed it as she cried. Her tears fell and ran down the casket's side. She wasn't able to see it, but Sophia had mimicked her mother and kissed the handle running along the side of the casket. It was as far as her small body could reach. Megan turned to Sophia, pulled her up and into her arms.

Mike watched as mother and daughter walked toward the limousine. He wondered what the little girl could be thinking at a time like this. Sophia looked back over her mother's shoulder at the casket as it was being lowered slowly by the cemetery workers into the grave. Her wrinkled brow communicated her confusion.

Chapter 19

Woodlawn Memorial Park
South Nashville

Still standing in the same place he'd occupied throughout the lengthy graveside service, Mike watched Megan as she helped Sophia into her seat inside the limousine. She glanced back toward the grave and paused before climbing in and closing the door, leaving her beloved husband for the last time.

Mike recalled how he felt after his sister Connie's burial. It was difficult, but this had to be so much more painful for Megan. The life they'd planned together—gone. Sophia, for the most part, would be protected by her youth and her failure to fully understand anything of what had happened, except Tim's absence from her life.

The detectives from the unit mingled, not ready to leave the grieving camaraderie of their Blue Family. They stood sharing small talk and trying to avoid discussions about Tim or their current proximity to his grave. Instead, they worked to find something cheerful or positive to talk about. Some shared sarcastic critiques on how their teammates looked in their dress blues. They all loved their contemptuous exchanges. They understood, it was simply their way of dealing with the grief. Cop humor. You had to had to be a LEO to fully appreciate it.

"Sergeant Neal?"

"Yes." Mike turned to see a man he hadn't seen in years. He laughed. "Grant Chambers."

Chambers smiled. "How are you?"

"I'm doing as well as Nashville will allow." Mike laughed.

This was a line Mike had learned from Chambers himself, years ago before his decision to become a Fed and accept his new assignment with the Bureau of Alcohol, Tobacco, Firearms and Explosives.

"What's it like working for the ATF?"

"It's a lot like working for Metro, only with a lot more people, a larger budget and a nicer retirement package."

"How long before that happens?"

"At least a dozen years," Chambers said. "So, I hear you got Tim's case."

"Yeah."

"He was a good detective. Almost as good as you."

"He was one of our best."

"If there's anything I can do to help, you need to let me know."

"Will do," Mike said. "It's good to see you again."

As Chambers walked away, Mike heard another voice. "Mike?" He turned to the voice.

"Hello."

"Hello, there." Mike shook the man's hand. "You're on my list."

"I figured I would be," Robert Franks said.

Franks was Tim Slater's partner before he and Dave Thurman hooked up.

"It's a sad day."

"It is," Mike agreed.

"So, do you have anything helpful yet?"

"I'm working some leads from his current cases, but nothing's firm yet. You and I will need to talk in the next couple of days."

Franks pulled out one of his frayed old cards and wrote his cell phone number on it. "Here's my cell number. Call me and we'll talk. I'll help you in any way I can."

"I don't suppose you have any ideas off the top of your head? Anybody who might have had a grudge?"

"I have been thinking about it. I'll give it some more thought before we get together and see what, if anything, I can remember."

"Thanks, Robert."

Mike turned and started for his car.

As he neared the car he could see what looked like someone leaning against his sedan. As he came closer, his suspicions were confirmed and he smiled. It was Carol.

"Hello there."

"Hi. You look sharp. I love a man in uniform." She gave him a big smile.

"Well," he looked back at the sea of officers as they were spreading out across the cemetery, "you have your pick of several hundred today."

"I've already made my selection, thank you." She smiled.

"I much prefer my slacks, blazers and Rockports. This stuff is not," he shrugged and shifted his shoulders, "comfortable."

"I think it's more for the look than the comfort."

"Yeah. Speaking of the look—." He scanned her up and down and then checked their surroundings before saying, "You have the look."

"Thank you."

Mike nodded. "It was a nice service, huh?"

"It was impressive. The department does it up right."

"Yes. It's sad we dedicate our lives to our work and then have to die to get this level of recognition."

"No one ever appreciates what they have until it's gone."

"So—you need a ride?"

"Maybe. I also wanted to talk to you."

"Okay. You going back to work?"

"Of course. You can give me a ride to my car. I'm parked over there." Carol pointed.

Mike unlocked the passenger side door and held it until she was inside. He circled the car, opened his door and tossed his hat into the back seat. He fired up the car and pulled away from the curb, but was unable to move forward due to the volume of traffic leaving the cemetery.

"What was it you wanted to talk about?"

"I—I wanted to ask you to please be especially careful out there."

"You said that last night. Is this bothering you more than usual?"

"Tim's killer is still out there. He's killed once. He could easily kill again. And, since you don't know anything yet for sure about his motive—." Carol stopped herself and pulled in a large breath to try and calm her emotions. "I don't want anything to happen to you. Okay?"

"I know. I don't think this is one of the 'let's kill all the cops' things. I think whoever did this had a definable motive and it was specific to Tim Slater. Otherwise, I think he would have waited five more minutes until he could shoot Thurman, too. I have to discover what the motivation was. With some luck, it'll take me forward to an arrest."

The cars began to move.

"You may be right. But the whole thing scares me to death."

"Let me explain something you may not want to hear. We are all in danger most of the time. Different degrees of danger, but in danger all the same. The crime scene work we do seems to be relatively safe since the action is typically over and the suspects are gone. But, we don't always know that for sure. I've worked crime scenes over my career when I felt for certain, the killer was still there, in the crowd, watching us. It's a sick voyeuristic thrill they get from watching us try to figure out what they did, who they are and why they did it.

"After a homicide, a shooter could easily set up on a rooftop or from a window and pick off you, me, Wendy or Carlos or the Lieutenant quite easily. I don't think it's likely, but it's possible none the less. This job we do is inherently dangerous. The best thing we can do is remain vigilant and learn to expect the unexpected. That's how my guys stayed alive in Iraq, and it is the best approach here in Nashville."

"You're right. You're usually right."

He held out his hands palms up as if to say, 'That's a surprise?'.

"I still worry about you," her facial expression turned sensual, "and I'd really like to kiss you right now and show you how much I care." She looked at all the cops walking by on both sides of the car headed to their own cars. "But, there are people here who may not understand."

"For that matter," Mike looked out at the crowd as if talking about nothing in particular, "if it wasn't for our fellow LEOs walking by, I'd throw you into the back seat, slowly remove your clothes, kiss every square inch of your body until your toes curl, and bring you to a point just short of losing your gorgeous mind."

Panting and obviously aroused, Carol looked at her watch, exhaled audibly and said, "I could call in; let them know I'll be a little late. We could be at your place in no more than ten minutes. It's easy from here. Just take Woodmont to a left on Hillsboro Road." She inhaled. "Whatdayathink?"

Mike started laughing. He covered his mouth and lowered his head. The cemetery was no place for laughter. "I'm sorry. I've got to get back to work on Tim's case and the one at the casket company."

"You know? You really shouldn't do me like this," Carol said with a serious glare.

Mike chuckled as they finally reached Carol's car. "I'm sorry. I didn't mean to—. What about a raincheck?"

"If you know what's good for you." She stared at him with a fabricated frown.

"I definitely know what's good for me. I just described it to you."

Carol nodded. "I'll see you later." She opened the door and climbed out.

Before she could close it, Mike said. "You bet you will."

Chapter 20

"Have you received anything back from the ATF on the two spent cartridges from Tony's place?"

"Nothing good," Wendy said. "The NIBIN search came back without any hits. The weapon the shooter used had no history in the database."

"Damn it. We needed that." Mike knew the unique markings on the brass were his best opportunity to locate the murder weapon.

"I know. Sorry."

"What about your vacuum's filter and the bark samples you found?"

"We're still analyzing, but so far we've identified bits of basil and oregano along with some fibers and GSR caught in the filter."

"Tony's cooks. Do you have anything definitive yet?"

"We know some of the fibers are cotton dyed dark blue and some are white 60/40 poly blend. They're all pretty short. The white fibers could be from the aprons Tony's guys wear. It's a common blend for work clothes. The fibers could have been transferred to the tree when they leaned against them during their breaks."

Mike immediately thought of the dark hoodie on the man Mrs. Jackson spotted and hoped it was the source of the dark fibers.

"The GSR is being tested by the TBI (Tennessee Bureau of Investigation) lab on their scanning electron microscope for percentages of antimony, barium and lead. With some luck, we may be able to identify a signature and match it to an ammo manufacturer, or if we have one, to a sample from a suspect shooter."

Mike wanted a suspect to test for GSR. He feared at this point, by the time he identified a suspect, there would be no residue remaining on him or his clothes.

"So, how did the analysis go on the hair you found on the tree?"

"If you have ten minutes, I'd like to show you something in hair analysis and also answer your question. This might even help some of your future investigations."

Mike checked his wristwatch. "Ten minutes? I'm game. Go for it."

"This," she tapped on a wooden case, "is our set of permanent specimen comparison slides from a series of one hundred and sixty-five different hair-producing animals known to be indigenous to our part of the country, the southeastern United States. Using these, we are able to determine, with a good degree of certainty, what animal provided the evidentiary hairs."

"Tell me you don't have to go through all one hundred and sixty-five slides every time you're looking for a match."

"For starters, we're not always looking for animal hair matches from a crime scene, so we only use this tool occasionally. And to answer your question, no thank goodness, we're able to narrow down the possibilities early on, thanks to our data from past cases.

"These twenty-four slides marked with the red trim on the ends, have provided eighty plus percent of our matches since I've been with the Nashville Crime Scene Unit, so we go to them first. If we can't gain a match there, we move on to what we call the bobcats, beavers, bison and bats."

"Bats? Bats have hair?"

"They're mammals." Wendy pulled a slide from the case labeled 'BAT' and handed it to Mike. "They have hair."

He held up the slide and squinted in order to examine a hair almost too small for him to see.

"Amazing. I feel like I'm back at UT Knoxville in Zoology 201."

Wendy laughed. "Did you pass?"

"Flying colors."

"I should have known. Let's move on to something I think you'll find even more interesting."

She handed Mike a paper evidence bag with a label telling him it contained hair evidence collected the night of Tim's murder at his crime scene. Next to the line marked 'Investigator' Mike saw his name. Inside the bag was the hair specimen Wendy had found caught on the bark warts of the Hackberry tree near Tony's Cafe.

"Recognize the contents?"

Mike looked inside the bag and then at Wendy. "Looks like the hairs we talked about—the ones I said looked like dog hair and you said you didn't think they were."

"Correct. So, why don't you check one against our set of slides and tell me what you think."

Mike looked at his watch again.

"Relax, we still have half of the ten minutes you agreed to. And, in the interest of time, I have set up one of those hairs here on the left stage of the comparison microscope. Now, using the slides I told you about, tell me which animal you think left us this sample of his, or her, hair."

"Uh—"

"I'll give you a hint. It's one of the twenty-four and since the specimen hair is rather large in diameter, you can narrow the possibilities down further using the naked eye."

Mike knew, for this to work he would have to pull out his magnifying specs.

"What are those?"

"These are my new eyes. Don't make fun."

"I'm not. In case you haven't noticed, I wear contacts myself."

"Okay." Looking through his glasses, Mike began his examination of the twenty-four high-probability options. "Looks like it could be one of these four larger hairs."

"Check them out against the specimen. You do know how to use the comparison microscope?"

Mike looked at Wendy over the top of his new glasses without commenting.

"The evidentiary hair on the left is at 260X."

"I can see that."

"Just trying to help."

He slipped each slide onto the matching stage across from the specimen and adjusted the magnification until the side-by-side images were clear.

"Well, you've looked at all four. Which one looks most like the specimen?"

"I'd like to say it's the dog hair #3 slide so I could be right, but I think it's the White Tail Deer."

"Thank you Zoology 201. We have a winner."

"So, if it's actually hair from a deer, how did it get on the tree, at that height, in the middle of a high-traffic area not far from downtown Nashville?"

Wendy shrugged her shoulders.

"I'd be willing to guess most people in this area of town have never seen a White Tail Deer, other than on television. And the ones who have seen one didn't see it in their back yard."

"Well, Sergeant Investigator, sir. I did my job by confirming for you what animal it came from. The question on how it turned up where we found it is, I'm afraid, yours to answer."

"Right again, and I have to get back to it if I'm going to be able to do that. Thanks, Wendy. You do good work."

"Good luck. Let me know if you need anything else."

As Mike left the Crime Lab, he couldn't help but feel anxious over the failure of the cartridges to produce a match from the ATF's NIBIN database. He was confident they were his best chance for a quick direction to take the case. This loss magnified the importance of all the other evidence they'd acquired. However, none of the remaining material evidence was offering him a clear direction.

Chapter 21

Peaceful Solace, LLC
Nashville

Mike watched the men and women of the night shift as they arrived for work. He knew the low slung Japanese coupes were generating all levels of throaty noise from their custom mufflers as their owners revved their engines in an attempt to impress their coworkers. From his position across the Cumberland River his binoculars gave him the full view of the facility, but without the sound effects.

He checked his wristwatch. He had eighteen minutes before his meeting with Elliott, Ross and the night shift supervisor. He left his current position and make his way back across the Korean Veterans Bridge and then east to the factory.

He turned into the company lot. It was 16:55. He parked near the rear of the building and walked in through the back entrance. He'd found throughout his career, doing unexpected things during his investigations frequently brought him unexpected results. As he rounded the corner of the building, he passed by more than a dozen young Latino men.

"*Hola,*" Mike said as he tossed his head back slightly.

None of the men returned his greeting. They only stared with questioning looks and added to the cloud of cigarette smoke encircling the area around the picnic table.

Mike walked past the red motorcycle, up the stairs and into the building as if he was an employee. Once inside, he scanned the shipping dock. In the distance he could see workers, no doubt day shift, collecting their belongings and lining up at the time clock.

The clock was mounted on the cinderblock wall beneath three bulletin boards, one with federally required documents posted in Spanish, one with documents in Mandarin and one in English. This seemed ironic to Mike since he wondered how many of the factory's workers were in the United States legally.

The people lined up to clock out gave him the same inquisitive looks as the group outside.

"Can I help you?"

Mike turned toward the voice to see a large bald man in jeans, a khaki work shirt with the short sleeves rolled up over his full biceps and wearing desert combat boots like the ones Mike wore in the Middle East. He was six foot one, maybe two, with muscled and tattooed arms folded across his swollen chest in an obvious attempt to intimidate. This display must have worked for him in the past. Mike was unaffected.

"I'm here to see Paul Elliott."

"He works up front, where you should have entered the building."

"I was running late and wanted to be sure I got in as soon as I could."

Ross gave Mike a look that said, 'Bullshit'.

"I'm Sergeant Mike Neal with the Nashville Police Department."

"I know. This way," Ross said, unimpressed. He started walking.

Mike fell in behind him and attempted to gather as much visual information as he could while the two men walked toward the company's offices.

Ross pulled open a black steel door and, rather than hold it for Mike, he walked through it and left it up to Mike to catch it before the hydraulic closer pulled it into him.

Nice guy.

Mike followed him down the hallway and turned left as they arrived at a cubicle area. It was the same area he'd passed through yesterday on his way to Elliott's office.

"Hello, Sergeant." Elliott stood as they entered.

"Is Mr. Puckett here yet?"

"We have not been able to reach him all day. We've called several times. We don't know if he's still ill, in the hospital, or what's the matter."

Mike looked from Elliott to Ross and back. "I need you to give me his phone number."

"Sure." Elliott picked up a sheet of paper and read the number for Mike.

Mike keyed the number into his cell phone and saved it. "I'll need his home address as well."

"I'll have to get it from Millie. One minute." He picked up the handset to his desk phone and pushed two buttons. After a brief conversation, he handed Mike a piece of paper with an address on it. "Here you are."

"Thanks. No one here has heard from him since he called in yesterday? Right?"

Elliott looked at Ross, who looked back and then toward Mike.

He shrugged his shoulders and said, "I haven't heard anything."

Mike stared at Ross for a moment. For years, he had dealt with people who were hiding information, acting as though they knew nothing. This guy was a classic example of the attempt, and the failure.

"Do you know if Puckett lives alone?"

"Millie says he's single," Elliott said, "but I have no idea if he lives alone."

Ross shrugged his shoulders, still striving to be of no help whatsoever.

"I'll be in touch." Mike turned and, without waiting for an escort, retraced his steps and walked back through the office to the warehouse door and exited the building the way he came in.

He knew Ross was following him, maybe ten or fifteen feet back. He could hear his heavy footsteps on the concrete behind him.

As he crossed the shipping dock, Mike saw on his left a large steel sectional door, much like the electric dock doors on the rear of the building, but this one was larger and mounted on an interior wall. There were tall stacks of empty pallets stacked in front of the door. This must be the access point for the facility's snake-ridden basement.

Mike called dispatch as he left the casket factory to request uniformed backup to meet him at the manager's office at Puckett's apartment complex. When he arrived, the officer was already there.

"Good evening," Mike said.

"How's it going? Curt Guidry." He said as the two men shook hands.

"We're about to find out, Curt. We're looking for a thirty-something man who lives here. I have no idea what he looks like. He's not answering his cell phone. He supposedly called in sick to his employer yesterday and failed to call or show today."

"Has this become a reason for police intervention?" Guidry asked with standard dry cop humor.

"It has when he's a suspect in a homicide investigation."

"I'd say."

"Let's get the manager to let us in."

The two men followed the signs to the manager's office. Mike pushed the door open. Seeing no one inside, he shouted, "Hello."

"Coming," came the response flavored with what sounded like a thick Spanish accent from the rear of the offices. A man who looked to be in his sixties stepped into the lobby. He appeared, at first, to be taken aback by the presence of the uniformed officer. "Hello, gentlemen. What can I do for you?"

"I'm Sergeant Mike Neal. This is Officer Guidry. We're looking for a Dwayne Puckett whose employer states he is leasing an apartment from you. Unit 19-B, I think it is."

"I will check. One moment." He stepped to a desk at the rear of the room and opened a black vinyl binder. After flipping through several pages, he said, "Puckett, Dwayne, Unit 19-B. You are correct. Would you like me to let you in?"

"If he is not at home, yes. We don't have a warrant, but under the circumstances, we need to determine if he is alive, safe or possibly in danger. It won't take but a few minutes."

"Oh, my. I hope he is okay," the manager said as he stepped outside.

"We do too."

"I am in this car here," the manager said, "If you would like to follow me."

Mike sat in Guidry's cruiser and the men drove past several buildings until they reached number 19.

The unit was on the bottom level in the rear of the eight unit building. The manager knocked. There was no answer. He knocked again.

Mike stepped forward and knocked firmly on the middle of the door. "Police, open the door."

There was no response.

"Open it."

The apartment manager checked the key ring and inserted his master key in the lock. As soon as the door opened, Mike took the manager's arm and pulled him back, away from the door.

"Stand over here, please." Mike brushed the right panel of his sport jacket behind his holster. "Dwayne Puckett? This is the police. We're coming in." There was no answer. Mike pulled his pistol from its leather holster and held it down at his side. As he stepped into the room, he brought the pistol up to a two-handed grip and began to survey the space along the pistol's iron sights. "Stay here. Cover the exit."

"Copy." Guidry pulled his Glock and stood in the doorway.

Mike moved through the front room, checking behind furniture as he went. He glanced into the small kitchen and quickly moved to the rear of the one-bedroom unit. The bathroom, including the tub area was clear. He looked into the bedroom before entering. It was a mess, much like the rest of the apartment. He flipped on the light with the barrel of his Glock and checked the walk-in closet thoroughly. He then checked behind and beneath the bed. Nothing.

"Clear," he shouted so Guidry could relax.

Mike returned his pistol to his holster and seized the opportunity to scan the bedroom for anything he could see that might be helpful to his investigation. The bed was not made and there was nothing on the sheets to indicate any struggle or other activity. It was difficult to determine the value of anything he was seeing, since so much of it looked to be trash or dirty laundry.

He stepped in front of the dresser. He wanted to open all the drawers and examine their contents, but he knew he could do it later if he needed to, after he obtained a search warrant. He looked in the smudged mirror at his reflection. His eyes moved to three photographs tucked into the left side of the mirror's wooden frame.

When he realized what he was seeing, he pulled his phone and tapped the camera app. He positioned the camera in front of the group and took a photo of the mirror with all three shots. He then snapped three close up photos of each one. When he'd finished, he checked the shots to be sure they were clear and then put his phone away.

He leaned over the dresser toward the photographs. Based on the surroundings in the images, the photos appeared to have been taken in the sewing department of the casket factory. Rows of women, sewing machines and frilly white fabric could be seen in the background. In the foreground, there was a petite and attractive young Asian girl. All three photos looked to be of the same girl. In two of the photos, she seemed unaware of the camera. In the third, the one near the top of the dresser's mirror, she was displaying a strained fake smile that said, 'take your picture and leave me alone'.

As he looked over the photos, his mind was bombarded with thoughts about Puckett, Lian Xiong, Ross and the entire odd group of folks at Peaceful Solace. He made one more pass through the small apartment.

He looked at Guidry and then the manager. "He's not here."

Chapter 22

Peaceful Solace, LLC
Nashville

Ross's cell phone rang, adding one more annoyance to his day.

"Yeah." Ross's aggravated tone made the single syllable sound like 'what the hell do you want?'

"What's got you so damned happy?"

"Nothing. What do you want?"

Briggs held his answer for a moment. "For starters, I'll take you with an improved attitude. You got a lot to be grateful for, but all I hear outta you is a grouchy-assed perspective every time I call."

"Give me a damn break. Would you?"

"I've been giving you breaks for a long time. I say it's time you give some back."

"You're not here fending off this pit bull homicide detective and putting up with Elliott's bullshit either."

"No. I'm not there in Music City USA, one of the most desirable destinations in the country. I'm in freakin' Bagram, Afghanistan, wearing kevlar drawers, dodging bullets and IEDs. I'm doing my damn job for the Army and for Uncle Sam. And on top of that, I'm locating arms wherever I can find them, to send to you so you can get them down to Central and South America so all the idiots down there can make us rich and do their best for population control by killing each other off. But, I ain't bitchin'. I'm doing my job and keeping my head down. So, why don't you give it a shot, Ross? What do you say?"

"Screw you."

"You see? That's what I'm talking about. Your Victor Ross visceral venom don't get you shit in the long run except the same thing thrown right back at you. Why can't you see it? It got your ass kicked out of the Army and, less than two years later, fired from a six figure job, likely the best paying gig you'll ever have with one of the premier private security companies in Iraq."

Ross held his response. He knew what he was hearing was not far from the truth, but he wasn't about to acknowledge it, not to Briggs. Besides, the episode Briggs was referring to was in 2006 when he was working for Leverage Security Group. And, it wasn't his fault.

He'd been working 14 hour shifts for over two weeks patrolling a supposedly strategic check point and listening to the irritating and unintelligible banter from the Iraqi's, both the Iraqi soldiers his team was attempting to train and the citizens moving through the checkpoint. He was trying to educate one group and simply communicate with and tolerate the other. Both efforts were failing.

It was late one afternoon after a day full of verbal confrontations and misunderstandings. Ross had been on duty going on twelve hours. A thirty-something Iraqi man approached the check point in a white Toyota Corolla at a high rate of speed. All these knuckleheads knew better than to approach a checkpoint at high speed. As he came closer, Ross thought he remembered him from earlier in the day. He looked like one of the troublemakers who started all the shit earlier.

Ross stepped into the middle of the roadway in front of the barrier with his left hand up indicating for the man to stop. He had his M4-M230 combination rifle-grenade launcher in his right hand and aimed at at the car which was still traveling at a speed which caused Ross to question the driver's intent.

Ross raised his rifle. With his thumb, he flipped the selector and fired one three round burst. As soon as he pulled the trigger, he realized he didn't have full control of the rifle's thermoset hand guard with his left hand and the rifle climbed out of his loosely cradled grip. The first round struck the ground below the car's front bumper. The climbing compound recoil elevated the barrel and sent the second round into the car's hood in front of the windshield. The third round, inches above the second, passed through the windshield and the front passenger compartment into the chest of the dumbfounded driver whose legs stiffened against the brake in response. The car came to an abrupt stop.

As the blood expanded across the man's thin khaki colored shirt, he placed his hand over the wound, pulled it back to look at the blood and then fell forward into the steering wheel. The horn blared, drawing unwanted attention to Ross who was still standing in front of the car with his weapon at his shoulder as if still prepared to fire.

All Ross could say was, "Shit—shit—shit." He walked to the car, grabbed the man by his hair and pulled him off the steering wheel and the high-pitched horn. Ross looked around hoping no one had noticed.

Iraqi's began running from doorways and climbing from every hole within a hundred yards in all directions. Men were yelling and women were screaming and crying. Ross stepped back from the car and, keeping his weapon horizontal, he walked away as if he knew nothing of what had happened. The people were shouting at him, no doubt calling him names in Arabic.

He keyed the microphone button on his radio as he continued to walk away from the scene. "Tac-two to base."

"Base, go ahead."

After a deep breath, he said, "We got an issue out here." Ross explained what had happened, laying full blame on the car's driver for not slowing and stopping in the manner he expected.

"Are you sure he's dead?"

Ross looked back at the crowd. "Affirmative. The Iraqis are loading him in the back of a truck now. I guess they're taking him to a hospital or something."

"Damn it, Ross." The radio was silent for a moment. "Do you have transport?"

"Affirmative."

"Use it. We don't need another Fallujah. Get your ass out of there now. See me when you get here. Out."

It didn't take much to get his commander, Art Railey, pissed off. Ross had a history of unwanted success in this area. The last time he was called into the head shed at Leverage Security Group, he was warned about the result of his next visit, should there be one. Looks like this could be what Railey was talking about.

The Iraqis subsequently put a bounty on Ross's head. Leverage, in order to avoid an expanding conflict and a media shitstorm, put Ross and his walking papers on a commercial flight back to the United States. In the end, Ross was not prosecuted, only terminated by Leverage.

"Listen," Briggs said. "You've got a tough box coming from Bagram with a false floor and a rear wall stuffed with all the AKs, M4s, and ammo in thick plastic bags we could get inside it. Do not screw this up. This one's a nice haul and the sergeant who owns the box has developed some potentially valuable connections here in Afghanistan. It could mean a monster supply for us in the future."

"When is it due here?"

"It's already on the way. Two, maybe three days, tops."

"I hope this son of a bitch detective is gone by then. Whose box is it, anyway?"

"Master Sergeant Hank Cody. It'll hit Fort Campbell and then be made available to him within 24 hours. You are already listed on the incoming docs as Cody's box hauler. Get it out of there before anybody gets nosey. He has your cell number, so be ready when he calls."

"Got it."

Chapter 23

Criminal Justice Center
Downtown Nashville

As he came down the stairs, Mike saw Meagan Slater pacing near the front entrance. She was, no doubt, an attractive woman and by Tim's own words, quite intelligent.

"Hello there."

Megan turned and smiled. "Hi, Mike."

He approached her and she opened her arms for a hug. "Did you find a good place to park?"

"Oh, yes. No problem there."

"I'm sorry to have to bring you all the way down here, but it usually works best in order for us to control the interruptions and such."

"It's no problem, really."

"Can I get you anything before we sit? A bottle of water, maybe?"

"I'd love one. Thank you."

"I'll get us both one up here." Mike started for the stairs.

He always used the stairs. He never asked anyone if they wanted to use the elevator. He knew if he started up the steps virtually everyone would follow and some would end up getting the most exercise of their day.

"Here we go." Mike handed her a bottle of water from the break room refrigerator and took one for himself. "We'll talk in here." He gestured toward a door across the hall.

He opened the door and held it for her. The room was small and bare with two club chairs and a small table. Megan sat, placed her water on the table and her purse on the floor.

"I'm sorry to have to do this so soon after Tim's funeral, but as a detective's wife, I hope you understand."

"Yes. It's okay."

"Let's talk about Tim's demeanor lately. Did he seem normal to you? Was there anything out of the ordinary in the way he'd been acting?"

She thought for a moment. "I can't recall anything. He was the same as far as I could tell. He was less energetic lately when he played with Sophia, but he had been to his doctor and he told Tim he had an upper respiratory infection. He'd been taking antibiotics and trying to kick it."

"Okay. In your discussions with Tim about his work or otherwise, did he mention anything new or odd which may have happened lately causing him any extra stress or concern? Or, were there any new names you hadn't heard mentioned before in recent conversations?"

Megan slowly shook her head. "Not really. Did you ask Dave Thurman about it? He spent as much time with Tim as I did and some days considerably more."

"Yes. All he could think of that might have bothered Tim lately was the news about Sophia's diabetes and your lack of knowledge about her family history on her father's side. Oh, and he also mentioned Judy."

"Judy. Now there's a reason for him to be stressed."

"Something tells me there's some indignation behind your statement."

"I'm afraid so. I've tried to be patient and caring and all those compassionate things for Tim's sake, but she has continued to take advantage of Tim's good nature ever since they divorced."

"What do you mean?"

"She calls him two or three times a week. At work, at home—she doesn't care. She somehow thinks Tim is still required to take care of her. If her faucet leaks, or an electrical breaker is thrown, or someone dings her car, she calls Tim to see what she needs to do, or more likely, what he can do for her. The woman is helpless."

"Wow. Tim should have shut her down a long time ago."

"I know. I tried to tell him the same, but—it was difficult. When their daughter, Becky was killed, I felt sorry for Judy. I held my tongue. Afterward, the social worker met with us and then met with Judy. When the judge gave us custody of Sophia and then allowed us to adopt her as our own little girl, Judy was devastated. I'm sure these are some of the things that drove Tim to want to be so patient and tolerate her clinging behavior."

"I understand his feeling sorry for her and being compassionate," Mike said. "It was his nature."

"Definitely."

"I have several fond memories of Tim, myself. You know he and I rode together several times when folks were on vacation or out sick for several days?"

"I didn't realize that."

"Yeah. He was a lot of fun. One of the best memories I have is a discussion he and I had at your house during your fortieth birthday party."

"Oh, really?"

"Everyone else was out in the backyard when Tim and I came inside to get more Jack Daniel's. We fixed our drinks and started talking. We ended up sitting in the den and chatting for quite a while."

"What were you two talking about for so long?"

"It started out as shop talk. I was interested in a case he was working and how they were getting it wrapped up for the DA. Somehow the conversation got around to talking about women, in general."

"Uh-oh."

"He was asking me how I had gone so long without getting hooked by some lady."

"Actually," Megan interrupted, "that's a question I had asked him about you. Several of the detectives' wives have been wondering. I mean, after all Mike. Look at you."

"What?" He looked himself over, knowing all along what she meant.

"You have virtually everything there is going for you. You're attractive head to toe, you're a gentleman and you're intelligent. You could have your pick of the eligible women in Nashville."

"You left out funny," Mike said with a dry expression.

Megan laughed. "Yes, and funny too."

Mike looked at his notes and intentionally avoided her question. "Getting back to Tim, I guess I danced around the answer long enough and he got impatient. He started telling me about how happy he was with you, how glad he was he'd found you at a time when both of you were ready for love and how important you were in his life."

Megan's face wrinkled and she reached for a tissue.

"He told me I didn't know what I was missing. He asked me how I dealt with the stress from our work without someone to love at home to share it with."

"I told him I had friends that help, but most of my stress monsters were burned up in the gym or during my runs. He agreed my method was good, but he assured me being able to talk out the job stress with someone who loved me, was totally different and much better. I knew he was probably right."

"He was," Megan said. "Did Tim ever tell you how we met?"

"No. I was going to ask you."

"I was working as a court reporter in Judge Abraham Stern's criminal court. There were two of us who shared those duties. The other reporter, Lynette Jarvis, came to me one day talking about this homicide detective who'd testified in the judge's court. She was beguiled by Tim's accent and his country gentleman ways. He was all she talked about for days. When the trial was over she did her best to talk him up and gain his attention, but sadly for her, he wasn't interested."

Mike was enjoying Megan's story and happy to see her smiling and talking about the man she loved.

"About three or four weeks later, I was assigned a criminal trial and was punching the keys on my stenograph when an MNPD homicide detective was called to the stand by the DA. The name rang a bell, but it didn't hit me until he walked in. This was the guy, the guy Lynette fell for. I had to smile when I saw him and thought about her dramatic display of spurned puppy love.

"This trial lasted almost a week and the DA wrapped it up with a settlement plea. When the judge adjourned court, I packed up my machine and stood to leave. That's when I heard the 'Hi.' I turned to see Tim standing behind me with his cute 'little boy' smile. He said, 'My name is Tim Slater.' I said, 'I know.' I typed your name, remember? He laughed and then I laughed. When he invited me for coffee, I accepted. That's how it happened."

"So, what did Lynette say when she found out?"

"Lynette was not happy. She asked Judge Stern to transfer her to another court. He did. I rarely see her anymore, but when I do, I can tell she hasn't forgotten or forgiven."

"That's a fun story," Mike said.

"Fortunately, Tim and I had a number of fun stories in our few years together. We enjoyed each other's company. We shared each other's joy as well as our pain. We had plenty of both. The joy seemed even better because of him and the pain seemed lessened for the same reason. So many memories."

"That's great."

"Mike, you never told me your answer."

"What answer?"

"The one to Tim's question at my birthday party. Why haven't you found someone and allowed yourself the chance at a shared and happy married life?"

As the detective, Mike wanted to claim the rights to asking all the questions because this was one he wasn't sure how, or if, he wanted to answer.

"You should be an interrogator."

Megan laughed.

Mike hesitated, but finally said, "You may not know this, but in the last twenty years, I've lost all of my family and several friends."

"I didn't know."

"It's been difficult. I lost my best friend to an ambush shooter in Iraq not so different from whoever killed Tim. He died in my arms. I couldn't save him. While still in Iraq and not long afterward, I received a call to come home. My mom was on her death bed with breast cancer. It had metastasized into her lungs. She wasn't expected to live out the week. She didn't. I went back to Iraq.

"The next year, my little sister Connie was raped and, along with three of her friends, brutally murdered while on a double date. She was seventeen."

"Oh, Mike. I'm so sorry."

He nodded. "I flew home to hear my dad's request. He wanted me to identify Connie's body for the police. I hadn't seen Connie in over a year. We'd swapped email almost daily. This was now to be how I would remember my only sibling the rest of my life." He shook his head. "It's still tough."

"Mmm." Megan shook her head.

"Ten years ago, after my father and I realized he and I were all each of us had left, we patched up our animosity and I moved him in with me. Then, one day I came home to find him dead in the shower. He'd fallen and struck his head. His dementia had been worsening, but he'd never have agreed to an assisted living environment."

"Mike, I'm so sorry."

"So, you see? I'm a bit gun shy when it comes to relationships. Frankly, I guess you could say I have a fear of losing people who are close to me. I watch daily as people suffer from the loss of their loved ones. Their sorrow keeps my own grief fresh in my mind; yet in a way, I think it helps me too. I'm better able to participate in their experience, understand their feelings and remain dedicated to helping them find justice.

"I see."

"I know you are quite capable of understanding my feelings about this, especially right now."

"Yes, I do. I understand."

"I know I'm being unrealistic to think I can avoid these losses in my life, none of us can. After all, death is simply a part of life." He paused. "I just don't like the hurt—when it gets in here." He tapped his chest with his finger.

Megan reached for Mike's hand and held it in both of hers. She looked at him with tear-filled eyes.

"Mike, there is someone out there for you, who wants to love you and build a family with you. The chance at a lasting and loving relationship and a full life together is well worth the risk. I don't regret a single moment I had with Tim. Not even one. And we will continue to love each other, and Sophia, until we're together again."

For years, he'd allowed his fear of more loss and hurt to trump his longing for a normal life. Megan's words made sense. But, he was still hesitant about exposing himself to the pain he watched others endure every day.

Chapter 24

Criminal Justice Center
Downtown Nashville

Megan descended the staircase to the lobby one step ahead of Mike.

"Judy," Megan said in a whisper over her shoulder.

"She's here to talk about what she may know to see if it can help us with the investigation."

"Megan," Judy acknowledged her as she approached.

"Hi, Judy." She turned quickly to Mike and spoke softly. "I enjoyed our chat. Let me know if there is anything else you feel I can help you with. And, thank you for your hard work and your support. Sophia and I appreciate everything you're doing for us."

"You're welcome." Mike held open the door for her. "I'll talk with you later."

"Goodbye."

The door closed behind Megan and Mike turned to Judy.

"I didn't know she would be here."

"Is there a problem?" He asked.

"No. I didn't know."

"We'll talk up here." Mike started up the stairs. He wondered why she would feel the need to say something like that. Maybe this was just the Judy that Thurman and Megan had told him about.

Mike couldn't remember when he'd first met Judy. It had been years and those years had not been kind to her.

"I'm not sure what it is you think I might know that could help you find Tim's killer."

"I'm not sure either. Most people know much more than they think they do about many things. Here we go." He gestured. "We're in here. Can I get you anything to drink?"

"I don't drink."

"I meant coffee, soda—a bottle of water."

"Oh. No."

"Okay." *She is definitely odd.*

Judy sat and held her purse in her lap with both hands as if she was afraid it might get stolen while she was in the Criminal Justice Center talking with an armed police detective.

"So, tell me a little about yourself. I remember when you and Tim were married. But, I don't know much about you since then. Where do you work?"

"I work for Kelly Equipment Company. I'm the office manager. I've been there almost ten years."

"You live here in town?"

"Yes. In the Berry Hill area."

"Can you tell me about your interactions with Tim over the last year or so?"

"We—we haven't exactly interacted. I've seen him a few times since our daughter's—funeral almost two years ago. But, I wouldn't call it interacting."

"Okay." Mike wanted to roll his eyes. "What were those occasions when you saw him or talked with him?"

Judy looked at Mike as though she didn't understand the question. She took a deep breath and exhaled. "I went to him occasionally when I was—having trouble, when I needed assistance or advice."

"What kind of assistance?"

"I'm really not sure this is any of your business."

Mike wanted to laugh, but he held back for fear it might be insulting.

"It's not. But, I'm not here to discuss what is *my* business. I'm here on behalf of Tim Slater and the citizens of Nashville to talk about *their* business. You're telling me you've gone to him for help, for assistance. I need to know what kind of help you're talking about. I need to know about anything related to the fact Tim was ambushed, shot twice in the chest and murdered.

"So, if you feel like I'm prying or being nosy, that's not it at all. I'm only doing the job I'm paid to do by the city, like Tim Slater would be doing right now if our roles were reversed and I was the one who'd been murdered.

"However, I want to find out who killed your ex-husband and why they did it because, beside the fact he was a sworn police officer deserving of my very best efforts, he was also my friend."

After a moment of thought, she said, "Okay."

"So, tell me what kind of assistance from Tim were you talking about?"

"Occasionally, I have trouble meeting my bills."

"Okay." He took notes.

"I have, on occasion, asked Tim for a loan."

"How much of a loan?"

Judy shifted in her chair and repositioned her purse. "I borrowed two thousand dollars from him."

Mike nodded and made more notes.

"Twice."

"Twice?"

"Yes. I asked him for it a third time, but he said no."

"What was this money for?"

She fidgeted again, and hesitated. "I have a brother who—who has issues."

"I thought you said *you* were asking for a loan, not your brother."

"Tim knew about Donny. He knew about him from when we were still married."

"So your brother has had this *trouble* since before your divorce?"

"Yes."

"What is his trouble?"

She looked up and then around the room. "Donny—is a gambler."

Mike stared at Judy. "A gambler?"

"He usually wins. Sometimes he wins big," she said in an obvious effort to convince Mike the issue was not so big.

"What do you call 'big'?"

"A few hundred dollars."

"And does he sometimes lose?"

"Yes."

"And sometimes he loses big?" Mike asked.

She hung her head. "Yeah."

"So, you're telling me you asked your ex-husband, a man who no longer had any responsibility to help you or your brother in any way, to finance your brother's addiction."

"What?" She sat up straight. "Donny's no drug addict."

"Gambling is as much an addiction as drugs or alcohol. How much of the four thousand dollars you borrowed did you pay back?"

"I was about to pay him something when he was killed."

It was all Mike could do to keep from saying, 'Of course you were'.

"So, you're telling me you had not paid Tim anything of what you owed him?"

She looked away. "No."

"Did Tim know what the money was for?"

She hugged her purse tighter and said, "I told him the first two thousand was to repair my car's transmission."

"And the second two grand?"

"Do we have to go through all this?"

"Yes. We do."

She shook her head slowly and looked at the floor. "I told him I needed it because my insurance wasn't going to pay all the cost of an operation the doctor said I needed. I told him I needed it for the deductible."

Amazing. Mike pulled in a calming breath and pushed back the words he wanted to say. He instead asked, "So, what happened when you asked him for the third loan?"

"He told me he knew what the money was for and he wasn't going to loan me any more."

"He found out?"

"Yes."

"He *was* a detective."

She sat, looking down. "He told me he was hurt I would have the nerve to ask him for money to finance my brother's gambling. The way he said it, he hurt my feelings."

"He hurt *your* feelings?"

"You asked him for money under false pretenses as if you

intended to pay it back. You repaid him nothing, and he hurt *your* feelings by refusing to give you more?"

"Ahh?" She was speechless.

Mike knew he'd already shown too much of his personal exasperation. It wasn't his place, but Tim wasn't here to do it and he knew she deserved to hear it.

"Tell me about your brother."

"What? What do you mean?"

"How old is he?"

"Thirty-two."

"Where does he live?"

"When he's in Nashville, he stays with me."

"How often is that?"

"Most of the time."

"Where does he work?"

"He's—between jobs right now."

"How long since he's worked?"

"He works periodically for a local agency."

"So, he's a temp?"

"He's trying out jobs to see what he wants to do."

"He's thirty-two and searching for what he wants to do?"

She tightened her lips and said nothing. Her look told Mike she realized how silly her excuses sounded.

"Does he have a telephone?"

"Yes."

"I need to speak with him. Can you give me his number?"

"Why do you need to talk to him?"

Mike forced his patience to absorb her naïveté. "To ask him some questions, like we're doing here, today. I thought we covered all this earlier?"

"He doesn't know anything about Tim or his murder. I haven't even told him Tim was killed. He's sensitive. He liked Tim."

Mike nodded as he wondered what else he would learn about Donny.

"Neither he nor you nor I know how much he knows. It's why we need to talk. So, please give me his phone number, so I can contact him and set up an appointment. Okay?"

She fished through her purse and brought out her cell phone. She scrolled a short list of contacts and gave Mike her brother's cell number.

"How well did Donny know Tim?"

"He knew him well. They did things together occasionally when we were still married. I have to admit." She paused. "Tim was good for Donny. Donny has never been the most mature man. He gets emotional sometimes and he's sort of selfish, I guess. Tim knew how to handle him better than I did back then, and still did for that matter."

Mike scribbled more notes. "Okay, tell me about the life insurance policy."

"What life insurance policy?"

"Attempting to be deceptive doesn't help. You know what I'm talking about. Just answer the question."

She sat, refusing to look at Mike. "What about it?"

"Judy, I already know the answers to many of the questions I've asked you today. I ask them for a number of reasons. One is to see if you'll tell me the truth. And two, I ask to find out what else I don't know. I need you to be a bit more forthcoming with your answers so we can move forward and hopefully uncover things that will help in the investigation. Can you do this for me?"

"Fine."

"So, the life insurance policy?"

"We bought it not long after we were married. When we divorced, my lawyer demanded I remain as the owner and beneficiary and Tim had to keep up the payments. Tim agreed."

"How much is the policy for?"

"One hundred thousand dollars."

Mike made notes.

"I know what you're thinking."

Mike finished his notes before responding. He looked up, anxious to hear what she knew. "You do?"

"You're thinking the insurance money was motive."

"Hmm. Actually, I hadn't gotten there yet," Mike lied. "But, since you brought it up, it is a potential motive since you are at least one of the individuals to benefit significantly from Tim's death, possibly the one who benefits most."

"I didn't kill him," she blurted. "I still loved him."

"That's good to know." Mike couldn't help himself. "Did Donny know about the policy?"

"Donny didn't kill him either."

"That wasn't my question." Mike stared at her. "Did he know

about the policy?"

"I'm not sure."

"That sounds an awful lot like a yes."

"He did not kill Tim."

"How do you know this?"

"He wouldn't do something like that? He's not that kind of person."

"Really?" Mike thumbed through the files he had on the table. "His record seems to tell a somewhat different story."

She was visually surprised Mike knew about Donny's past.

"In fact, it reflects a rather violent history."

"Donny is not a violent person."

Mike opened one of the files he had with him and thumbed through the pages to a form and read, "Did you feel this way on August 12 of last year when you made a 911 call to request the police come to your home to take one intoxicated Donald J. Knox away because he'd struck you? It says here, you told the officer you feared he would do it again and you couldn't control him. Your words."

"That was different. He'd been drinking then. He wasn't normally that way."

Mike wondered if she truly believed what she was saying or if this was only the pitch she was throwing at him.

"What about October 3rd of 2011 in Robinsonville, Mississippi when your brother was expelled permanently from the Galaxy One casino after a loud verbal altercation which ended with him climbing across a counter and taking a swing at a sports betting agent? How do you explain that one?"

She looked down and hugged her purse, without answering his question.

"What about January, 2012 in Metropolis, Illinois at Harrahs—"

"Okay," she shouted. "He's passionate about his gambling."

Mike almost laughed out loud, but he managed to remain professional and keep his response to himself.

"Passionate about his gambling? If your brother is passionate about his habit, he is most likely passionate about the money which allows him to feed his habit. This is where you, Tim Slater, and now Tim's life insurance, comes into play."

Her brow wrinkled and she looked Mike in his eyes.

"Tim was a source of funds for your brother's habit and you

were the vehicle to secure those funds. I'd say the two of you were somewhat important to Donny in his quest to maintain his habit. Who knows what a man might be willing to do to feed his addiction."

She stood. "I don't have to sit here and listen to you talk about me or my brother this way. I'm leaving."

Mike folded his files, placed them on the table and stood. "I'll show you out."

He walked the halls toward the staircase with Judy on his heels. When they reached the bottom of the stairs, he turned to her.

"Thanks for coming in," he said to her back as she passed him on her way to the door.

Chapter 25

Exposure Men's Club
Downtown Nashville

Mike's discussions with the ladies in the Peaceful Solace sewing department were marginally successful. Rather than wait to seek out a police department translator who spoke both Mandarin and Cantonese, he decided to see if there might be ladies in the sewing department who knew enough English to translate and answer a few questions about Lian Xiong and the women she lived with.

He met four of Lian's roommates who also worked in the sewing department. One of them was most helpful and her English was semi-intelligible. She explained Lian was young and shy and kept to herself most of the time, rarely speaking unless it was necessary. The roommate did, however, tell Mike that Lian's best friend was one of the other roommates. She told him her name was Mei Zhou and she worked at *Exposure*, a men's club near downtown.

As he drove toward the club, Mike thought about where he was with Lian's case. The Crime Scene Unit found nothing of value at the scene of the girl's murder. She'd reported to work on Monday evening and worked the first half of the shift without issue.

According to the other women in the sewing department, she did not go out, but always brought her lunch. She had apparently been killed somewhere on the premises at a time close to their nine o'clock lunch period and dropped at the dumpster. The act of placing her next to the trash was possibly a symbolic gesture of her killer's opinion of her.

Victor Ross was uncooperative. Elliott was of little use and her supervisor, Dwayne Puckett, was missing. Mike needed this roommate to share something in order to push him in the direction of her killer.

Inside the entrance to *Exposure*, Mike was met by a large man sporting a huge mustache and dressed in all black. "I'm Sergeant Mike Neal with the Nashville Police Department. I need to see Mei Zhou."

"Can I see your ID?"

Mike handed the man his badge wallet.

"Let me check to see if she's here yet." He returned Mike's wallet, turned and walked toward the rear of the club.

Mike scanned the large darkened room with matte black walls and ceiling. The raised walkways were lined with running lights along the edges, presumably so the girls would not fall off when they danced.

He watched the bartender as she restocked the bar and the beer coolers. He recalled the first time one of his investigations brought him inside this depressing dungeon.

Like so many others, a young girl from West Virginia had come to Nashville to make it in the music business. She was said to have possessed a beautiful voice. Mike didn't get to hear her sing.

When interviewed, the other dancers in the club at the time told him the money she brought with her from West Virginia ran out and she started doing something she knew how to do—dance. She was a cheerleader and a member of the dance troupe at her high school not so long before her trip to Nashville.

One night after she had been working at *Exposure* for a couple of months, she left with a man. Some said he was twice her age, clean cut, nice clothes, diamond ring. He'd been stuffing her garter with cash every time she danced close enough he could touch her. The bills were not singles. She couldn't help but be appreciative. It was in her upbringing, they said.

She was found less than two miles from the club in a respectable motel. She had been raped and beaten to death. The Medical Examiner stated her toxicology scan revealed Rohypnol, the date rape drug.

Her killer was still out there, possibly guilty of other such murders by now.

"Sir."

Mike's memories were interrupted. He turned toward the voice.

"Yes. Hello. I'm Sergeant Mike Neal with the Nashville Police." He handed her his card. "Are you Mei?"

"Yes. I am Mei."

"I'm investigating the murder of Lian Xiong."

She lowered her head. Her jet-black pageboy cut hid her face. She pulled out a chair and sat.

Mike did the same. "I understand she was one of your roommates?"

"Yes."

"Did you know her to date anyone on a regular basis?"

"No. Lian did not date. She was shy and afraid of the ugliness in the world."

The girl's accent was strong, but Mike had no trouble understanding her English words.

"She did not see anyone?"

"No. No one."

"How long did you know her?"

"Maybe a year. She moved in this time last year." The girl pulled a crushed pack of cigarettes and a plastic lighter from the pocket of the flimsy Oriental robe she was wearing. She lit the cigarette, held her head back and blew the smoke straight up as if trying to avoid having it bother Mike.

"She moved in as soon as one of the other girls moved out."

"One of the other girls?"

"Yes. They come and they go. Most do not stay for long, a year maybe."

"I'm told there are eight of you in the apartment."

She looked at Mike, took another drag on the cigarette, but said nothing in response.

Mike was suspicious these Asian girls could be involved in trafficking, but he had to move forward on Lian Xiong's murder before stirring up anything with the TBI.

"Is there anything you know about Lian that could help me find out who might have wanted her dead? Anything she may have said or done to indicate she felt someone was a threat to her?"

"Lian came home from work in the mornings. She slept in the day time and went to work at five o'clock in the evening. We had almost the same schedule."

Mike took notes.

"She did not go outside the apartment except to go to work. She was afraid of people she did not know." Mei sat for a moment smoking her cigarette. "Lian told me a few weeks ago, she was scared. I ask her why. She told me her boss at the factory would not leave her alone. She said he was always stopping at her machine and pressing her to go out with him. He made her nervous. She was afraid she would lose her job. She did not trust him." Mei looked up at Mike. "Lian was a beautiful little girl.

"She told me she may have to quit her job to get away from him. He was scaring her. I told her to go to the jerk's boss, but she said if she did, he would only get worse."

"Did she ever tell you her boss's name?"

"No." Mei shook her head. "She always called him her boss. I miss her. She was an innocent young girl." She took a long drag off her cigarette and stared off into the black distance.

Mike nodded.

"She was my friend." She turned to face him. "Can you find out who killed her? Do you think it was her boss?"

"We don't know yet. We're talking to the people who knew her and worked with her, hoping someone knows something."

"Find him, please? She was such a good person. She did not deserve this."

"We'll do our best. Thank you for your time."

She nodded.

Chapter 26

Marked Cruiser #1801
Nashville

Vincent Gordon had been a Field Training Officer for the last two of his eleven years with the MNPD. As an FTO, he had the opportunity to effect positive change on the new officers before they had a chance to develop their own collection of bad habits. He'd griped for years about the rookies hitting the streets too early, sorely unprepared for the changing world they agreed to protect and serve. He could now help them benefit from his years of experience and be better equipped to face today's growing challenges to all those in law enforcement.

Officers who'd been fortunate enough to have Gordon as their FTO knew how valuable those months had been as they were getting started and would continue to be throughout their career.

Gordon's current challenge was Alan Flowers. Rookie Flowers had graduated the academy ranked ninth in an small class of ten recruits. He was to be Gordon's biggest challenge to date.

Gordon knew early into Flowers's training, if this rookie was going to make it past Field Training, he would have to locate something deep inside himself capable of transforming a LEO wannabe into a man passionate about his public service. He felt

Flowers *could* do it, but he wasn't sure he wanted it enough.

On an afternoon two weeks ago a call came in to Dispatch from a concerned citizen who'd spotted a group of young men gathering on a street corner where drug sales were known to have been conducted. Flowers and Gordon weren't far away. They took the 10-78 call, possible criminal activity.

Flowers was driving when he abruptly turned onto a side street next to four young men standing on the street corner and talking.

"You might want to—."

"I got this." Flowers interrupted Gordon as he pushed the shifter into park. He threw open the door and, intent on impressing his FTO, he approached the young men.

"I think you guys need to move along. Your loitering here is disturbing the neighbors and you need to take this somewhere else. Okay?"

The men looked at Flowers and then toward each other. They looked back at him with confused looks.

"Maybe you didn't hear me." Flowers put his right hand on his Glock and his left on his Taser. "I said move along, *now*."

The men shook their heads and started to walk down the street away from Flowers, complaining as they went.

Flowers returned to the patrol car and took his seat behind the wheel. "Well. How'd I do?"

"Other than the fact our dispatched location is about six blocks that way and this corner is an MTA Bus Stop, I thought you did a good job of taking charge and convincing those young men to change their plans to take a bus."

The rookie's facial expression went from confident and proud to defeated in an instant. He sat for a minute looking down and likely feeling sorry for himself.

"What do you want me to do?" he asked with a look of total defeat.

"I want you to think before you act. You won't always have someone sitting next to you to tell you what to do. You won't always have a lot of time to think before action is required of you. This time, you had plenty of time to be observant and take in the situation. You didn't do it. You jumped to a conclusion without collecting any evidence, other than you had a group of men who resembled the dispatcher's call. Cops can't do that. We're not allowed the luxury.

"If you had been observant, you could have easily noticed the bus stop sign and the street signs telling you that you are not at the proper dispatched location. Being observant is possibly the best tool a cop has in his toolbox. It can save your life and possibly the lives of others. These types of situations are common. You will encounter them frequently. You must think. You must look. You must observe and interpret what you see. Assumptions are unpredictable. Do not act on them."

"I understand."

"I certainly hope so."

Since that event two weeks ago, Flowers had worked to improve his level of observation, but Gordon's concerns for the young man's chances remained.

"Thirty-nine," the radio barked after several minutes of inactivity.

Gordon held the steering wheel in his left hand and keyed his epaulet mic with his right. "Thirty-nine."

"We have a 10-64 at the Pulley Road NES substation near the intersection with McCrory Creek Road. Respond Code 2."

"Thirty-nine, 10-4."

"I haven't been on a dead body call yet," Flowers said.

"You won't be able to claim that after today."

Flowers took a breath, looked out the side window and exhaled slowly.

"How many did you say were in your class at the academy?

"Seventeen to start."

"How many of those are still with us."

"Ten, I think."

"A little less than sixty percent. Not the best percentage I've seen."

"Your class went to the morgue for an autopsy didn't they?"

"Uh, yeah."

"What does that mean? Uh—yeah."

"I, uh—tossed my cookies."

"Seriously? Oh, shit. When we get up here, do not stand behind me. Do you copy?"

"Copy."

"I just polished these shoes and I'd like to keep 'em clean. So, keep your distance."

Gordon's doubts about Flowers making the grade were mounting.

Gordon drove for close to ten minutes without a word from Flowers. The rookie's complexion looked like it had lost some color, but then it was normally pale.

"If my memory serves me, the substation is around this curve. There's the road." Gordon took the gravel road leading up the substation.

The smell of burned meat was in the air, but it was mixed with other burned odors that were less familiar and much less tolerable.

As Gordon drove, he tried to condition his rookie for what he was about to experience. "The smell of our burned insides, blood, guts and stuff, is worse than the smell of our muscles." Gordon glanced over at the rookie, knowing it was a burned human that had put a sustained wince on Flowers's face. He looked as if he would retch at any moment.

"Hey. Do not hurl in my car. If you do, I'll mark you low on all evaluation points and they'll wash you out before the week's over. Roll down the window and get your head outside, now."

Flowers did as he was told. As the patrol car shifted back and forth on the uneven gravel, Flowers's chin bounced on the car window sill adding to his queasiness.

When they reached the end of the gravel drive, Gordon spotted two pickup trucks. One was white with Nashville Electric Service markings and the other was a sporty red truck with high dollar wheels and a Tennessee vanity plate that read 'RELOADN'. Gordon ran the plate and then exited the car. Flowers hesitated, but followed his FTO.

"Morning. Jim Harrison, officers. I'm the one called it in. I live about four tenths of a mile up Pulley Road there. Power went out. Figured a dang varmint of some kind must have got in here like once before and arced the dang thing. Shut us down."

Gordon smiled at the old man's animation when he spoke.

"Had no idea it would be a dang copper thief. I thought that crazy stuff went away when the price of copper dropped back a few years ago."

"Maybe this fellow didn't keep up with the commodities section in the *Tennessean*," Gordon said.

"I'd say so. That there," the old man pointed, "is Herb Walters."

The NES man approached. "Morning officers."

"Good morning. What can you tell us so far about what you've found?"

"Well, I got the inbound power to the substation shut off, but he's still a cookin'. Might take a while for the body to cool down. A lot of damage." He rubbed his chest. "A lot of damage."

"Let's take a look," Gordon said after turning toward the rookie. "You up for this?"

Flowers shrugged. He still sported the winced expression and the pale complexion.

Walters led the officers through the gate and around the monochrome gray equipment to the spot at the rear of the substation where the intruder met his maker.

"As you can see, the chain link fence along the back has been cut to make a hole the guy used to get inside. His bolt-cutters are laying there, outside."

An eight square foot section of the fence had been cut away and bent outward to allow the intruder access to the substation.

Gordon walked closer to get a better look. Before he reached the body, he turned in response to the sound of Flowers projecting his pancakes through the chain link fence and onto the tall grass outside the substation's crushed rock base.

"At least you didn't do it on my shoes."

Gordon reached to his epaulet microphone and called in a request for homicide detectives. He kept his eye on Flowers in case there were any secondary tremors following the main quake.

"Go ahead and notify the Crime Scene Unit. The detectives will call them anyway when they get here. This will give the criminalists a little more notice."

When Gordon finished his radio call, he asked, "Flowers, are you back among the living yet?"

The rookie cleared his throat and spit. "I think so."

"You still look sorta green to me, so keep your distance. Let's go back to the car and see if you're as good at bringing up forms on the laptop computer as you are at bringing up breakfast."

Gordon glanced at Walters and winked to punctuate his attempt at cop humor. "Mr. Walters, if you would close the gate, I'd appreciate it. Touch it only on the chain links, please.

"Flowers, I'm going to stretch some crime scene tape and secure the area while you're starting on our favorite thing about being police officers—filling out forms."

Chapter 27

Charlotte Pike
West Nashville

The morning's first episode was a dispatch call on a body, female, black, twenties, five feet three or four inches, wild red hair matted with dried blood on the left side, apparent head injury or two, double dose of makeup, clothes half on-half off, no purse, no ID, some tattooing, discovered at the rear of a liquor store on Charlotte Pike by the manager as he was taking out the previous day's trash.

She was likely a prostitute who had a conflict with one of her business associates who took issue with something she said or did or didn't do and he chose the easy way out. Easy for him, anyway. He apparently pistol whipped her, ended the confrontation and moved on without concern. Now, the results from their hostile encounter was the newest addition to the day's task list for Detectives Cris Vega and Jerry Rains.

The two detectives were now front and center in hour number four of their investigation into the brutal slaying of another Jane Doe. They'd spoken with business owners and managers in the area surrounding the liquor store, shown the photo Rains took with his cell phone and uncovered nothing fruitful other than a few comments such as 'Yeah, I think I've seen her around'.

The detectives were now walking the residential streets of the area behind the commercial development where the liquor store was located. They were attempting to speak with folks who may have been in the area or who know something about this young woman and the ugly fate that took her. So far, they'd had no luck.

Several doors had gone unanswered. When Cris and Jerry knocked, they always held their badges up in front of them so the residents could see who was there. They wanted them to know, this pair was not selling, or buying, anything.

Cris insisted their response rate was increased by the fact that one of the plain clothes detectives, and always the one nearest the home owner's front door, was a woman. This fact still had not netted them any valuable information today.

Jerry was confident their response rate was diminished in this type of neighborhood by the badges they were holding up for the people to see through their peep holes. He'd told Cris more than once, if they would stand to the side and hold up a dime bag of grass, they'd get a lot more doors opened for them.

The door to their most recent attempt was opening. A stocky woman in a very large flowered house dress filled the opening and pushed out on the storm door. She held on to the storm door's handle with an unyielding grip. Her frown announced her intended level of cooperation.

"Yeah?"

With her badge still held out in front of her, Cris said, "Good morning, ma'am. Thank you for speaking with us. I'm Detective Cris Vega and this is Detective Jerry Rains. We're investigating a homicide which occurred last night near here. We were hoping you'd be willing to look at a photograph and tell us if you know who the young woman is."

"Uh, okay. I guess." Her exaggerated frown relaxed a bit as she looked beyond the pair and out into the street.

Rains reached his long arm forward with his over-sized cell phone in his hand. The photograph was on the screen.

"Oh! You didn't tell me she was dead in the picture. Oh. No. I don't know her." She shook her head violently and jerked the door closed in Vega's face.

Vega turned slowly to face Rains. "We're batting a thousand. With all this rejection, I think I'm developing a complex." She cupped her hand over her mouth and sniffed. "My breath isn't that bad."

Rains chuckled. "For sure. I can't remember when I've had this much fun," he scoffed as he followed her down the front steps.

"I hope the Medical Examiner's group can get us something—." Vega stopped when she heard her cell phone's chimes.

The detectives faced each other on the sidewalk.

"Vega." She stared into the distance. "Okay. Yeah. Yeah. No." She looked at her wristwatch. "Probably twenty to thirty minutes, depending on traffic. Okay. Got it." She ended the call and looked up at Rains.

"Well?" He asked with an anxious accent on the word.

"We have received a reprieve from our current exciting and highly productive investigation." Vega started walking back toward the liquor store where they'd left their car. "We have another body, an electrocution."

"Electrocution? Aren't those normally accidents?"

"This one is in the outer reaches of the Donelson area, at an electrical substation near the county line. The first officer responding is an FTO with his rookie in tow. The FTO has been around several years. He says he has serious doubts about it being accidental."

"Hmm. This one *has* to offer us a better chance at resolution than Jane Doe," Rains said.

"No doubt."

"But, I'm confident Jane will still be there waiting in the morgue when we're finished with the *shocking* new corpse."

"Dead hooker cases almost always seem hopeless. The lack of family or anyone to help connect the dots creates so many limitations. But, we don't get to give up easily. We're her only hope."

"You're right. As usual, you're right."

Vega patted him on the back. "Those are the two most important words you'll ever use."

Vega and Rains had been partnered for almost three years and were beginning to experience some of those long term partner events such as finishing each other's sentences and knowing when the other one is thinking about lunch.

Rains was ready to admit to anyone, Cris Vega was a damn good detective and a good role model for a young detective like him. He had learned so much from her during their time together. He'd readily admitted to Sergeant Neal, and to Vega herself, the thing he valued most from working with the two of them was the way they had helped him to become more compassionate and more thoughtful about the victims and their families, no matter their station in life.

The driving force, for him, was no longer about solving the puzzle and how he could be sure the killer received their just reward. Each case was about bringing the ugliest episode possible in a family's life to a conclusion that produced some level of justice for them.

He no longer believed in what some people called closure. Closure, in his mind, was not a realistic target. He didn't believe it was possible, or even desirable. Closure meant an ending and a moving on. The victim's family didn't normally want that. Frequently, they didn't want to forget *or* move on. They wanted justice. Some wanted revenge. Helping those families to obtain justice had become for him, as it was with Sergeant Neal and Detective Vega, his inspiration.

Chapter 28

Pulley Road Substation
Donelson Area

On the drive to the substation, Cris Vega spoke briefly on the phone with FTO Gordon about what to expect at the crime scene. He assured her the area had been secured and, despite their walk inside the fence, nothing was touched or disturbed other than the gravel and a small section of fence with the contents of the rookie's stomach. She offered her thanks for his ordering of the Crime Scene Unit and gave him her estimated time of arrival.

The trip up the gravel drive confirmed Gordon's warning of the scene's acrid fumes. When Rains had parked the car, Vega held out her jar of Vicks as she applied a small amount beneath each of her nostrils. He accepted the jar and gave himself a thin VapoRub mustache causing his dark brown lip to shine.

The classic salve with the strong menthol smell had been used for decades by detectives entering crime scenes where noxious smells, mostly from the putrefaction of the human body, were common and sometimes distracting.

As she approached the officers, Vega saw the thin plume of smoke leaving a black mass near the rear of the substation. She knew this had to be the victim.

"FTO Gordon, I'm Detective Vega and this is Detective Rains."

Gordon nodded, but failed to introduce Flowers. Vega suspected it was out of fear the pale young man might still have something left on his stomach.

"This older man up here," he pointed, "is the neighbor who found the victim and called it in. The other gentleman by the white truck is Mr. Walters with NES. He is the only person, other than the two of us, who has been inside the fence."

"Good. You guys can stay here. We'll talk with Mr. Walters and then get a closer look. Why don't you check on the CSU and see when we can expect them."

"Will do." Gordon motioned for Flowers to follow him back to their cruiser.

"Mr. Walters?"

"Yes, ma'am."

"I'm Detective Cris Vega. This is Detective Jerry Rains." Both flashed their badges.

"Good to meet you."

"Tell us what you can determine as facts about what has happened here."

Walters went through the short list of known events from the power outage and his call up to exactly what he found on his arrival at the substation.

"What do you think about all this based on your experience?"

"Well. I don't think this fellow could have had much expertise harvesting copper out of substations. Normally, when we find thieves have entered a substation like this, we see missing ground wires. This is the source of copper easiest to harvest and least likely to do this kind of damage." He gestured toward the body. "There are lots better places to find copper than a substation. And, they're much less dangerous. Forget the fact it's against the law."

Cris nodded her head and turned to Rains. "Let's walk around the outside of the fence and see what we can determine without entering the substation."

"You might want to keep an eye out for the young man's breakfast there outside the fence."

"Thanks for the warning," Rains said, as he raised the crime scene tape for his partner.

Vega and Rains tromped through the tall grass a few feet out from the chain link fence. When they'd reached the area near the body, Vega covered her nose and mouth with her left hand holding in the menthol aroma and hopefully blocking out the stench.

"Whew. That's pungent."

Rains nodded as he also covered his nose.

"I've never seen anything like this." Vega squatted close to the fence. "The current has consumed his chest cavity from his collarbone down to his abdomen and the internal organs as well. The continued flow of high voltage power must have simply burned up his thoracic area."

"Look at the position of his hands and arms," Rains said.

"I know. If he was attempting to steal the copper, his hands would have likely been the first part of him to contact the juice."

"Even if he'd tripped and fallen, his hands would have been out to catch him. It's a self-preservation reflex."

"His hands should be under him and based upon the way his chest looks, his hands would have been burned off. Instead, his hands are by his side, away from the current and still intact."

"Even if he was pushed into the power," Rains said, "he would have reached out to catch himself."

"Unless he was unconscious at the time."

"And thrown onto the power," Rains added.

"In an attempt to cover up the fact he was already dead?" Vega speculated.

"That's my guess."

Vega stood. "Let's get a look at the truck."

The detectives approached the officers as they were leaning against their cruiser.

"Can I assume you ran the vanity plate on the pickup?"

"Yes ma'am. The search said it belongs to a Dwayne Puckett."

"I'm going to take a look inside the cab while we're waiting on the crime scene unit."

She pulled on a pair of nitrile gloves and gently opened the passenger side door. Without climbing inside, her visibility was limited, but her eyes caught sight of something easy to see. She stared at the lanyard hanging from the truck's rearview mirror to be sure of what she was seeing. She backed away from the truck and pulled out her cell phone.

Chapter 29

Criminal Justice Center
Downtown Nashville

Mike was reviewing his notes from his interviews with Megan and Judy when his cell phone rang. He was focused on the data Tim's two wives had shared with him and didn't want to be interrupted. He chose to let the call go to voicemail and call them back later.

When the phone rang again within seconds of the previous call, he considered it might be important. He checked the display to see who it was.

"Hey, Cris. What's up?"

"Mike, the case we talked about after the funeral home the other night involving Victor Ross. What was the strange name of the company you said he worked for?"

"Peaceful Solace."

"That's what I thought. I'm at a crime scene in the eastern reaches of the county where we have what looks to be a male victim who has been electrocuted at a substation on Pulley Road. The body has been badly damaged by the electrical current."

"Workplace accident?"

"Not a chance. The vehicle at the scene is a large red pickup truck and it has an employee security tag on a lanyard hanging from the rear view mirror. The employer is Peaceful Solace."

Mike's adrenaline shot up. "What's the name on the tag?"

"Puckett, Dwayne Puckett."

"Shit. I'm on my way. Freeze the scene. Don't let anyone do or touch anything."

"Got it."

Mike left his desk as it was and hurried to his car.

The limestone rocks banged against the car's undercarriage like a machine gun as Mike impatiently accelerated up the substation's inclined gravel drive. He parked and scanned the area outside the fence. The Crime Scene Unit was there, but Vega had instructed them to stand down until he arrived and gave them the go ahead.

"What's our status?" He asked Cris as he climbed from the car.

"CSU is on hold, but ready to go through the truck on your call."

"Let me take a look," Mike said, as he stepped toward the truck.

He pulled a pair of nitrile gloves from his jacket pocket and wiggled his fingers into their respective positions until he had them on. He approached the truck's passenger side. After opening the door with two fingers, careful not to touch printable surfaces any more than necessary, he pulled the door until it was open to its widest point.

He stepped toward the door's threshold stopping short of his shins touching the truck. From this position he was able to lean his body into the cabin for a cursory inspection without touching anything inside.

"Did you see those?"

"What?"

"Blood spatter, there, about midway of the bench seat and again here on the passenger's seat belt."

"Cris craned her neck, but couldn't see from her position what Mike was talking about."

"I didn't see it. As soon as I saw the security access tag from the company, I backed out and called you."

"No problem." Mike kept scanning the truck's interior. He pulled out his small, but exceptionally bright, LED flashlight and shined it down onto the floor. "There could be more blood down there on the carpet. He may have been killed here in the truck or maybe earlier and placed in the truck for the trip here."

Mike held his flashlight so the beam shown across the surface of the floor mat from the threshold creating oblique lighting, meant to accentuate small items protruding up from the mat's surface. He then held the light in a position to create the same effect across the bench seat. He oscillated the beam from side to side. He turned back to Cris and Rains.

"I'm pretty sure we have some soil on both sides of the floor mats. The seat has several hairs, and possibly some fibers too. Let's make sure the criminalists know about these and collect them for analysis."

"Copy." Cris made a mental note.

"Also, be sure they collect prints from the steering wheel and gear shift, as well as interior door handles and any push buttons on the dash. I have my doubts our victim drove here, so check for prints on the rear view mirror and the buttons for side mirror adjustment."

"Got it." Cris made notes on her pad, this time.

"Okay. Tell the CSU to get started on the truck and let's get a look at the body."

Mike ducked under the yellow tape and started for the back of the substation fence while Cris spoke to the criminalists. He followed the trampled path made earlier by Vega and Rains.

Mike covered his nose and mouth with his hand. He stepped along the outside of the fence inspecting the body from different angles.

"What a mess. He had to be unconscious, maybe dead, at the time he went onto the current. He would have tried to catch himself otherwise."

"That's what we thought," Cris said as she caught up with Mike and Jerry. "Jerry and I think there's a good chance he was killed and thrown onto the current in an attempt to burn the body and cover up the murder."

Mike squatted and Vega followed suit.

"I wouldn't be surprised. I only hope Dr. Jamison has enough of him left to work with in order to determine what happened. Little of his ribcage is there anymore. He's missing a quarter to a third of his body mass. But, it looks like we'll have fingerprints to confirm his identity. This is—unreal."

"Do you have any ideas about who could have done this?" Vega asked.

"Yes. I'm almost certain of it. But, proving it now," he pointed at the body, "could be difficult, unless CSU can locate some definitive trace evidence in the truck or around the area here." Mike continued to inspect the body. "I'll try to remain hopeful. Keep the gate closed until the ME's team gets in here. I don't want to take any chances on losing any more parts or pieces of our friend here."

"Copy that."

"Also, tell the criminalists to pull soil samples from several areas around the truck and the substation and especially in the area behind the opening in the fence. And be sure they check this entire area back here for shoe and tire impressions, especially motorcycle tires."

Chapter 30

Criminal Justice Center
Downtown Nashville

Mike was reviewing some searches from NCIC and the MNPD databases when he received the call from The Bubble. The enclosed location in the center of the CJC lobby where the guards were based, in a way, resembled a large bubble with windows. Hence, the nickname.

"Sergeant, you have a guest in the lobby."

"Thanks. I'll be right down."

As he walked the hallway toward the stairs, Mike considered Donny Knox was at least getting off on the right foot by arriving at his appointment on time.

Mike looked around and then crossed the lobby to a rather small man in jeans and a plaid shirt. He was sitting on one of the wooden slat benches lining the walls on either side of the entrance. His hands were on his knees and his nerves had both his legs bouncing. This had to be Knox.

"Mr. Knox?"

"Yeah." He looked unsure of what to do. He was slow to stand.

"I'm Sergeant Mike Neal." Mike offered his hand.

Knox hesitated, then held out his hand as if he was fearful Mike would clasp a handcuff over his wrist. Knox failed to exchange a handshake grip. Mike recalled the old adage, 'Like shaking hands with a fish'.

"If you'll follow me please. We'll talk upstairs."

Knox appeared uncomfortable. The weak handshake told Mike a lot about him. He climbed the stairs consistently six to eight steps behind Mike. His head, with his greasy hair, looked like it was on a swivel, as he checked out everything within his line of sight. His behavior reminded Mike of someone who'd recently been released from prison and was amazed at all the changes since he went in.

"We'll go this way." Mike pointed. "Would you like something to drink?"

"Huh?"

"A drink. Would you like a soda or bottle of water, coffee?"

"Uh, no. Caffeine gives me the jitters."

"We'll talk in here." Mike stepped into the interview room where he'd left a stack of files.

The men took their seats facing each other.

"So, tell me about yourself, Donny. Are you from Nashville?"

"Uh, no. I grew up in Kentucky."

"Where did you go to college?"

"I didn't."

"What did you do after high school?"

He shrugged. "I worked for a while with a company doing data entry."

"Did you like that kind of work?"

"Yeah. I did. I didn't have to talk so much with people."

"You like working alone?"

"Yeah."

"Why do you think you like it, Donny?"

"What? Working alone? I don't know. I don't like a lot of people around. I like it when it's quiet. I don't like when people talk loud, laugh a lot and yell at each other. I like computer work. It's quiet."

"Good. We need folks who like that kind of thing. There's a lot of computer work to do nowadays, isn't there?"

"Yeah."

"What do you like to do on the computer, Donny?"

"I like to play games and gamble."

"Really? Tell me about it. I don't know much about gambling online."

"Well. You can do on the computer almost anything you can do in a casino without all the noise and the people. You have to know the right websites to go to."

"Sounds interesting. Where do you get the money to make your bets, since you're on the computer and not handing anyone any cash or using chips?"

"You use credit cards."

"You have credit cards? I thought you had to have a steady job to get a credit card? Do you have a job?"

"I work for an agency. They send me out to work whenever I call them."

"When you want to?"

"Yeah. Some days I don't feel like working."

"Really? What is it you do on those days, Donny?"

"I usually gamble some on those days."

"I guess this takes us back to the credit cards, huh? Where do you get them?"

"I use my sister's cards."

"She doesn't mind?"

"I pay her back when I win."

"Do you win very often?"

"Yeah." He looked away as he answered, confirming the likelihood his response was a lie.

"Do you lose very often?"

He hesitated. "Sometimes." He hung his head.

"Did you go to work this past Monday?"

"Uh, I don't think so."

"You don't know, or you don't remember?"

"I didn't work Monday."

"Donny, where were you Monday evening between eight o'clock and ten?"

He thought for a moment. "I was at home, on my PC checking on the horses at Keeneland in Lexington. Judy will remember. I like to go to their website on Mondays. I've even been to the track. The atmosphere is interesting and it's not so loud there, at least not until the horses come across the finish line. Then some folks yell because they won, and some yell because they lost."

"So, you like to gamble on the horses?"

"Yeah. They're so beautiful the way they run. You can win some decent money with the horses, sometimes."

"I've never done that. Tell me, what happens when you lose and you don't have enough money from your winnings to pay back your sister?"

He looked down. "She gets upset with me when the credit card bill comes."

"So, she has a big bill to pay because of your losing. Right?"

"I guess so."

"How do you feel when she gets upset with you?"

"I don't like it." He spoke up with an irritated tone. "I don't like it when she gets mad. It makes me mad."

"Really? You get mad at her because she wants you to pay a bill you created and for which you owe her?"

"She wants me to stop gambling."

"I can understand why. You're asking her to foot the bill for your habit, aren't you? Isn't that what you're doing?"

He looked at Mike with anger in his eyes. He leaned forward. "I'll pay her back."

"Unlike your sister, the credit card companies don't take IOUs. She has to pay them when they want it or she gets in big trouble."

"You sound like her." Donny's face was wrinkled and he began breathing heavily. "Stop yelling at me."

"I'm not yelling at you Donny," Mike said softly. "I'm simply telling you what you need to hear about the way you are mistreating your sister. She deserves better than this. Aren't you living with her most of the time?"

"Yes."

"Isn't she buying the groceries, paying for your Internet and paying the mortgage? Isn't she taking care of you?"

"I guess so." He looked at Mike beneath a wrinkled brow.

"You might want to think about getting a steady job and start paying her back for her generosity. I'd say you owe your sister that much."

Knox squirmed in his seat. "Are we finished?"

"No, Donny. We're just getting started."

Chapter 31

Peaceful Solace, LLC
Nashville

Ross looked at his vibrating phone. He'd turned the ringer off earlier when he became irritated by it. Briggs was relentless. Ross decided he may as well answer it. The guy wasn't going to stop.

"What?" He could hear Briggs angered breath blowing into the phone.

"What the hell is wrong with you?"

Ross pushed his lips together to avoid offering an answer.

"Are you incapable of doing what you've agreed to? Has this become so difficult, you can no longer manage to pull your end of the agreement?"

"I'm doing my damn job. What's *your* problem?"

"What's this shit I'm hearing now about you selling to gang members?"

"What?"

Obviously without Ross's knowledge, Briggs had a connection with someone there in Ross's group. Otherwise, he had no way to know about this.

"You know what I'm talking about. And I know all about it. You're selling guns to the damn gang bangers. And since I'm just now hearing about it, I have to assume you're trying to keep all the proceeds and screw me out of my share. Am I right?"

"Wrong. You didn't know about this because it doesn't involve you."

"What's *that* supposed to mean? Doesn't involve me? Since when are you doing shit that doesn't involve me?"

"I started my own business with my own money. It ain't got nothing to do with nobody else but me."

"Please." Briggs laughed. "Won't you share with me what this is all about?"

Briggs's laughter was pissing off Ross.

"Seriously. I want to know."

Ross hesitated, but finally began, "Our straw buyers who've been buying AR15s, AKs, shotguns and other long guns for us at all the gun shows in Tennessee, Kentucky and around here, started coming back telling me they had met independent individual sellers with large quantities of semi-autos and large caliber revolvers. They told me these guys were complaining because we weren't interested in their handguns.

"So, I told them the next time they were approached, buy some of the guns, as long as they're in good condition and 9mm or larger. The next team came back from their show with 35 pistols and revolvers they'd bought from individuals, not gun dealers. Some were bought for less than half what I can get for them. The next gun show brought in 23 more. So, all the straw buyers, in addition to buying our rifles, started buying pistols and revolvers for me using *my* money, not yours."

"Hmm." Briggs grunted.

"I couldn't care less if you're impressed or not. Like I said. This shit ain't got nothing to do with you."

"I can understand you think your little enterprise has nothing to do with me, but once again, you're wrong. Anything you do exposing you or our straw buyers to the risk of being caught by the authorities, involves me because it also risks exposure of my involvement with you."

"Well, you're crazy if you think I'm gonna stop. This stuff is too profitable."

"It's also too dangerous. You're dealing with people who cannot be trusted. These are not business people with ongoing business interests, concerns and risks. Surely you know this. They know where you are and how to get to you. It puts you, and ultimately me, at extreme risk."

"They don't know where I am or where the guns are coming from."

"How the hell do you make that work?"

"See? You don't know everything, smart guy. The gang I'm selling to isn't even in Nashville. They're in Memphis. They're bigger and they got more cash. All they know about me is they text their order to a blind cell phone number and within a week they wire my money to a numbered account and then they get their guns. First time I don't get my money, they stop getting guns. Too easy."

"Got it all figured, do you?"

"You're pissed cause it ain't your idea. It's working."

"That's debatable. This gang in Memphis, you say they're big? Into a lot of shit and got a lot of money?"

"Yeah. That's right."

"You ever hear of the Mongols Motorcycle Club out of California?"

"Yeah. I heard of them."

"Well, they were into some serious shit like these guys you're dealing with. Big time enterprise—drugs, guns, protection, you name it. Guess what?"

Ross said nothing.

"They were infiltrated by an ATF agent and when he was done 53 of them were convicted of everything from the possession and sale of narcotics and illegal guns to rape and murder. You sure this big time gang you're working with is secure and they're not putting us at risk?"

Ross was quiet.

"I don't think you have any way of knowing if they're secure or pose a risk. I don't think you've done your share of due diligence. Therefore, you can't be sure of anything. So, once we move the inventory you have there now—we're done. Understand? You and I are finished. I can't afford your kind of risk." Briggs disconnected the call.

Ross sat back in his chair. Briggs brought up some things he hadn't considered, things which could blow everything up. Maybe he was right. Maybe it was time to wrap it all up and take off in a different direction. Things were getting hot in Nashville.

Maybe it was time to head back north, back toward home.

Chapter 32

Criminal Justice Center
Downtown Nashville

"So, Donny. Tell me what you know about Tim Slater."

"He's a cop. He's my sister's husband—was my sister's husband."

Mike's radar went up when Knox used 'was'. Judy said Donny didn't know about Tim's death.

"They got a divorce, a while back."

"Yes, they did. How long since you've seen Tim?"

"It's been a long time. I didn't like it when they got a divorce. I like Tim. He's always nice to me. He's the one who took me to Keeneland racetrack, the first time, to watch the horses run. We had fun. We left Judy at home. We had so much fun."

"It sounds like you and Tim got along well."

"Oh, yeah. He's a nice man. I think he got tired of my sister's complaining, always unhappy about something. She can be a real bitch sometimes."

"Really?"

"Yeah. Tim used to tell her, she needed to get me some help with my gambling and my anger problem. I can't help myself sometimes." Donny looked down. "I heard Tim tell her. He said, 'Donny needs professional help'."

"Tell me about your anger issues."

"Well. Sometimes I get mad when people get upset with me and start yelling. I don't like it when people yell. Sometimes I get so angry I start yelling back and then it all gets worse and—and then I get in trouble. I don't know why I do it. I—I just don't. I can't help myself."

"Did you ever get mad like that at Tim Slater?"

He hung his head. "Only once. He was trying to get me to calm down after Judy and I had a fight. I didn't want to calm down. I was mad at her. I got mad at her a lot during the time of their divorce." Knox hesitated. "He was trying to talk to me and I hit him. I didn't mean to. I couldn't help it. He was trying to hold me and I—I screwed up. I hit him. I was so stupid."

Mike could see the tears forming and they finally ran down his cheeks.

"Tim stood there. He didn't hit me back. I wished he had. He just looked at me. I ran away. I didn't want to take a chance on hitting him again. He was good to me." He cried.

"Did you come back?"

"Not right away."

"When?"

"When I calmed down later, after dark. I was ashamed of myself. I didn't want to see him. I didn't want him to be mad at me. I wanted to apologize, but I was afraid. A few days later, he came to talk with me. He said—he said he forgave me. He said he understood I had a problem. He told me I needed to get help. He said he wasn't going to be able to stay with me and my sister and Judy was going to have to get me some help. That was right before he moved out."

"Did your sister check into getting you an appointment with someone who could find out about your issues and help you?"

"No. She said there was nothing wrong with me." His forehead wrinkled again. She said I was only being selfish and irresponsible. And besides, she didn't have the money to pay for that kind of useless crap."

"She doesn't have the money to pay your gambling debts either. Donny, based upon what you've told me today, you may have what's known as Bi-Polar Disorder."

"I've heard of it. I think it was Tim who said he thought it might be my problem."

"I know a doctor over at Vanderbilt Medical Center who works with people who have issues like yours. If I can get you an appointment with him, would you be willing to talk with him for a few minutes about how you feel?"

"How am I supposed to pay him? I don't have enough money, and Judy won't pay for it. She's already said it."

"Donny, I almost forgot to ask you. Did you know your sister has a life insurance policy on Tim?"

"Uh, I think I heard her say something about it one time when she was talking to her lawyer during the divorce. She told him," he stopped, recalling what happened, "she wanted it even if she didn't get anything else. That was it."

"Okay. Is that all she said about it?"

"Yeah. I think so."

"Do you know how much the policy was for?"

"No sir."

Mike was a pretty good judge of body language and the tells cops look for in liars. Donny looked to be telling the truth.

"I think I can get the doctor to talk with you the first time or two without a charge. There may be some programs he knows about which could help you take care of the charges."

"Do we have to tell Judy about this?" He pleaded.

"I don't think so. Not at first, anyway. Let's see what he can do to help you, then we'll talk about who needs to know about it. Okay?"

"Okay. Can you do me a favor?"

"Sure."

"Can you tell Tim the next time you see him. He'll want to know I'm finally gonna get some help."

Mike closed his notebook and laid it on the table. "Donny, there's something I need to explain."

Chapter 33

Criminal Justice Center
Downtown Nashville

Mike knew, if he was going to resolve Lian Xiong's murder, he needed to find out more about the illicit activity going on inside the casket factory. Both the Latino population and the Asians, even the ones residing here legally, were skeptical about sharing anything with the police. The law enforcement agencies in many of their home countries were tainted with corruption at virtually all levels. Cooperating with the police was not something that came natural to these people.

With Puckett dead, Mike was confident his best chance to find out the truth was gone, parked on a cold stainless steel gurney at the county morgue.

Each time he was asked, Paul Elliott acted as though he was oblivious to anything happening at the shop floor level of his company. Victor Ross wasn't about to divulge anything to anyone, intentionally or otherwise.

When it came to collecting covert data from inside any nefarious group in Music City, Mike knew his best chance always began with a call to his most reliable confidential informant, Orlando Reese. Lando had connections. He had experience. He had methods. He had ways to get to the people who knew things and ways to find out what they knew. He was good at what he did. Lando was an information broker and well worth what he cost.

"It's yo nickel, homey," Reese said, answering his phone.

"Lando."

When he heard Mike's voice, Reese must have pulled his phone away from his head and looked at the display. "Wait a minute. Is this who my cell phone tells me it is?"

Mike laughed and let Lando be himself.

"Is this the famous Sergeant Po Po of Nastyville, Tennis Shoe? What's up, Sarge?"

"Hey, Lando. How's the high life?"

"How the hell would I know?"

Mike laughed. "I thought you were still one of the major players here in the Musical City."

"Shiiiit, man. There was a day when what you say was the gospel. Man, I was filet mignon in a Vienna Sausage world. Mm, mm, mm. Those were the days."

"And it's not like that now?"

"Watchutalkinbout, man? Everything's saggin'. I'm startin' to get gray hair. I have to put Grecian Formula on my hair and my whiskers so I can go out on the street without hearin' derogatory critiques from the brothers *and* the sisters."

"It's a cruel world, Lando—a very cruel world."

"You ain't lyin' cuz. It's gettin' tight out there."

"It looks like my timing may be good for you."

"Yeah? Lay it on me."

"You'll be glad to know; I have a job for you."

"Praise be. That good green city money is some sweet stuff."

"You get me what I need and I'll get you what you want," Mike promised.

"Music to my ears. We got us a deal, my brother. What is it you need Lando to find out for you?"

"Do you know anything about a place down by the river on Visco Drive called Peaceful Solace?"

"Peaceful what?"

"Solace."

"Is it a new nightclub? One I haven't had the pleasure to visit yet?"

"I'm not sure you want to visit this place."

"Oh? Why zat?"

"It's a burial casket company. They make caskets. You know, coffins."

"Oh, that's some creepy shit, man. Whatchu got yourself into that involves a casket company anyhow?"

"A young Chinese girl was murdered in their parking lot. She worked there at night."

"Mmm. What is it you need me to find out? Want me to find out who killed her?"

"I have a line on that now, but I need more to lock it down. And, I'm pretty sure there's more going on in the factory than people building caskets. There's either a drug operation or maybe human trafficking to stock the place with workers, or both.

"Almost all the employees behind the front office are either Asian or Latino. There are too many and there's no way they're all legal. Impossible. Also, I'm interested in knowing more about a big bald headed American who works there named Victor Ross. I'm suspicious he's involved in whatever questionable activity is going on there."

"Okay. I know a guy who does business with a lot of the Latino and Asian folks in town. He hangs with a group of Asian car freaks. He does a lot of those car conversions for them. He may know somethin'."

"More than half the cars in the parking lot at this place are customized, lowered with performance mufflers and such."

"Sounds like his kinda stuff. He works at one of the Honda dealers in the daytime and runs his own conversion shop out of his garage at home."

"As always, stay discreet and you don't know me. You copy?"

"10-4, Sarge. I won't have any choice with this guy. If the info you need blows a bunch of these foreigners out of the water, he could lose a bunch of business. I'll have to stay undercover."

"See what you can find out and call me, the sooner the better. Talk to *me* only."

"I'm up for the sooner part. I'm in need of some of that PD money, brother."

"Talk to you soon."

"Sarge."

"Yeah."

"If you see my main man, big Norm, tell him I said hey. I

haven't seen him in a long time. I like the big guy."

"I'll tell him, Lando."

"Cool. Back to you, soon."

Chapter 34

Davidson County Morgue
North Nashville

Mike checked his wristwatch. He knew he was late, but cross-examination from the defense attorney in a second degree murder arrest from almost six months before his vacation was in day two of the prosecution's presentation. He'd not allowed enough time for the long-winded defense attorney's rigorous cross examination.

He knew the Davidson County Medical Examiner, Dr. Elaine Jamison, wouldn't mind if he was a little late. However, he didn't want to miss anything, especially since this would be his first autopsy of an electrocution victim where the body was damaged to such an extensive degree.

Mike had found a convenient excuse to miss Tim Slater's autopsy. A commitment involving a prior investigation provided him the excuse he needed to avoid the uncomfortable event. Attending these distressing dissections when the victim was a stranger was unsettling enough. Watching a friend's body being eviscerated was different—quite different.

He noticed the strong smell emanating from the autopsy theater was not the same as he was used to. The formaldehyde aroma was always pungent and irritating to his nose, but today it smelled as if there had been a fire in the morgue. He knew why.

Mike fought with his personal protective equipment in the outer room as he prepared to join the ME. The faster he tried to pull on the PPE, the more trouble he had getting it on over his clothes.

The pungent aroma was causing him to wish he'd brought in his jar of Vicks. He didn't have time to go back to the car.

Suck it up soldier. His 'go to' command for those having issues with their assigned tasks, learned from his commanding officer in Iraq, Colonel William Timothy Lee, seemed appropriate for him today and this somewhat uncomfortable mission.

He pushed open the double stainless steel doors leading into the large autopsy theater where everything was either stainless steel or painted with bright white enamel. The stench was strengthened by his increasing proximity to Dr. Jamison's patient.

"Sorry I'm late, Doc." Mike reached behind his head and adjusted the rear tension knob on his face shield.

"Our guest here has been patiently waiting for you, but I could not."

"I understand. I know you're busy. You're always busy."

"Unfortunately—yes, like you. Thanks to your street clientele, our schedules seem to always be full." She continued to work as she spoke.

Dr. Jamison was a Nashville native and a graduate of arguably the area's finest medical school, Vanderbilt University.

As Mike reached the tilted autopsy table holding the victim, he had trouble looking at the body. He had just as much trouble looking away. He spotted sections of charred material lying along side the body on the table and wondered what part of the body they'd come from. "What are these?" He pointed.

"They are pieces of the victim's burned—leather jacket."

"Oh, that's good. I have to tell you. I've never seen a high-voltage electrocution victim, at least one who'd been burned so badly on so much of the body."

"This victim is one of the worst I've seen in a long while," she said. "The body must have been in contact with the voltage for a considerable period. The chest and upper abdomen, even the ribs, have been virtually destroyed by the persistent flow of high voltage power. The chest cavity has split open and much of the internal organs have been cooked as if left on a rotisserie for days.

"My normal analysis of most of the internal organs will, of course, be impossible due to their condition. I've already weighed and measured the body even though neither of those measurements bear any resemblance to normality. I have also X-ray'd and found no bullets or other foreign matter within what's left of the body. The dental x-rays will be compared to those at Mr. Puckett's dentist to see if he is who we think he is. Fortunately, we were able to obtain good fingerprints. Those have already been sent to AFIS (Automated Fingerprint Identification System)."

"We were talking at the scene about his hands not being burned. We felt confident he was unconscious at the time he contacted the power."

"It does appear this electrocution may have been a staged scene meant to cover up a homicide. Fire has long been used as a fairly effective method to conceal murder and its evidentiary traces. In this case, as in most fires, the destruction of forensically useful evidence is quite significant."

"The one organ here that may be preserved sufficiently for productive analysis is the brain. The distance from the flow of electrical current could provide us some opportunity."

Mike looked at her as if to say, 'Can we hurry up?'.

She smiled, perceiving his angst from his body language. She knew him well. She and Mike had over ten years of shared experience in the autopsy theater attempting to resolve homicide cases in Nashville.

Under normal circumstances, this point in her exam was the time when she would request help from Mike or one of her assistants in relocating the plastic body block from beneath the victim's upper back and place it under the back of the neck. Due to the condition of the corpse, she was unable to perform a traditional autopsy and harvest the internal organs from the thoracic cavity. Therefore, the normal 'Y' incision from each shoulder down to the sternum and a single incision from there to the pubic bone, was unnecessary.

Once she'd placed the plastic block beneath the victim's neck, she used a scalpel to dissect the charred scalp from the front of one ear across the vertex of the skull to the other ear. Hoping not to tear the somewhat charred skin, she carefully pulled both the front and rear flaps of the scalp down and away from the internal structure of the head, exposing the skull.

She readied her Stryker oscillating saw, used to remove the skull cap and provide access to the brain. The special saw worked in a way no other did. It was the same saw used to cut away plaster casts used to stabilize broken bones while they heal. When used by an experienced operator, and the blade of the vibrating saw met a hard surface, it cut through it. When the blade met a soft surface it did not cut, but backed off without damaging the soft tissue. It worked the same way when used to remove the top of the skull.

She pressed the saw blade against the discolored skull. It made an unnerving sound much like a screaming cat who'd been caught against it's will, a normal sound from the saw both of them were prepared for. The smell of the heated brain matter was not as familiar.

The aroma caused Mike's breakfast to stir and begin a vertical climb toward his esophagus. He turned away from the doctor and her patient. With a few deep breaths through his mouth, he managed to coax the granola topped yogurt and orange juice back where they belonged.

"You okay?" The high revolution sound of the saw wound down and Dr. Jamison suggested, "You may want to stand back and toward his feet a bit. Lately, my saw has been acting up. Occasionally, it jerks and causes me to press too hard and—well, the outer layer of the meninges sort of splatters out through the skull cap kerf. Just a thought. You may want to avoid the spray."

"Thanks for the warning." Mike side-stepped and reached up to check the position of his face guard. "Why don't you requisition a new saw?"

"Not in the budget, Sergeant. Besides, none of my patients have complained—so far."

Even after all these years he wondered how she did this stuff day in and day out.

She rested her hand on the top of the skull and moved the saw slowly as she cut around the circumference of the cranium leaving a single piece of bone resembling a beanie setting atop the head. She stopped the saw and set it aside. After prying the dome-like piece loose using a chisel-headed key, she made a series of incisions which allowed her to remove the brain from its resting place. She placed it on the scale and recorded the weight.

She held up the darkened gray-beige mass for Mike to see. She indicated with her finger, a spot on the right side of the brain where blood had collected.

Mike nodded. He could see markings in the right Temporal Lobe that reflected the introduction of an object small in diameter, but with unknown length.

"I'm going to speculate, based upon these signs of penetrating trauma, someone shoved an ice pick, a screwdriver, or possibly a drill bit into the victim's ear canal creating a hemorrhage and ultimately death. We'll know more for certain in a couple of weeks after the brain has completed its 'formalin fix' and we can move it to the forensic lab for sectioning and tests."

"The killer may have taken some type of pleasure from this theatrical act, something similar to when killers cut the tongue from their victim when the reason for their murder was their inability to keep quiet about something."

Mike nodded. "Just when you think you've seen it all."

"Exactly how I feel much of the time, Sergeant. Do you have any suspects on this one?"

"Yes, and this unfortunate soul may not be his only victim." Mike lifted his face guard. "I'm going to have to run. Thanks, Doc. As always, you do great work."

"Anytime, Sergeant. You're always welcome here, much like all my other guests."

"No offense, but I think I'll keep my visits here as infrequent as possible."

Chapter 35

Criminal Justice Center
Downtown Nashville

Mike was studying Dwayne Puckett's autopsy report he'd just received via email from Dr. Jamison. There were no real surprises beyond what they'd discussed while together at the morgue. The results from the brain analysis was yet to be determined, but the ME's prediction about the introduction of a long sharp object into Puckett's right ear canal was clearly evident as the probable cause of death. The electrocution was likely an attempt to conceal the murder.

Mike's vibrating cell phone began to dance on his desk. The display read: Terry Moses.

"Mike Neal."

"Mike. You have a few minutes?"

"Always for you, Captain."

"It seems your friend Mr. Victor Ross has constructed for himself quite a menacing background. Obviously, one which has motivated someone in power within the Army to make an attempt to hide it."

"Sounds like you've broken the block on his military history. Can you tell who initiated the block?"

"My colonel assures me he plans to determine who did it and unless he's presented with a justified explanation, he will reward the individual appropriately, regardless of rank. He said the name will remain a 'need to know' item. I know my colonel well enough to accept his comment as the end of the discussion."

"I understand. I've been there."

"However, since this data on Ross is part of a criminal investigation, I was able to gain his approval to share what I've discovered with you. He has asked for you to refrain from sharing any more of it than you have to with others, outside your superiors and the District Attorney, of course."

"Not a problem."

"It seems Mr. Ross had a difficult time getting along with folks. He's made his share of enemies over his time with our uncle's Army as well as afterward when he took a job with Leverage Security Group in Iraq.

"I'm going to email the documents to you now along with a timeline. It won't take me but a minute."

Mike wondered how someone with Ross's demeanor and history could be hooked up with a person at the higher ranks of the U.S. Army who was capable of putting a block on his background, unless of course the individual possessed a similar malicious intent and simply used his rank to protect Ross.

"Okay. I'm back."

Mike could hear the rustle of papers in the background.

"The records showed Ross was inducted into the Army in September of 1995. He took basic training at Fort Benning, Georgia. In late 1996, after his assignment to Fort Hood, TX for Logistics Training, Ross was charged with domestic assault and soon afterward an order of protection was filed against him. Both charges were filed in Killeen, TX. The fact he was in the Army at the time may have bought him some lenience from the conservative local Texas judge."

Mike opened the attachment and began to scan the timeline as Moses talked.

"In 2001, while in Basra, Iraq there was an altercation between Ross and one of his reports. He was given a warning, busted back to E4 and relieved of his leadership duties.

"For the next few years afterward, he must have tolerated his assignments and limited his pushback until early 2004 when he threatened a physician who was attempting to give him a physical exam. When all was done he found himself with a General Discharge and a flight home."

"He somehow escaped the Army with only a General Discharge?" Mike asked. "I can't understand how." Mike suspected someone of influence connected to Ross had a hand in that indulgent decision.

"Less than two years after his discharge Ross was accepted as an employee at Leverage Security Group, making a six figure salary. He managed to stay out of trouble for several months until one afternoon outside Ramadi when he screwed the pooch. He let his exhaustion allow him to ignore procedure, become reckless and cost a young Iraqi man his life while locals watched."

"Brilliant."

"I used one of my connections to continue Ross's background search past his service. It seems that following the Ramadi incident, Ross returned to the U.S.. He worked security jobs such as an armed bodyguard for a global company's Chief Executive Officer who traveled extensively. Ross was discharged from this job after a security confrontation in the United Arab Emirates escalated beyond what was necessary. The CEO lost control of him and rather than put his company through further risk and embarrassment, he cancelled Ross's employment agreement on the spot.

"After this, he worked for a local Tennessee company for a few months as a security consultant. They fired him after he gave their customer an ass chewing for not adopting his security recommendations for their facility."

Mike listened as he followed along the timeline.

"He worked for a second security company for three months, at which time he walked off the job with no communication whatsoever. He simply left. They said they had no idea why.

"He worked at a local public gun range as an instructor until he was fired for fondling one of the students while supposedly showing her how to hold and aim her weapon. He said it was a misunderstanding. The fact it was the third time they'd received the complaint told them it wasn't.

"Following this episode of lewd behavior, I don't see him employed anywhere until you show him at this Nashville casket manufacturer. That's all I have."

"Terry, you are still the player I thought you were."

Moses laughed. "I'm not sure that's a title I'd like to get out."

"Not a chance. It's just between you and me, buddy." Mike laughed.

"I wish you good luck with this Ross character. I'm glad I could help you a little. Call me anytime."

"You were a big help. Thanks, Terry."

Based on the research Mike had done and which was supported by Terry Moses's work, it looked to be impossible for Victor Ross to function for long periods within society's established parameters. For some reason he seemed to see himself and his desires as exceptions not bound by the rule of law.

Ross was not the first of his kind to cross Mike's path. While with CID in the Middle East, Mike investigated several of these delinquents who had been created and fostered by inadequate corrective consequences for their criminal or near-criminal behavior. The military was famous for inadvertently rewarding warring behavior bordering on malfeasance.

On more than a few nights, fueled by quantities of inexpensive beer, Mike and his CID peers could be found discussing the Defense Department and the fact that, for too long, they had allowed an environment of semi-permissive violence with regard to private security contractors. Incidents of gross misconduct within their ranks were well-documented, but were rarely dealt with properly.

The rules of engagement given to these contractors told them when, where and how they could apply force. The application of these rules and the consequences for their violation remained conveniently vague. This perceived flexibility fabricated the gray area where most of these private contractors operated. When it came time for them to fess up to their failures, their hands went in the air, their shoulders shrugged and no one remembered anything.

Mike's years investigating for the Army's CID exposed him to numerous incidents where soldiers acted outside their orders, failed to seek guidance and took matters into their own hands.

In the Middle East, as in Vietnam, some people attributed our active duty soldiers' mistreatment, even killings, of noncombatants to stress from the conflict and vengeance for the deaths or dismemberment of their fellow soldiers. Their ever increasing anger within the war environment simply enhanced the likelihood soldiers would disregard military ethics and assault civilians whenever they thought it was justified.

For some folks, following extended or multiple deployments where they'd been neck deep in destruction, dismemberment and death, the line between war and murder became a difficult one to draw.

Mike wasn't so sure this was Ross's problem. He was confident Victor Ross was simply a sociopathic loose cannon.

Chapter 36

Mike was reviewing his notes from his call with Captain Terry Moses when his cellphone announced he had an incoming call.

"Mike Neal."

"Sarge. How's things on the blue side of the crime world?"

"Hey, Lando. We're still trying to protect and serve. You have some good news for me?"

"Man, I got all kinda news for the PD."

"Spill it."

"You know, my man who does the car conversions on all those rice burners? We had us a nice chat. He told me he's done a couple dozen conversions for the dudes at the factory you told me about on Visco. He said the Latino and Asian dudes like their rides to be low, glow and go. He said—."

"Lando." Mike interrupted. "I'm in sort of a time crunch here and really don't care about the automobile preferences of the *dudes* at the factory. I need to know about what criminal activity, if any, is going on inside the factory."

"Okay, cuz. I'll cut to the chase."

"Excellent idea."

"I told my man this discussion is top secret and is between him and me. I told him I had a brother who was screwed out of some cash by a dude who works there and I need to know what he'd be facin' if he was to go out there to try and recover it.

"He told me he'd think twice before gettin' aggressive with anybody at the factory. He said he had been offered some guns in payment for his services out there. He likes guns so the offer made him interested. He was given two AR-15 type rifles in exchange for his work on a Honda Civic. They were full freakin' auto."

"Interesting." Mike knew, since the rifles were full auto, they were likely M4s stolen from the military.

"Yeah. And, he said when he got the guns he asked if there were any others for sale. He was lookin' for some handguns for him and his brother. The guy told him he would check with his boss and see if he wanted to talk with him.

"This dude arranged for my man to meet him in the parkin' lot one day and this big bald dude with these huge guns, I mean biceps you know, came out and talked to him. He said the big guy asked him if he was in a gang in Nashville. My man told him no. The big dude asked him if he liked to shoot guns. He told him, 'hell yeah'. He said he and his homeys go out to the woods where there's an outdoor range and punch a lot of holes in shit.

"Then this big dude showed him a couple of Berettas, M9s I think he said. My man said he made the big dude an offer, he came back with a counter offer and my man got him two pistols for cheap. It was that damn easy."

"Hmm."

"Yes, sir."

"What else did you learn? Anything?"

"That big dude told my man if he needed any more guns, to let him know cause he could get him about anything he wanted."

"Okay. I mean about the number of Latinos and Asians working there."

"My man wasn't too interested in talkin' about the illegals thing. He said he had too many customers at the factory for him to get involved in that. He said he gets a lot of steady business out of there with all the new workers comin' in from time to time."

"Sounds like there's a pretty good turnover at the factory."

"He told me he sees more changes in the women workin' there than the dudes."

"Oh?"

"Yeah. He said some times he test drives one of his new conversions out there to try and drum up some business and all the dudes are talkin' about are the new chicks that just arrived."

That doesn't sound good. "I don't suppose your man said anything about where all these new folks are getting their documents in order to work here?"

"He did not. He didn't want to talk about the stuff, but you do raise a good question. How can these folks work here if they're illegal?"

"They're getting their bogus documents somewhere, probably somewhere around here. I'll take care of that later." Mike knew as soon as his homicide investigations were complete, he had to share this information with ICE and the folks at the TBI.

"Did you ask him about copping some dope there at the factory?"

"He said there is some grass changin' hands out there, but it's nothin' on a large scale, just some of the Latino guys sharin' blunts with their amigos, you know. He said the real action there is with the guns."

"Thanks, Lando. I'll give you a call tomorrow and we can meet up somewhere outside your world, so I can give you your compensation."

"I'm all about the compensation, Sarge. You can call me anytime."

Chapter 37

Davidson Street
North of Cumberland River

"It's too quiet," Mike adjusted the focus on his binoculars as he scanned the rear of the casket factory. "The red Ducati is still parked in Ross's dedicated spot."

"I thought you said this Ross guy didn't work nights," Norm said. "I think 22:00 qualifies as nights."

"Another one of his lies," Mike said, still scanning the factory.

Mike, Dave Thurman and Norm Wallace were parked on the north side of the Cumberland River in Mike's car facing the back side of the casket factory.

"Nothing's happened since we got here." Norm straightened up in his seat. "I think I'm getting blisters on my ass."

"So sit still."

"I can't. My hemorrhoids are getting pissed off at me."

Mike took his eyes from the binoculars and looked over at Norm. "I guess if I put that much weight on my ass, mine would revolt too."

"Ha. Remind me again why we're sitting here like we're at a drive-in theater. You said my man Lando told you things were getting hot in there?"

"He said one of his 'homies' told him prices were down and the guns were flying out of there like pigeons from a coop. Before I call in the ATF, I need to have some better evidence. I know Lando is reliable, but they don't know him from Adam. I don't need them doubting me if his information fizzles."

"I agree," Thurman said from the backseat, in an attempt to find a way into the conversation.

"I talked to Grant Chambers, with the ATF," Mike said. "He wasn't anxious to move on the word of our CI. He said they'd been burned too many times by confidential informants and he was apprehensive. So, I told him we would attempt to get a better picture of what's going on here and call him back. He assured me they could react quickly. They just needed some solid evidence so the honchos upstairs don't go off on them for jumping the gun."

A group of welders who had been outside smoking for the last several minutes were beginning to stroll back inside. The door at the top of the concrete steps next to the motorcycle was propped open.

"Break time must be over." Mike turned to Norm. "What do you say we move in before any more guys come outside and get into a position to warn Ross of our arrival?"

"Let's lock and load, partner. You have my hemorrhoid's vote."

With almost no traffic, Mike made the trip across the river without lights or siren in less than five minutes. He pulled into the far end of the employee parking lot and drove to the area outside the shipping docks. No one was outside. He pushed the shifter into park. The three detectives left the car and climbed the steps into the warehouse through the open rear door.

Inside, the crunch of metal stamping and bending along with the whirr of electric grinders, filled the space. The incessant beeping of forklifts in motion, the smoke from welding, and the acrid smell of burned metal completed the irritating environment.

"No wonder they wear earplugs." Thurman put his fingertips in his ears.

"Do they make nose plugs, too?" Norm asked. "This shit burns my nose."

Mike scanned the floor for Ross, but did not spot him anywhere.

Everything looked similar to the way Mike remembered it from his last visit, except the large white steel sectional door was no longer blocked by the stacks of pallets. The door was currently closed, but Mike was confident this was the access point for the basement Elliott had told him they never used.

He walked to the right edge of the door with Wallace and Thurman trailing him. On the wall next to the door was a small gray box with three control buttons labeled Up, Down and Stop. Mike looked at Norm, pulled back the right side of his jacket and removed his Glock. He held it tight against his outer thigh. The other two detectives followed his lead. Mike pressed Up and the door's electric operator began to pull the door along its screeching track, dragging metal against metal to the top.

The motor pulled the door up rapidly and stopped when it met the limiter. On the other side was a dark forty degree concrete ramp pitched down to the left. It had to be at least fifty feet long, dropping to the basement floor. The detectives walked the ramp side by side, guns in hand, unsure of what they'd find on the level below the factory.

"Thurman," Mike said, "stay near the bottom of the ramp in case anyone tries for an early exit through this doorway."

Thurman nodded.

The florescent lights were on and the air in the more than twenty-five thousand square feet of concrete-floored expanse was filled with what looked like smoke. Two Latino men were sweeping the area with push brooms, creating thick clouds of dust. The space was much cleaner than Mike had been led to believe. Other than the eight I-beams evenly spaced to support the upper floors, a single workbench and a chair, the space was empty.

"Well, well. We have visitors." Ross stood and tossed a men's magazine onto the workbench. "No need for armament, gentlemen. We are all unarmed here. To what do we owe this visit?"

"We came by to see your snake collection. Norm here likes snakes. He prefers them fried for breakfast, but any meal will do."

Mike returned his pistol to his holster. The other two detectives did the same.

"Really? The ones we have here may bite him back."

"Norm doesn't usually have anyone or anything bite him back. Besides, no one I've spoken with has seen any snakes down here. Only you."

Ross laughed. "Every threat is not always in plain sight."

"And, sometimes the snakes of the world are really only overconfident worms with inflated egos."

Ross maintained a smirk. "Why are you here, Sergeant? Is there something else we can do to help you with your investigation into the girl's death?"

"The girl, as you referred to her, had a name. Lian Xiong was trying her best to make a living using the skills she possessed. Someone in this building made the decision to take her future from her."

"Now, what does all this have to do with me?"

"I'm not completely clear on it yet, but I'm convinced you're involved, somehow."

"Whoa. Sergeant. It's not nice to make unsupported accusations. I didn't even know the girl."

"That's what they all say. And, who said they're not supported?"

"If you had anything other than speculation, you'd have already made your move."

"That's where we differ, Mr. Ross. As detectives, we're not allowed the luxury of making assumptions. We're required to gather facts, not conjecture. Regrettably, unlike the miscreants of our society, we are required to play by the rules."

"Now you're calling me names?"

"If the shoe fits ... ."

Mike strolled the space as he spoke. When he came to one of the gray plastic trash cans the two men were using to collect their trash, he stopped. He bent to look inside. He waved away some of the flying dust, and grabbed a piece of wood from the container. He stirred the contents, but it was too dark to see down into the depth of the container.

He tucked his hand beneath the handle of the large container and dragged it to the workbench. He bent and lifted the trash can with both hands, carefully dumping its contents on the top of the workbench, spreading it over the entire surface.

"What the hell are you doing?" Ross complained. "We just cleaned all that up. We're getting ready to use this space for new orders' finished goods storage."

Mike ignored him. He took the piece of wood again and began to push the larger pieces of identifiable and unimportant trash off to the outer edges of the table. This left in the middle of the workbench surface only the miscellaneous small pieces and sweepings from the bottom of the trash container. Mike examined the items scattered throughout the dust and dirt and pushed the insignificant ones to the outer edges along with the wood and plastic he'd already discarded.

He looked around, reached up to a shelf mounted above the table, and took hold of one of the extendable plastic-cased speakers with a wire running back to an inexpensive stereo. He turned toward Ross and asked, "Can I use this?"

Ross looked at one of the Latinos and said, "I guess so. It's—."

There was a loud crash as Mike smashed the speaker down onto the edge of the table, shattering the plastic case.

Chapter 38

Peaceful Solace, LLC
Nashville

"What the hell?" Ross shouted.

"I heard you say 'I guess so'. Where I come from, that's the same as a yes."

"Jackass." Ross whispered, but in the empty basement his statement could be heard by all those present.

Mike almost laughed. His back was turned to Ross as he positioned the broken speaker in his hand so the magnet was exposed and away from his palm. He began to move the magnet back and forth through the floor sweepings. After a minute or so of pushing around the residual mixture, he lifted the speaker and held it up in front of him.

He turned to Norm. "You ever see anything like this Detective Wallace?"

"As a matter of fact I have, Sergeant Neal. If I'm not mistaken that shiny three inch metal shaft is from a Dremel carborundum bit. From the looks of the metal shavings surrounding it there on the magnet, I'd say the bit was used to remove serial numbers and ownership markings from government owned weapons in order to minimize their traceability. At least it's what we found the dozen or so times we saw those things when I was with the Military Police."

"I think you're right Detective."

Mike turned to speak to Ross, but the man had already made his decision to run. He hit Thurman with his right forearm as if he was an offensive lineman blocking a linebacker for the Titans. Thurman hit the concrete floor hard and stayed there. He was gasping, lungs trying to secure their next breath.

"Son of a bitch," Mike shouted. "Secure those two." He sprinted for the ramp.

"Copy that." Norm shouted and then turned to the two Latinos. *"No problemo."*

Mike reached the top of the ramp as the door was closing. He hit the stop button and was able to squat and duck walk under the door. As he straightened up, he heard the revving motorcycle as it pulled away from its spot at the rear of the building.

Mike's car was facing the opposite direction from the way Ross had gone. He started the car, put it in reverse and floored the accelerator. He backed out of the truck lane and into the parking lot as he scanned his mirrors in hopes of spotting the Ducati's tail light. He didn't see it at first, but when he spun the car around and accelerated toward the entrance, he saw the single red light brighten in the distance to his left as Ross hit his brakes. He was confident Ross was taking Visco Drive east so he could turn right on Omohundro Place and then left on Lebanon Road to head out of town.

As Mike neared the traffic light at Lebanon Road he lit up the cruiser and turned on the siren. He slowed and looked in both directions. No traffic. He was sure he could see the red tail light in the distance to his left, getting smaller. Again, he pushed the accelerator to the floor, made a hard left and headed east toward Donelson in hopes of catching the Ducati's red light.

"46 Delta to Dispatch." He waited.

"Dispatch 46 Delta, go ahead."

"Detective needs assistance. In pursuit of homicide suspect on red motorcycle east bound Lebanon Road at high speed west of Donelson. Need immediate backup in Donelson."

"Copy, 46 Delta." The dispatcher paused to check her screen. "23, what's your twenty?"

"Donelson Hills Drive and Lebanon Road."

"Be on the lookout for a red motorcycle east bound on Lebanon Road at high speed approaching your location."

"10-4. I've been here a while. Nothing of your description has passed so far."

Mike continued his high speed trip into Donelson. When he saw the marked cruiser sitting only a few feet off Lebanon Road on Donelson Hills Drive with his parking lights on, he killed his emergency equipment and pulled up next to the patrol officer.

"You haven't seen a red motorcycle?"

"I haven't seen any motorcycles, red or otherwise, in the forty-five minutes or so I've been here."

"Shit. He must have taken one of the residential roads back there." Mike backed out onto Lebanon Road, squealed his tires as he accelerated back toward downtown.

He turned right on Lisa Lane into the residential area and slowed to begin his search for signs of Ross or his Ducati. The longer he spent cruising the subdivision, the more he realized his chances of spotting either were slim.

He drove the streets of the more than fifty year old subdivision looking for signs of Ross or any single high-speed tread marks at the street corners. He circled a dark cul de sac and parked facing outward with his lights off.

He pulled out his cell phone and scrolled to Paul Elliott's name and tapped it.

Chapter 39

Donelson Area
East of Nashville

"Mr. Elliott? This is Sergeant Neal. I need to get some information from you."

"Uh—okay."

"About an hour ago, I was at your factory with two other detectives. We were talking with Victor Ross and a couple of his minions down in the basement."

"The basement?"

"Ross said they were cleaning it up so you folks could use it for finished goods storage since you have a large number of new orders to stage before shipment."

"New orders?"

"That's what he said."

"Hmm."

"Listen. I need information on anyone who's known to have been associated with Victor Ross in more than a casual way since he came to work at your company."

"I'll—I'll have to go to the office and call Millie from HR. Why do you need this?"

"Sir, this is a murder investigation. I really don't have time for questions. I need this information from you immediately. Can I trust you to act on this situation promptly?"

"I'll call Millie now."

"I'll be waiting. Can I assume you have my number?"

"Yes. I've captured it."

Mike disconnected the call, scrolled through his contacts and dialed Lieutenant Burris.

"Burris."

"Lieutenant. I've got a suspect on the run. It's Victor Ross from the casket factory. I need air support."

"Where?"

"Just west of Donelson. He got away on the high dollar crotch rocket I told you about. I followed him and lost him in this area."

"Hmm. I overheard Captain Moretti telling someone earlier who had requested air support the pilot vacations and mechanical issues had grounded two of the units."

"Can you check on it?"

"I'll call you back." Both men disconnected the call.

Mike checked his wristwatch and mentally asked Burris to hurry and call back with ETA on his air support.

His phone interrupted his thoughts. It was Elliott.

"Sergeant, I was able to log onto the company mainframe from home with my laptop. Millie walked me through the employee database. She said Ross wasn't known for connecting socially with hardly anyone at work other than Dwayne Puckett."

Mike didn't see that one coming.

"She remembered he did have a relationship with one of his direct reports for a while. It was common knowledge, according to her. I didn't know it. She was a shipping clerk. Dawn Morris was her name. She left the company abruptly a few months back with no call in or any type of notice. At the time, Victor said he had no idea where she went."

"Do you still have her address?"

"Yes. I looked it up. It's 1916 Coyne Court."

"Hang on, please." Mike felt his luck may be changing. He was currently parked three blocks from Coyne Court. He put Elliott on hold to take an incoming call from Burris.

"Tell me you've got good news."

"Sorry. Helicopters are not available."

"Damn."

"Is there anything else I can do?"

"You can get me a SWAT team out here. I have an address where I'm certain we'll find Ross."

"What is it?"

"1916 Coyne Court. Tell them to arrive Code 2 and hang back from the location at the command post. Tell them to look for my car."

"I'll get them on their way."

"Thanks."

Mike yanked the shifter into gear and drove toward the girl's address as he reconnected Elliott's call.

"Mr. Elliott, you've been a big help. I need you to give me Ross's cell phone number."

"Okay." Elliot hesitated, no doubt scrolling to the number.

"Thanks. Keep your phone close. I may need you again."

"O—Okay."

Mike scrolled his contacts again until he reached names starting with the letter M. He highlighted Dean McMurray's name and made the call.

Mike parked at the entrance to Coyne Court as the phone rang. He got out and stood looking across the car's roof at the wooded area around the girlfriend's house which sat toward the rear of a deep pie shaped lot, at least seventy yards from the street. Mike could see the home's eve and porch lights through the thick grove of trees. The light illuminated the entire front of the house.

"Hello."

"Deano."

"What's up, Mike?"

"I need your help."

"You got it."

"You still have the drone you bought in Atlanta?"

"Ariel? Of course. She's my favorite new toy."

"Ariel?"

"I named her. I thought it fit."

"Yeah, I get it." Mike said. "Can I assume you have cameras on it, I mean her?"

"Night vision and thermal image."

"Perfect. Have you flown that thing at night yet?"

Chapter 40

Remington Lane
Donelson Area

Mike called Ross's cell phone at least a dozen times. There was no answer. At his request, an officer back at the CJC searched for the home's land line. There was none. It had been disconnected four months ago.

As Mike had instructed, all responders arrived Code 2, emergency lights off—no sirens. He established a command post back on Remington Lane, two blocks away and hidden behind a large berm covered with trees. Ross couldn't see the officers or their cars.

With radios on low volume, Mike heard, over the chatter from at least two dozen cops, someone bitching about having to park so far away. He looked up the street to see officers walking on either side of a man in a wheelchair, who was shaking his head and pumping his narrow wheels.

"You guys have obviously not heard of the Americans with Disabilities Act. I am supposed to get a parking place for my van near my destination. Not three blocks away."

Mike waved Dean over. He could see the drone resting in his lap and the controller next to him in his chair.

"I think I'm getting a cramp."

"Suck it up soldier. Is that thing ready to fly?"

"Ariel is not a thing. Yes, she's almost ready."

"Get it up. I need to see what's going on in the house."

"Here. Place her on the pavement for me."

"How do I—?"

"Pick her up with one hand here and the other here. Then set her down on her skids. She's fairly rugged, actually tougher than she looks."

Mike picked up the aircraft, held it above his head and checked out the three cameras suspended beneath it. "Night vision, thermal imaging, what's this one?"

"A camera."

"Smart ass."

Soon after Mike placed the drone on the street, the propellers started spinning. The whirring sound gradually ramped up in pitch. Four small red LED lights, one atop the shaft of each propeller, flashed on.

Dean laughed. "Cool, huh?"

"Yeah. You never answered my question."

"What question?"

"Have you flown it at night?"

"Well, not really. But, I don't see it as a problem. I'll keep her above the tree canopies, and the power and phone lines."

"Good idea. Let's do this."

Dean held the controller in both hands, stared at it like it was his newborn baby and began to move the joysticks. The drone left the pavement with a jerk. The on board night-vision camera signal was displayed on the controller's five inch monitor. The bright green display showed Mike, Dean and the others looking up at the drone and their images getting smaller as it climbed. The speed of the drone increased and it moved toward the house.

Mike stood next to Dean and stared down at the display.

"Take it up higher. I don't want him to see it coming."

"Done." Dean pulled back on the joystick and the drone responded.

"Can you kill those red lights? I'd prefer not to announce our presence."

"Done."

"When you get above the structure, I want to see a thermal

image. I need to know if the girl friend, or anyone else, is in there with him."

"Will do."

Dean stared at the screen. As the drone hovered in place above the house, he switched from night vision to thermal. The green screen was replaced by a dark background with bright white images wherever there was a source of heat.

"Okay. I've got one human heat signature inside the home— moving occasionally. It looks to be male. Let me get the entire structure on the screen." Dean worked the controller and widened the camera angle in order to see the entire house.

"Is that it?"

"Wait. I've got a second signature."

"Where? Near him?"

"Here." Dean pointed to the screen. "It looks to be at the other end of the house."

"Well?"

"It's not moving. Maybe it's the female and she's tied up."

Mike bent over for a closer look at the controller's screen. "And maybe it's his motorcycle. That's the garage."

"You didn't tell me he was riding a motorcycle."

"You didn't tell me you couldn't tell the difference between a motorcycle and a woman."

Dean had a constipated look on his face. Mike could tell he was dying to make a comeback comment, but he was at a loss for words. Not something Mike had seen before.

"I need to know for sure whether he's in there alone."

"There are no other readable human signatures inside the house," Dean said.

Mike looked back toward the area where the SWAT unit was staged and waiting.

The Special Weapons and Tactics unit was prepared. They trained just to be *ready*. SWAT team training was constant. This was also the main reason why they sometimes found themselves charged with the use of excessive force. The command to *go* was a positive reward for their training efforts, one they all anticipated. The command to stop was one which sometimes needed to be given more than once.

Mike raised his left arm and pointed up with his index finger. He checked to be sure he'd caught the SWAT commander's attention.

He began waving his hand in circles above his head. The team boarded their BearCat armored personnel carrier and readied themselves for the take down. Lieutenant Dirk McGrath made his way toward Mike for final communications.

"I'd like to take this scumbag alive if possible," Mike said. "His history tells me it may not be so easy."

"It's our preference, but as always, the decision belongs to the suspect."

Mike thought of the SWAT actions he'd been involved in over the last dozen or so years. He wasn't so sure all the guys in SWAT back then felt the same way. He doubted it was any different today.

"Based on Ross's history and his access to weapons, he is most likely heavily armed. Don't let him injure one of our guys. I'd rather see his ass in a body bag."

"10-4, Sergeant. We'll bring him to you in whatever condition he allows. It's up to him."

"I understand." Mike turned to Dean. "Deano, what's Ross doing now?"

"I can't be sure. He's not moving."

"Where is he in the house?"

"Front room. Looks like he's by a window about midway of the home near the front door. If he's smart, he's probably watching for us."

"If he was smart, none of us would be here right now." Mike turned back to McGrath.

"He's all yours, Lieutenant."

Mike checked out McGrath's gear as he walked toward the BearCat. The body armor the team wore was a balancing act between protection, heat and freedom of movement. The vital areas of their torsos were safeguarded with Kevlar or ceramic panels and their heads were protected with Kevlar helmets. Depending on team members' assignments, other areas of their bodies were also shielded.

McGrath joined his men and the BearCat started down the driveway slowly with its lights off. The armored beast ran quieter than Mike expected. The driver veered off the gravel and onto the grass. He assumed it was done in order to eliminate the sound of their approach made by the popping of the oversized all-terrain tires on the driveway gravel.

"SWAT 1 to team. Confirm 10-2."

Each officer responded in numerical sequence to verify he was receiving and transmitting properly. Following the last team member's confirmation, Mike spoke into his radio, "Base, 10-2."

"Swat 1, Copy. We are go on my signal."

The BearCat climbed the sloped terrain and slowed near the front corner of the structure. The right side door of the BearCat opened and a dozen men exited rapidly from the side of the vehicle away from the home.

The plan was to set up positions at the front and rear of the home and each group be ready to move on McGrath's command. Each man confirmed his position.

"Go," McGrath gave the signal.

Within seconds of his command, the large living room window exploded from the inside out. Glass showered the front lawn as a rocket propelled grenade was launched through the window. The familiar rush of air from the rocket jacked up the adrenaline of the entire team.

"Oh no." Dean lifted the controller for a better look.

Chapter 41

The BearCat rocked up onto its right side tires, almost tipping over. After a moment, the massive weight of the armored truck brought it back down onto all six tires. It bounced once and settled.

"What the hell was that?" Mike looked toward the house and the billowing smoke rising in the distance, beyond the trees. He looked at the small screen on Dean's controller, but could not make out anything. The smoke had engulfed the drone.

"I don't know." Dean adjusted the reception. "I have to get Ariel out of the smoke." He pulled the right side joystick and took the drone up and away from the house while the smoke thinned.

"Base to SWAT 1. Do you copy?" Mike asked, wanting a situation report. The only thing he heard was chatter among the team. After a moment, he received his answer.

"SWAT 1 to Base. The Cat took a direct hit, left side. It's dented and charred, but it appears the armor held. The team was outside at the time, no injuries."

"Roger that."

Officers in the front of the house fell back to positions behind

178

the larger trees and filled the shattered window with full-auto fire from their H&K MP5s. One officer, who came from the garage area, moved tight along the home's foundation to a place beneath the window from where the RPG was fired. He pulled the ring and tossed in an M84 type flashbang stun grenade and then dropped to cover. Two seconds later, a window in the rear of the house was broken and a second flashbang was thrown into the home.

"He's moving. He's moving." Dean shouted as he stared at the controller screen. The smoke had cleared enough to drop Ariel in for a closer look.

"He's going to the garage." Mike shouted into the radio as he stood, looking over Dean's shoulder. "It looks like he's headed for the bike. Be ready. Don't let him get away on that thing."

"Four, five and six—move to the garage and cover the door."

The electric garage door began to rise and the guttural sound of the revving Ducati peaked the team's readiness.

As soon as the door was high enough, Ross surged from the garage lying flat across the fuel tank of the red rocket. He came out with his rear tire spinning in the gravel and he used the spin to turn the bike tight around the corner of the house and aim for the street.

The motorcycle straightened and began to pick up speed. Ross used his left hand to pull from his waist band a full auto Glock 18 with a 30 round magazine. He forced the men around the garage to dive for cover as he sprayed multi-round bursts in their direction.

Before he cleared the front corner of the house, one of the younger SWAT team members dropped his rifle and started running from his post in the front of the house. Ross was still looking and firing his pistol behind him. He didn't see the officer until he entered his peripheral vision from about three feet away.

The athletic officer used a flying clothes line tackle to take Ross off the bike. The Glock went airborne. Ross's gorilla grip on the bike's handlebar caused the Ducati's front wheel to come up and the bike flipped over backward, just missing Ross who went airborne along with the officer. When Ross landed on his back, there were two SWAT officers on top of him before he could get to his feet.

Ross was so strong he was able to fight his way to his feet and spin out of their control. As soon as Ross broke free, the officer standing next to the Lieutenant fired his Taser. The barbs found their target in his massive chest and the fifty thousand volts stormed his body. Ross grimaced and yelled. He yanked out the barbs mid-jolt and pulled an assisted-opening knife from his back pocket. He slung the five inch steel blade from the handle and started toward the closest cop, Lieutenant McGrath.

The young cop who took Ross off his bike came at him from his blind side and leaped into the air. The outside edge of his right boot struck the side of the big man's left knee and Ross went down. As he was attempting to fight his way back to his feet, Lieutenant McGrath, without emotion or warning, lowered his MP-5 and shattered Ross's right kneecap and fibula.

Ross collapsed and grabbed his leg. "Son of a bitch!"

"If you want the left one to remain functional, assuming it still is, I'd stay down if I were you." McGrath gestured to one of his team, who stepped forward and trained his weapon on Ross's left knee.

"Get the cuffs on him now and empty his pockets," McGrath said, "so we don't have to waste any more ammo on this bastard."

"Yes!" Dean shouted, pumping his fist.

Mike and Dean had watched the takedown from Ariel's airborne perspective.

"Are we done with Ariel?"

"I think so."

"She's pretty cool, huh?"

"Yes. She is very cool, but you and she were not here tonight. Understand? We had no authorization and we don't need to jeopardize this arrest."

Dean moved the controls and stared at the screen. "I don't know what you're talking about. We were less than five miles from here, out in Two Rivers Park tonight, for her inaugural night flight."

The high-pitched buzz from the drone's propellers became louder. It dropped in front of Dean and touched down on the pavement like a pup answering a 'Come' command. Mike picked it up and placed it on Dean's lap.

"Thanks, buddy. Good job."

"I was never here." Dean bumped fists with Mike, rotated his chair and headed for his van.

Mike watched as the BearCat approached with the SWAT team. Some were riding on the running boards, others were walking.

"He's inside," McGrath said as he took Mike's extended hand.

"Great work, Lieutenant. Thanks. I'm glad none of our guys were hurt."

"Our pleasure, Sergeant. Here's his cell phone. I thought you might be able to pull some helpful numbers from it."

"Thanks."

"See you around, Mike."

"Lieutenant."

"Yeah."

"Dean and the drone weren't here tonight. We didn't have approval."

"Who?" McGrath smiled. "No problem. My guys know discretion." He turned and headed back toward his car and at least a dozen departmental reports that would have to be completed by tomorrow morning for MNPD leadership.

Mike walked to the rear of the armored truck. He watched and waited while one of the officers opened the rear doors. The EMTs, who had been on site since before the take down, rolled their gurney into position and began to treat Ross's leg and stem the blood loss. One of the men checked his vital signs, another inflated an air cast to be applied prior to transport. Once ready, they lifted him onto the gurney amid several grunts and curses.

"He'll be okay," one of the EMTs said to Mike as he passed by.

"I want two officers inside the ambulance and with him and at all times, understand?" Mike stared at Ross as he winced in pain.

"Got it." McGrath's sergeant said.

"I'd hate for him to not enjoy his extended stay at one of Tennessee's picturesque iron-bar institutions."

"Kiss my ass," Ross managed to utter between grunts.

"No thanks." Mike pulled his cell phone from his jacket and walked away. He wanted to check on the two Latinos Norm and Thurman were babysitting.

"Wallace."

"Norm. We got him."

"Excellent."

"How are the minions? Have they taught you to speak Spanish yet?"

"No. Unfortunately, I don't *habla*. However, over the last couple of hours, these two have themselves become bilingual."

"You're kidding."

"At first, they wanted to act like they didn't speak English. 'No habla. No habla, señor,'" He mocked the Latino men. "I figured Ross wasn't the type to spend time learning Spanish, so they had to be able to communicate somehow. I left them alone for a few minutes. When I came back, I told one of them rather casually, there was a Brown Recluse spider crawling on his collar. I thought this was a very believable possibility down here in this hell hole. But, one you could not relate to without some ability with the English language.

"When he started jumping around, flailing his head and shoulders about, rather limited by the handcuffs behind his back, I asked him what was wrong. He spoke some rather loud and fluent English words such as 'Get it off. Get it off me, you big bastard.' After that, I was amazed at his ability to pick up the English language so quickly. Astonishing as it was, both men learned to speak and understand English at a rate unmatched by anyone I've heard of. We were able to communicate easily afterwards. It's fascinating isn't it?"

"It is." Mike laughed.

"I told them we could deport their entire families as accessories to a massive criminal enterprise as well as send the two of them to prison as accessories to murder, never to see their families again. I told them their family members who didn't also go to prison for a long time would be deported back to wherever they came from and never allowed to return to the United States.

"The one guy who looked like he's in his late-forties, possibly a grandfather, started spilling his guts about everything he knew. He told me about the trucks, how many, what color, the trailer numbers, gave me the shipping documents, told me what time they left, what guns are inside the caskets, everything."

"That's great."

"He said Ross was in charge here, but he had someone who told him what to do and when to do it. He said he'd heard Ross getting instructions on the phone from somewhere. He said he didn't know who it was, but he heard Ross call him Colonel.

"I knew you were busy, so I called Lieutenant Burris. He called the Tennessee Highway Patrol and gave them everything. He said THP told him they would contact ATF while they pursued the trucks, but wouldn't be able to take the trucks down until the Feds approved it. So, who knows if we'll get the guns stopped. Hell, by the time somebody actually does something, they'll be delivered in New Orleans and Houston. Damn bureaucrats."

"Thanks, Norm. I'm going to check and see where they are on making something out of this mess. I'll talk with you later. Thanks for your help."

"10-4. *Hasta luego.*"

Mike laughed at Norm's limited Spanish as he hung up the call. He scrolled to the Lieutenant's number and pressed send.

"Burris."

"Lieutenant, it's me. Ross is on his way to jail after a stop at the ER escorted by a couple of our guys. He won't be walking for a while. McGrath took out his knee."

"Good for him."

"What do we know about the trucks so far?"

"I just got off the phone with Captain Sheridan with the Alabama Highway Patrol. He is working with the ATF to covertly intercept the trucks at the Athens, Alabama weigh station. It's about a hundred miles south of Nashville. AHP is currently following the trucks in an unmarked cruiser. When the trucks stop for their weigh-in, they plan to delay them long enough to attach magnetic GPS devices to each trailer so they'll be able to back off a bit as they track them to their destinations. When they arrive, they'll bring in the troops and arrest everyone involved."

"Great. When we catch our breath a little, I need to talk with you about the number of Latinos and Oriental folks working at the casket factory. I can't help but think, that many people can't all be legal. And, I'm suspicious those Asian girls could be part of a trafficking operation feeding labor to Paul Elliot. I'm not sure he's as clean as he wants us to think."

"I'll text you my contact at ICE. It'll help cut through some bureaucratic muck. Once you talk to him, you can forget about the casket company and focus everything on Tim's case."

"Thanks. So you'll know, I'm having two of our uniforms remain here at the house where we tracked Ross and I'm going to call in for an officer to guard Ross's office so Norm and Thurman can leave for the CJC with the Latinos. As soon as we can get a warrant to bring in his computer, his files and anything else we can find involved in his operation, we'll cut the officer loose.

"Paul Elliott told me this property where we found Ross is owned by his former girlfriend. We're doing an exigent search of the place now. We haven't found any signs of her presence here, so based upon what we know about Ross, I've ordered cadaver dogs to also search the surrounding property tonight. The lot looks like maybe five or six acres."

"Good work. I'll see you tomorrow. Get some sleep."

"Yes sir. I could use it."

Mike disconnected the call when he was sure the lieutenant had hung up.

He was glad this part of the ordeal was almost over. He wasn't so sure Ross was involved in Tim Slater's murder, but he knew somehow he was tied to the deaths of the Chinese girl and Dwayne Puckett. If his gut was on target, the dogs would likely add a third.

Mike heard a strange cell phone ring and realized it was Ross's phone in his jacket pocket. He pulled it out and looked at the display. The caller was from the 931 prefix. He decided to answer it. "Hello."

"Hey. This is Cody."

"Cody?"

"Sergeant Hank Cody at Campbell, you're picking up my tough box, remember?"

"Oh, yeah. Sorry," Mike played along. "I've been covered up and forgot. I'm glad you called."

"So, when can you get to Campbell with a lift-gate truck big enough for this box?"

This was beginning to sound interesting. "What about 08:00 tomorrow morning? Does that work?"

"Yeah. Okay. Listen. I got some shit in there besides the guns and ammo you're getting, so don't plan on running off with it before I get my stash. You copy?"

"Oh, Roger that. No problem. Where do I meet you?"

"Call me back in the a.m. on this same number before you get to the main gate. I'll know better then which hangar it'll be in. You gonna have my payment with you?"

"Yep. Cash money. Got it right here."

"Cool. What was your name again?"

Mike knew what the man was doing. "Ross, Victor Ross."

"Yeah. That's what the Colonel told me."

"See you at 08:00, Ross. Don't be late."

"Not a chance, Sarge. Wouldn't miss it."

Mike disconnected the call and pocketed Ross's phone. He

pulled his phone from his other jacket pocket and scrolled his contacts to the new number he'd added for Grant Chambers.

"Hello."

"Grant. It's Mike Neal. I have some information I think you're going to want to hear."

Chapter 42

Mike Neal's Home
Green Hills Area

With Ross safely locked up, Mike slept in to try and catch up on his recent deprivation.

He was confident he would have ample opportunity to make the case against Ross for Puckett's murder and also as a conspirator in Lian Xiong's death. Once Lian's fellow workers discovered Puckett was dead and Ross was in jail, they would surely choose to share more of what they knew and suspected. All their testimony, along with the physical evidence would be enough to convince the DA, Dwayne Puckett killed Lian Xiong.

Mike sipped his coffee as he once again called Grant Chambers's number. As he listened to the phone ring, he wondered what it would be like to work for the 'Feds'. There was no way Grant's high bureaucracy job could be any more fulfilling than putting away murderers and bringing some sense of peace and justice to a family who'd lost their loved one.

"Hello."

"Grant. Mike Neal."

"Hey, Mike. You calling for a Sit-Rep?"

"Guilty. What do you know so far?"

"Well, when my guys reached Fort Campbell, the guards at the gate didn't know why they were there, but they were expecting their visit. So, we had no trouble getting in. The hangar number Cody gave us on the phone this morning was good and he was there waiting with the box."

"Great."

"My guys maintained their acting roles until they got the box on the truck and followed Cody to an old storage warehouse in Clarksville where he'd rented some space. When they arrived, they met another guy who was a friend of Cody's. Seems he owed Cody some money in exchange for what Cody had sent himself from Afghanistan."

"Oh?"

"When they helped Cody pop the box, he dug through a bunch of personal junk inside and pulled out a small tactical bag. About this time is when our backup team rolled in and the odds turned heavily in our favor."

"What was in the bag?"

"Heroin."

"You're kidding?"

"Nope. Over a kilo, uncut, worth about a quarter million. This part of the bust went to the Military Police riding with my guys. They hauled both Cody and his friend back to Campbell. I'm told he was singing the entire way wanting to make a deal to roll over on some Lieutenant Colonel still in Afghanistan. Thanks to you, we could end up with quite a haul, Sergeant Neal."

"Sounds like it, but you'll have to get in line for the arms smuggler here in Nashville."

"How's that?"

"I've got him locked up downtown charged with murder, conspiracy on a second victim after the fact, assault with intent on our SWAT team using an RPG, as well as assault and battery on one of our detectives. He isn't going anywhere until we convict him. Then I may let you have him for international gun smuggling."

"Seems fair. By the time we're finished, the U.S. Army may be short a few soldiers."

"I don't think they'll mind. Thanks, Grant. I'm glad I ran into you again earlier this week."

"Me too, Mike. Take care of Tim's family and let me know if

there's anything I can do to help you."

"Will do."

With his case drawing to a close, Mike thought today would be a good day to honor his promise to Jennifer and spend a few minutes with Mason.

He pulled on some long-legged basketball shorts, a blue and white Memphis Grizzlies jersey with number 15 and Vince Carter's name in blue letters on the back. On the way out the kitchen door, he grabbed his Titan's ball cap and reversed it on his head. With his basketball in hand and three pieces of bubble gum working in his jaw, he jogged up the steps.

At the top, he spun the ball on his left index finger and put his face against the storm door. He pushed the doorbell.

"Yo." He spun the ball again to keep it going.

Jennifer came to the door laughing.

"Can Mason come out to play. I need to beat him unmercifully at some roundball."

"Hang on. I'll get him." She shook her head, laughing as she walked away.

Mike leaned against the metal railing and continued to spin his ball. Mason came to the door smiling.

"Homie, you up for a butt-kickin' on the court?"

"Not a chance, old man."

"Let's go." Mike moved down the steps and out onto the driveway, dribbling. He passed the ball to Mason and he shot. The ball went in and then Mike took a shot. Mason got the rebound and dribbled out to the free throw line. He dribbled twice and dropped another one.

Mike grabbed the ball. "So, you want to talk about some stuff?" Mike drove the basket with a layup.

"Yeah. I—I had some questions about some stuff."

Mike bounce passed the ball to Mason and said, "Shoot."

Mason dribbled twice and made a jump shot.

Mike grabbed the rebound and walked over to Mason. "No. I meant shoot with your questions."

"Oh. I don't know. There are some things I don't understand, I guess."

Mike looked at him as concerned as any father would be. "What is it?"

"I was told there's this girl who likes me."

"What's her name?"

"Rachel."

"Who told you?"

"A friend of mine."

"A good friend?"

"Yeah. He's a good friend."

"Cool." Mike shot the ball and missed. "Do you like her."

"I don't know. I guess. She's nice. She's quiet. She's real smart. She has a 4.0 average. That's pretty smart."

"Yep. You can't get any smarter than that. Okay. So you have this girl—who likes you—and you think you like her?"

"Right."

"Sounds like a good thing to me. So, what's the question?"

Mason hesitated and took a shot. "What do I do next?"

"Does she talk to you at school?"

"Yeah, we sit at the same table at lunch. We ride the same bus."

"That's good. Does she sit with you on the bus?"

"She sits with her friend, but that's okay."

"So she lives around here?"

"Yeah. She lives over on Sharondale."

"You said your friend told you about her liking you. Do you talk to your friend about her?"

"I mostly listen. He talks more than I do."

"Okay. Let me share something with you. This is very important when it comes to dealing with girls and emotions. You need to remember this if you forget everything else."

"Okay." Mason stood still, ready to hear the secrets to dealing with women.

"You never, ever kiss and tell. Do you know what that means?"

"Don't tell anyone who you kissed?"

"That's part of it. It means don't tell your friends or anyone about everything you do with the girls in your life. The girls expect you to treat them as if they're special, and if they care about you, they *are* special." Mike could tell Mason wasn't exactly sure of what he meant. "If you shared some personal things with a girl you liked, what would you think if one of her friends told other guys and girls what you'd said and all the time you thought it was only between you and her."

"Wow. I think I'd be upset."

"I think you would, too. So, always try to be considerate of other peoples feelings and don't discuss with the guys or other girls the things you did or talked about with the girl you're dating. It's just the right thing to do."

"What about if you know someone who likes one of your friends, but the person isn't comfortable telling your friend. Is it a bad idea to tell your friend about the person who likes them?"

"You mean sort of like your buddy who told you about Rachel?"

"Yeah. Like that. I might never have known she likes me."

"That's different. Sharing something along those lines is a good thing. Some folks are shy and too hesitant to make their feelings known. So, it can be a good idea to make your friend aware he has an admirer. It made you feel good when *you* found out, right?"

"Yeah. Cool," Mason said. "I guess you ought to know. My mom likes you."

Mike almost swallowed his wad of bubble gum. He coughed it back up from his throat and began to chew again.

"Uh—I like your mom, and I like you. You guys are my friends. You always have been." Mike was trying to come up with the right thing to say in response to Mason's announcement, but nothing coming out of his mouth sounded particularly appropriate.

Mason came closer and spoke softer. "I hear her talking to my aunt Barb. She closes the door to her room, but I can still hear her. She talks about the way you look, your smile, your muscles and," he looked back toward the stairs and then back to Mike, "your butt. I've heard her talk about your butt a bunch of times."

"You probably shouldn't be eavesdropping on your mom's phone calls. That's not very nice. You wouldn't like it if she listened in on your calls to Rachel."

"Yeah. I guess. Hey, what's the deal with girls checking out boys' butts anyway?"

Mike laughed. "It's natural. Girls like boys with tight jeans and cute butts. It's always been that way since Eve looked at Adam's butt and said, "Nice cheeks, dude."

Mason laughed.

"You look at the *girls'* butts don't you?"

Mason hesitated. "Yeah, I guess so."

"Well, sounds natural to me."

Mason turned sideways and looked at his reflection in Mike's kitchen storm door.

"Do I have a good looking butt?"

Mike caught himself and held the laugh. He walked over to Mason and pretended to examine his butt. "I think you have an exceptional butt. What about mine?" Mike laughed at himself, but tried to not let Mason hear. "I think you and I both have superior butts and the girls simply can't help themselves."

Mike extended his hand for a high five and Mason slapped it.

"I have a question I wanted to ask you." Mike stood still and let Mason know this was a serious question.

"About what?" Mason shot the ball and made it.

Mike grabbed the rebound, held the ball and walked over to Mason.

"You're getting older and I was curious. Have you ever been offered any drugs?"

Mason slapped the ball from Mike's hands, grabbed it up, dribbled to the hoop and made a layup. He turned around and said, "Yes. I've been offered marijuana a few times."

"What did you do?"

"I told them I didn't want to smoke anything because I was planning on trying out for the cross-country track team and I didn't want to do anything to hurt my lung capacity."

"Wow. Great answer."

"It's true."

"I didn't know. That's cool. I love to run."

"I know. Maybe we could run together sometime."

"Definitely. We can run together anytime you want to." Mike put his arm around Mason's shoulders. "I'm so proud of you. Please continue to avoid the drugs and the people who use them."

"No problem. They're not my kind of friends."

"I'm glad." As he said it, his cell phone played its intrusive tones.

"Mike Neal."

"Mike, it's Megan. I need you to come over."

"Okay. Right now?"

"Yes. I've found something you'll want to check out."

"What is it, Megan?"

"Did you know Tim used a personal digital recorder."

"He may have started using one after he and I partnered for a couple of weeks back when Thurman went on vacation. I've been using one for several years."

"You're going to want to hear what's on this one."

Chapter 43

Home of Megan Slater
Nashville

The front door to the modest ranch style home swung wide. Mike was greeted by a beautiful face with a weary smile.

"Hi."

"Hello. Come in."

Mike could see a redness in Megan's eyes as he crossed the threshold, he guessed she'd been crying.

"I hope I didn't interfere with anything important when I called you. I was certain you'd want to know about the recorder as soon as possible."

"You did exactly as you should have, and no. The only thing you interrupted was a one-on-one basketball game between me and my 15-year-old neighbor. We were finished and just talking."

"What can I get you to drink?"

"I'm good, actually." Mike began to scout the house. "Where's Sophia?"

"She's back in her room playing with her dolls. I asked her to play alone and allow us some time to talk. The recorder is in here." She started for the rear of the home.

Mike followed and they took seats across from each other at the modest kitchen table.

Mike spotted the recorder and picked it up. He reviewed the controls and the screen. There was only one recording showing on the display. He looked at Megan and pushed Play.

> *"You confessed. Damn it. You admitted you killed Vanessa Kemp. You need to man up and turn yourself in."*

Megan looked at Mike. He could see an accumulation of tears at her lower eye lids, likely in response to hearing Tim's voice again. He wondered how many times she'd played the recording before he arrived, only to hear his voice.

> *"I only admitted it to you, asshole and only after I was acquitted by the court. In case they don't teach you knuckleheads the law, you can't indict me twice for the same crime."*

> *"A flaw in our system; I assure you."*

> *"Just because you and the DA screwed up on this one, don't mean you get a second chance at me. And, if you don't stop harassin' me, I'm gonna take care of your irritatin' ass like I took care of her. And, like her, nobody will know who did it."*

There was a moment of silence on the recording.

> *"Listen. I know you pukes ain't that sharp. Hell, if you were, I'd be in jail right now. You ain't got nothin' on me. So, leave—me—the hell—alone. I ain't warnin' you again, Slater. You got it?*

> *"Oh, I got it. I definitely got it."*

Mike was sure he knew what Tim meant when he said he *got it*. Tim meant he got exactly what he wanted, the threat captured on the recorder.

"That's all of it," Megan said.

Mike stopped the recorder and returned it to the table. "Do you have any idea who Tim was talking to?"

"I'm not sure." She hesitated. "I remember quite a while ago overhearing him talk to someone on the phone about a case he and Robert Franks worked back before he and I met. I asked him about it when he got off the phone. He told me the girl was young, about twenty. I could tell there was something about her case that got to him, but he didn't want to talk about it in depth. This could be related to it. I don't know. But, I would think only Robert Franks could confirm it."

"I'll talk with him later. I need to take this with me."

"I know."

"Would you like me to get you a copy of the recording?"

"Uh—"

"I don't mind." He knew she was afraid he would think she was strange for wanting it. But, he also knew it may be the only recording of Tim's voice she might ever have.

"If you don't mind."

"Not at all," Mike assured her. "I can't be sure yet how valuable this is, but locating it has to help. Thank you for calling me as soon as you found it."

Megan nodded. "I pray this can make a difference and maybe play a role in finding Tim's killer."

Mike stood. "Me too. I'd better get going. Call me anytime." Mike started for the front door.

"Mike."

He turned back to Megan.

"Thank you." She put out her arms and hugged him.

"You're welcome. Give Sophia a kiss for me."

"Okay. Call me when you know something?"

"I will."

Chapter 44

Criminal Justice Center
Downtown Nashville

Mike stewed all the way back to the CJC. He was going to call Thurman on his cell as soon as he left Megan's house, but he knew he needed to calm himself before making the call. He decided to use the drive to try and let his anger dissipate before he said something he might regret. All he could focus on was why Thurman would keep something like this to himself. He made the call.

"Hello."

"Were you aware Tim had been threatened?"

"What are you talking about?"

"You know what the hell I'm talking about. I'm talking about your partner. Your dead partner. Were you aware he'd been threatened?"

"If you're trying to find a way to blame his death on me, you can go to hell."

"I'm the one investigating this case and no one is above suspicion. So, if you know something, anything you've been holding back for whatever reason, you'd best start talking real soon."

"How about you tell me what the hell you're referring to?"

"Megan told me what little she knew about the murder of a young girl a few years ago when Tim and Franks were together. She wasn't sure about the details because Tim wouldn't talk about it. She said he told her it was one of those cases that get to you. Surely, as long as you two were together he had to have talked about it at some point."

There was silence on the line.

"I'm going to presume you're talking about a case Tim had obsessed about for years, much longer than he and I were together. And wouldn't you think if he refused to talk to his wife about it, he probably wouldn't talk to his partner about it either? Doesn't it sound logical?"

"Maybe. What case?"

"He wouldn't tell me any details about it. He told me it was no concern of mine and I needed to stay out of it. But, he was definitely obsessed with it, whatever it was."

"In all the days you rode together, he never told you?"

"No. He wouldn't talk about it. He said it was for my own good. He said it was something that happened years ago. I remember him saying it was a case that touched him like no other he'd ever worked."

"And you weren't curious?"

"Hell yeah, I was curious. I bugged the hell out of him several times. He got pissed off and told me to drop it. I assumed—"

"Wait a minute." Mike's frustration was surfacing. "You're a homicide detective for the Nashville Police Department and you're making assumptions?"

"This wasn't an assumption made about a case, damn it. It was made about my friend, *my* partner. I assumed the best thing for me to do, based upon the passion in his voice, was leave it alone and trust him, much like I would have asked of him if the roles were reversed. I *honored* my partner. I *trusted* my partner. I—. Damn it, I cared about my partner. If you don't believe me, you can kiss my shiny blue ass."

"Partners don't keep secrets from each other."

"Exactly what *I* told him, but he said partners honor each other's requests. What I'm telling you is the truth. You can believe it or not. I don't care. It doesn't change anything. I got tired of bugging him about it and being told to butt out. That's it. Take it or leave it."

"Why didn't you tell me about this when Tim was shot?"

"What? How in the hell am I supposed to put an old case I didn't work, and about which I know shit, together with Tim's murder? I'm not clairvoyant, you know."

"You should have told me something."

"Give me a freakin' break."

Mike gave Thurman's responses some thought. "I have a recording on a personal digital recorder Tim was using. On it, some guy who was acquitted of a homicide he was obviously guilty of committing, threatens Tim's life if he doesn't stop following and harassing him. It sounds like Tim is pressing this guy to confess even though he has already been found not guilty by the court.

"What's the date of the recording?"

"I don't know, but logically I'd say it was recorded since the two of you have been together. Megan didn't realize Tim was using a recorder. If this was recorded recently, you should be in a position to know something of value whether you realize it or not. Do you not have any idea who this guy might be?"

Thurman thought for a moment. "There were times—when we were headed somewhere, and he was driving, he'd drive through an area over by Twelfth Avenue South and scan the streets. I asked him what he was doing. He said, 'Forget it. Just enjoy the ride'.

"One time he stopped and told me to stay in the car. He got out and approached some guy who was walking."

"What did the guy look like?"

"He was maybe five eight or nine, kind of a small to average build. He wore jeans, a cammo hooded jacket and a ball cap. He walked like he was selling himself as a badass. Anyway, they talked for maybe four or five minutes. I rolled my window down when he left the car so I could hear what it was about. I was only able to catch some of the words until they started yelling at each other. The shouting only lasted a few seconds before Tim came back to the car and we left. The guy shot us the bird as we drove away. I asked Tim again what it was about. He said it was a lovers quarrel. I rolled my eyes and dropped it. I knew he still wasn't going to talk about it."

"What did they say when they were yelling at each other?"

"I heard the guy say something like, 'Leave me the hell alone. I'm getting sick of you. I was acquitted. I'm innocent.' Then Tim said, 'You may have been acquitted, but you are not innocent. I'm not going to give up until you man up and confess.' There were several expletives shared and Tim walked back to the car."

"You said there were other instances?"

"A few times when I was driving and we were in this same area, he told me to drive through Twelfth Avenue slowly. One time, only a few days ago, he saw this guy and jumped out before I could get the car stopped. Again, he told me to stay in the car. It was like Tim was stalking the guy, trying to irritate him, or intimidate him. It's like he *wanted* to piss him off."

"What was said this time?"

"The same basic stuff, more threats from both of them. I expected them to come to blows any minute. The guy said something this time that made me feel like Tim was maybe taking this thing a bit too far."

"What was that?"

"The guy said something to the effect of 'If you don't leave me alone, I'm going to give you some of the same shit she got. You got it? and Tim said Yeah, I got it.' The whole thing didn't seem to bother Tim as much as it did me. He got back in the car and said 'Let's go.' We left."

Mike sat quietly processing Thurman's story. "This sounds a lot like what's on the recording."

"So, play it so *I* can hear it."

Thurman listened as Mike held the recorder next to the phone and played the threatening message.

When the recording stopped, Mike said, "Well?"

"I'm sure it was the same guy, and I'm almost certain it was the same conversation I heard a few days ago. So, who is this guy?"

"I don't know yet. If this is related to a case from Tim's days with Franks, I can't figure why it's still an issue after all these years, unless there's something about it that's still open?"

As he and Thurman were talking, Mike flipped through Tim's murder book looking for something to connect, to trigger a thought, or provide an answer. He pulled out the manila envelope from the back flap of the blue binder. He turned it over and realized he'd never opened the autopsy report when it came in from Dr. Jamison. He must have been in a hurry or focused elsewhere and simply shoved it into the back of the binder, where it would normally be kept.

He slipped his finger beneath the flap and pushed it across the top of the envelope separating the adhesive. He looked inside, turned it upside down and dumped the report into his left hand. Thurman was still talking and Mike was half listening as he began to casually read over the ME's report.

"I don't know," Thurman said, "I saw this guy twice, maybe three times, all the times were at night on the street. I told you everything I remember. I know you're frustrated. I am too, but brow-beating me isn't going to solve Tim's murder. Talk to Franks. I assure you—."

"Oh, shit! I gotta go." Mike disconnected the call before Thurman could respond.

Chapter 45

Davidson County Morgue
North Nashville

When Mike pushed the doors open to the autopsy theater, Dr. Jamison was up to her elbows inside the chest of a man who must have weighed more than four hundred pounds. His chest was so deep, she and her assistant were both standing on stepladders in order to access the thoracic area and the internal organs, make the necessary incisions to free them for removal, and then lift them out *en bloc,* or as a unit.

Mike approached them. When he got a closer look at the voluminous task before them, he chose to wait until Dr. Jamison addressed him and was able to come down from the ladder.

"Hello, Sergeant. If you'll give me a minute, I'll be right with you."

"No problem," Mike said, even though he had a big problem and he wanted some answers fairly soon in order to resolve it."

Dr. Jamison knew Mike well enough to know when he was upset. She could see his wrinkled brow, arms folded across his chest and his frustrated pacing across the tile floor.

"Ted, can you work on the rest of this for a few minutes, so I can talk with Sergeant Neal?"

"Sure."

"Thanks."

She carefully stepped down the ladder to the floor, removed her face shield, mask and her gloves and laid them on the edge of a stainless steel table. As she stepped toward Mike, he passed her and started walking hurriedly toward her office.

"Can we talk in there?" He pointed as he marched.

"Yes."

The door swung shut and Mike started before she could even get seated. "I need you to explain this."

"What is it?" She took the envelope from him and removed the contents. After looking over the front page, she said, "This is Tim Slater's autopsy report." She looked up at him.

"I know."

"What's the problem?"

"I was here with you during Dwayne Puckett's autopsy less than forty-eight hours ago. You said nothing."

"Well—I said a lot while you were here, but none of it had anything to do with Tim. We were discussing Dwayne Puckett at the time, as I recall."

"That's what I'm talking about. Why didn't you tell me?"

She looked at Mike and took in a breath. She was confident she knew what he was referring to. "What was there to say? I prepared the report and, as the lead investigator, I gave it to you immediately after I completed it. You received it much faster than normal, because of who it was."

"You didn't think it was peculiar enough to say anything about it?"

"Mike, I deal with this kind of thing every day. It was inconsequential. Nothing is unusual in this building. I put everything in my report. Besides, everyone knew the cause of death was the two gunshot wounds to the chest and abdomen. You received my report, didn't you?"

"Yes." Mike admitted after a large exhale.

"Don't you guys normally read them? That *is* why I spend so much time writing those things, you know. They're not a lot of fun to prepare."

"Yes. We read them. I guess—this time I got distracted because it was one of us who was killed."

"I understand. So, what do you want from me?"

Mike rubbed his face with both hands as if trying to wipe away his frustration. "Nothing. I wish I'd known sooner."

"Maybe you should have read the report. You didn't read it did you?"

"Not until today." He hung his head and looked out her window at her assistant balanced on the step ladder over the massive corpse.

"I'm sorry. I'm not sure what else I could do. I followed procedure."

"I know you did." Mike paced. "It's my fault. I didn't mean to beat you up or say you did anything wrong. You did everything by the book, like always. I wish I had been aware sooner about his lung cancer. Forgive my rant. Okay?"

"You're forgiven," She said, immediately. "Do you think he'd kept this from his wife?"

"Yes, I'm sure of it. I don't even know if he knew."

"Oh, he knew. It was much too advanced for him not to know. He had to have been in some considerable discomfort, at least periodically."

"Mmm. I'm not sure he ever showed it."

"Honestly, from what I saw, I don't think he would have lived more than a few months."

Mike shook his head and rubbed his left temple in an attempt to massage his headache away. He couldn't figure why Tim would have kept this to himself.

"Thanks, Doc. I'll—see you later. I have to try and locate his personal physician and find out as much as I can about this. There could be something related to his death."

Dr. Jamison nodded. "Good idea."

Chapter 46

Mike Neal's Car
Nashville

"Hello."

"Megan, it's Mike. I have a quick question for you."

"Sure."

"I need the name and phone number, if you have it, for Tim's primary care physician."

"Why would you need that?"

"We have to talk with everyone we can who knew Tim and who may have heard him say something that could point us in the direction of his killer. It's standard procedure."

"Okay. I'll be right back."

Mike hated to lie to her to get what he needed, but it was Saturday and the ladies in Human Resources were off today. Besides, what he'd said to Megan was mostly true anyway.

"Here it is."

She gave Mike the data he needed and he wrote it in his notepad.

"Thanks, Megan."

"You're welcome."

"Call me if you need to." He ended the call and keyed the

physician's number right away.

"Doctor Eric Baugh's office."

"Hello. This is Sergeant Mike Neal with the Nashville Police Department. I'm sure the doctor isn't in today, but it is imperative I speak to him as soon as possible."

"Uh, Sergeant, Doctor Baugh is not available. Can you speak with Doctor Hartford?"

"This an emergency. I need to speak with Doctor Baugh, *now*."

"Sir, if this is an emergency, you should hang up and call 911."

"It's not that kind of emergency. Do you have Doctor Baugh's cell phone number?"

"We're not allowed to give it out. This is his day off. He's playing golf today."

"Good for him. I still have to talk with him."

"He left word he didn't want to be disturbed."

"Let me make myself clear. I'm investigating the murder of one of Doctor Baugh's patients. If it becomes necessary, I can call a judge and obtain a warrant for you to release his cell number and the location of the doctor's golf course to me. Do we really need to go there?"

She hurriedly informed Mike the doctor was playing Gaylord Springs and she gave him the doctor's cell number without pause. He saved the number and aimed his car toward the golf course.

Unlike the negotiations with Doctor Baugh's receptionist, once Mike identified himself and flashed his shield, he had no trouble convincing the cordial course pro to loan him a golf cart for a half hour. Once he selected the cart, he took his seat and called Doctor Baugh.

"This better be good," Baugh said.

"Doctor Baugh, this is Sergeant Mike Neal with the Nashville Police Department. I am currently at Gaylord Springs and I've borrowed a cart from the course pro in order to locate you for a brief discussion. I need to know what hole you are approaching."

"Sergeant, this is my day off. I play golf every Saturday here at Gaylord. Can't this wait until Monday?"

"No sir. It cannot. One of your patients was murdered earlier this week and there are things I, and his family, need to know in order for me to investigate his homicide properly. We need your cooperation."

"Oh, my goodness. Who was it?"

"Detective Tim Slater was ambushed as he was leaving the restaurant where he and his partner had dinner."

"We're finishing number twelve. I'll watch for you from the back of the thirteenth tee."

Mike held the accelerator pedal to the floor of the electric golf cart as he sped from the ninth hole's green, next to the clubhouse, out to the thirteenth tee. He could see four men standing together in the shade of a large Oak tree as he approached. Dr. Baugh had his hand in the air, waving to Mike. One of the men was standing with his hands on his hips. The other two had their arms folded across their chests. They did not seem glad to see Mike.

"Doctor," Mike said, as he offered his hand. "Let's talk over here." He gestured toward a spot away from the other men. "Can I assume you were aware of Tim's cancer?"

"Yes. He came to me about four months ago concerning a pain he had in the left side of his chest. I asked him several questions and scheduled him for an MRI. When I received the results, I arranged a meeting for him with one of Nashville's top Oncologists. After their meeting, I called the doctor and asked him about his diagnosis for Tim. He told me he'd recommended an aggressive campaign of chemotherapy in an attempt to buy him some time."

"But?"

"He said Tim's cancer was advanced and he didn't have very long. He said Tim had chosen to avoid the side effects of the chemo and attempt to enjoy what time he had left before the cancer caused him to be bedridden."

"That's a tough decision."

"Yes, and I'm afraid it's one too many today are being forced to make."

"Eric. Please. The next foursome is putting. Hello?"

"Wave them through, Jack."

"Eric? Geez. Come on."

"What happened? How was Tim killed?" Baugh asked.

"He was shot, ambushed."

"He had a wife and a little girl didn't he?"

"Yes. I don't think they knew."

"He told me he was going to tell his wife at some point. He wasn't sure when. He seemed hesitant. He said he wasn't ready yet to break the news."

"How bad was it?"

"Bad. Stage 4. It had metastasized and had moved into his lymph nodes."

"How was he able to work?" Mike asked.

"I don't know. He was tough, I guess. Tougher than me. That's for sure."

"His partner told me he'd had a chest cold for quite a while. An upper respiratory infection, I think he said."

The doctor nodded. "Some similar symptoms. He was hiding the truth from you guys. I told him after he'd met with the Oncologist, he could bring his wife in and we would discuss the progression of the disease so they could be prepared for the things he would have to face in the near future. He didn't want to go through all the standard protocols a disease like this calls for. Did you know he watched his father die with this same disease?"

"No." Mike closed his eyes momentarily and shook his head.

"He said he didn't want to go through all the chemo and treatments his father did. He said they didn't help him. He believed they were pointless and caused a lot of prolonged suffering for his dad. Tim's case was fairly advanced. He would have had a similar experience. Obviously, the difficulty from watching his dad influenced his decision making."

"I'm sure it did. Thank you, Doctor. Mike offered his hand. I'm sorry to disrupt your game. Please offer my apologies to your friends."

"That's not a problem. Tim seemed like a very caring man. I'm sure he was a good detective."

"He was an excellent detective. A good husband and father, too."

"No doubt."

"We're going to miss him." Mike sat in his cart. "Thanks again."

As he drove back to the clubhouse, he thought about how difficult it would be to discover you are going to die soon and then decide not to share it with your loved ones.

Tim had a beautiful and loving family. What could have possibly driven him to want to keep this from Megan?

Chapter 47

Home of Robert Franks
West Nashville

"Hello, Mike." Robert Franks stepped back and held open the front door to his home. "Come in."

"Sorry to impose on you with such short notice."

"It's not a problem. Retirement affords a man certain flexibilities, you know."

"I'm looking forward to finding out what it's like."

"Don't rush it. You're a young man and Burris needs you too much to let that happen."

"I don't feel so young sometimes."

"That's the stress talking. Have a seat."

Mike sat at the dining table.

"Can I get you something, a Jack Daniel's or single barrel scotch?"

"Don't tempt me. I'm good. Thanks. I wanted to talk with you about a recording Megan Slater found on a personal digital recorder Tim had been using."

"Okay. I wonder when he started using one of those?" Franks pulled out a chair and joined Mike.

"I'm not sure, but he and I rode together for a few weeks during the years after you retired. I've been using one for quite a while now. He may have picked up the habit."

"Makes sense."

"I'd like you to listen and see if you can tell me who Tim is talking with on the recording."

"Sure." Franks sat forward in his chair.

Mike started the recorder, turned up the volume and laid it on the table close to Franks.

As the voices started, Franks angled his left ear toward the recorder and his mouth opened a bit. After a few sentences, his facial reactions told Mike he had recognized the voice.

The recording finished and Mike pressed the stop button. Franks sat back in his chair. He shook his head slowly as if in disbelief and then looked at Mike. "I thought that son of a bitch was history."

"Who is it?"

"It sounds like Buck Kessler."

"Who is he?"

Franks took a breath and interlaced his fingers on the table in front of him. "Around September of 2004, Tim and I caught a case involving a young girl, twenty-something, who'd been strangled with a ligature in an apartment stairwell. The ME said the pattern of neck impressions told him it was a length of military type paracord.

"We hadn't been at the crime scene more than maybe five minutes, Tim started acting sort of odd based on his normal behavior. He squatted next to the body like he did normally, but he stayed there for a while longer than usual. I watched him. After a few minutes, it looked like his upper body was shaking. I walked over and stood next to him. He flinched when he realized I was there. He was crying. I asked him what was the matter. He waved it off; said it was nothing.

"After a bit he spoke, 'Just such a damn shame,' he said, 'for someone so beautiful to die like this—so young.'

"I nodded and accepted his explanation, but I sensed there was more to it. He was avoiding telling me something. I knew better than to push him. I let it go, confident he would loosen up and talk about it later.

"We didn't have an ID on the girl, no purse or wallet or anything. I thought she was going to be another Jane Doe. But, this girl was dressed too well for that. Later when the ME's team took the body and the CSU finished up at the scene, we left.

"I was driving, heading back to the justice center. He was sitting over there, real quiet, looking out the side window. I knew he couldn't stay that way for long. We were always able to talk. Even when he and Judy were going at it, I heard about each argument blow by blow, as they say. I guess I was his sounding board. I didn't mind.

"Pretty soon, he cleared his throat and finally started to talk. 'The girl back there—'. He stopped and was quiet for a few minutes, trying to collect his emotions I think. I waited. Out of nowhere he said, 'Her name is Vanessa Kemp.' I looked over at him. I wanted to ask how he knew, but with his emotional response earlier, I was pretty sure I needed to just listen. I was sure the information, and probably much more, would come out on its own. He broke down and sobbed. I let him take his time. I drove. I wanted to help him. I couldn't imagine what was going on inside him.

"In a couple of minutes, he wiped his face with his handkerchief. And then he said, 'I knew her father. He was a good man—a good friend—an Army buddy of mine.' He looked at me without saying anything. I looked across the car at him. His face wrinkled up. I felt so sorry for him.

"He said, 'She was my Godchild.' Then he broke down and I almost wrecked the car. I pulled into an empty retail parking lot. I asked if he was sure it was her. He looked across the car at me with this—this expression on his face. I nodded.

"Seems Tim and her dad had remained close for several years after their discharge. His friend discovered he had pancreatic cancer, and didn't have long to live. The girl was only eleven years old at the time. Tim said his friend asked him to watch out for her since he wouldn't be there to see her grow into an adult. He didn't have any other family in the area to help, only his wife. Tim said he remained in contact with the girl and her mom until they moved to some place up around Goodlettsville. Somehow he lost touch.

"He was regretful for not keeping tabs on the girl and honoring his friend's wishes. It was really causing him some grief. I'd never seen him like this.

"I asked him if he thought we should recuse ourselves since he was so close to the case. He insisted we shouldn't. He was afraid no one else would do the job we could to clear her case and put her killer away. He decided we would keep it to ourselves."

"You didn't get a vote?" Mike asked.

"She was *his* Goddaughter. I didn't feel I could say no to him." Mike nodded.

"Everything went well with the investigation. We found there was this guy, Kessler, she'd dated who, according to friends, was overly possessive. Typical story, she broke up with him and she moved on, but he didn't. The more people we talked to who knew her and the more information we collected, the more guilty this guy looked.

"We submitted our case to the DA and he said he felt good about it and was willing to run with it. We picked up Kessler, booked him and the familiar game began.

"During our investigation, we discovered Kessler worked at a local gun shop and target range, Precision Arms, I think it was. But, it had no bearing on our case since the Kemp girl was strangled. I would think this could have some considerable pertinence in Tim's case."

"Definitely." Mike noted the name of the gun shop.

"We also found out Kessler was a hunter and a member of a local gun club up in Smith County where he spent much of his free time. The members occasionally hunted together, frequently held competitions, shooting contests for cash prizes. They told us Kessler was a frequent winner in their pistol competitions and occasionally in the rifle shoots too.

"Since he was acquitted of all charges in the girl's murder, there was no law preventing him from owning or shooting a gun. So, I'm confident he went back to his normal life with the target range and the gun club."

"What was Tim's response to Kessler's acquittal?"

"Oh, boy." Franks shook his head as he recalled Tim's anger. "He went off. I had to physically restrain him in the court room when the judge hammered the gavel down on the block. Tim was livid. He felt totally responsible for Kessler getting off. It was his idea to withhold his relationship. That, along with the secondary DNA he didn't want to include, is what led to Kessler being found not guilty."

"How did that happen?"

"At the crime scene, the criminalists were collecting evidence from all over the place. Tim made sure they were all in full Tyvek and being as thorough as they'd ever been. He was checking and triple checking their photography, documentation, their collection of hair and fiber, bagging and labeling, everything. He was obsessed with it. He was beginning to irritate the techs. And, I was going behind him apologizing to them for the stress he was creating. I understood his motive. They were trying to understand.

"Later during the trial I discovered, along with the jury and the judge, there had been a third sample of unidentifiable DNA found near the right knee of the girl's jeans. It didn't belong to her or Kessler. Seems one of the techs told Tim about it in the lab and he told her to forget it. He said it wasn't a significant sample, and rather than piss Tim off and suffer more of his wrath, she followed his instructions and didn't report it. Though she failed to report it, she didn't fail to discuss it with one of the other techs who ended up on the stand facing Kessler's attorney, Ann Culbertson.

"I'm not sure if the defense team's investigator found out about it, or if Culbertson was just fishing and got lucky, but she hooked a big one when she asked the lab tech if she was certain all the evidence found at the crime scene had been documented and submitted to the court.

"The DA told me afterward the tech hesitated when asked, looked at him, and then admitted to what the other tech had told her. She was asked why she didn't tell someone before now. She said she assumed the detective knew best. By the way, after the trial, both techs received written warnings.

"At this point, Culbertson must have smelled blood. She went for the kill. She magnified the importance of this new DNA evidence to her advantage. It was obviously enough to create a degree of reasonable doubt in the minds of the jury. Not only did she use this to assure the jury the prosecution was selectively hiding evidence that could damage their case, she added the new information her investigator had uncovered when he researched connections between Tim and the Kemp family. She announced to the jury Tim was Vanessa Kemp's Godfather and should have recused himself from the case. Instead, she said, Detective Slater chose to declare himself judge and jury and then manipulate the evidence in his favor."

"How did the defense find out she was his Goddaughter?"

"We estimated Culbertson's investigator must have been

watching Tim and saw him, at some point, make eye contact with Mrs. Kemp. We thought they became suspect and had the two of them followed. She and Tim were talking outside a coffee shop near the courthouse in what they assumed was a private conversation when Tim said she hugged him and started crying. He thought he spotted the investigator across the street looking at them. I remember him saying right after it happened, he knew no good would come of it."

"What made Tim think the third DNA sample wasn't enough to enter into evidence?"

"Beside the fact the sample was so small, I think he knew there was a chance it could blow our case against Kessler. He was obsessed with solving her case and bringing her mom and her deceased father the justice they deserved. We were both certain of Kessler's guilt.

"The acquittal gave Kessler an overdose of confidence and he actually admitted to Tim later, after he was released and they were alone, he did in fact kill the girl. Tim said Kessler laughed about it as he walked away.

"I think his admission did a number on Tim. He began to feel his decision to ignore the minute sample of DNA and his being seen with Mrs. Kemp were blunders on his part which cost us the case. It really messed him up. Kessler is lucky Tim didn't take him out back then, but Tim had his family and his job to think of."

"That's disturbing," Mike said. "It's sometimes hard to know where to stop with evidence. So Robert, what are your thoughts on the recording?"

"I'm confident it's Kessler. I'd know the jackass's voice anywhere. It's obvious, his intent was to threaten Tim, or worse. But, knowing Tim and knowing his unceasing concern about this case, I would not be surprised if Tim was giving Kessler as much grief as he was getting. Regardless, what this asshole is saying here should park him atop your 'person of interest' list."

"He's easily my number one, but like you guys, I have to give the DA a complete and viable case in order for him to be able to nail his ass this time, without fail."

"Remember, I told you Kessler is a big hunter?"

"Yeah."

"The way you described the shots that took Tim out, I'd say he's more capable of that kind of marksmanship than most."

"I think I know my next stop. Thanks, Robert."

Chapter 48

Criminal Justice Center
Downtown Nashville

With an arm load of files and a cup of hot coffee, Mike pushed open the door to the interview room. He normally brought with him a stack of files or binders. Sometimes they all applied to the case being discussed. Other times, they were from other cases, merely props for the purpose of implicit intimidation.

The impact of this display of information, had at times been surprisingly beneficial, causing the interviewee to stare and wonder what was inside such a pile of printed papers. Often, the stack created uncertainty and even fear in the minds of the suspects. This time, all the files and murder books were indeed related to Mike's current guest in one way or another.

A relatively small Buck Kessler looked even smaller slumped down in the straight back chair with his eyes closed and his tattooed arms folded across his chest. He glanced at Mike with a look on his unshaven face that said, 'Who the hell are you?' Mike parked his files on one of the small table's corners nearest to him so the names on the files and binders faced Kessler.

The two officers who visited Kessler's duplex had fortunately been able to convince him he was not under arrest, and it was in his best interest to follow them. He voluntarily agreed to meet with Mike to discuss what he might know about Tim Slater and whoever could have wanted him dead. The officers explained the alternative of not agreeing to speak with Mike. It could make it look like Kessler was being uncooperative and acting suspicious. Kessler chose the first option and followed the officers to the CJC in his pickup truck.

"Buck, my name is Sergeant Mike Neal. Can I get you anything to drink before we get started? A Coke or water? Coffee?"

Kessler looked at Mike as if trying to figure out if he was serious. "I'm good." He grunted.

Mike glanced at Kessler as he pulled out his cell phone and pushed down the slider button to change the ringer to vibrate so he wouldn't be interrupted while in the middle of his interview.

Kessler was looking at the stack of files.

"Can I assume you don't have a cell phone on you?"

"They took it, out there." He gestured toward the door. "And everything else from my pockets, too. They even took my damn snuff. I guess they thought I might dip myself to death in here while I waited."

"You'll get it all back when we're finished."

Kessler frowned.

Mike removed his sport coat and draped it over the back of his chair. He pulled out the chair and sat. Mike's chair, unlike Kessler's, had arms and was padded on all surfaces. It was on wheels so he could move about as he pleased.

The walls and ceiling of the interview room were covered with soundproof acoustic panels. One of the two longer walls had a large mirror heavily framed much like a window in a house. Anyone who didn't know this was a one-way mirror would surely have to be from another planet.

"Can I assume by your cammo baseball cap you're a hunter?"

Mike noticed Kessler wore a braided bracelet made of olive green 550 paracord. The same type of cord, declared by Dr. Jamison in Vanessa Kemp's autopsy report, was used to strangle the young girl.

"Yeah," he finally said.

"Deer?"

"Yeah, mostly. And a few others."

"My dad and I hunted together when I was young," Mike

shared. "I'm from Rutherford County, near Murfreesboro, originally. We hunted a lot of deer, rabbit, squirrel, sometimes quail and doves."

Kessler gave Mike a weak nod.

"Where do you hunt?"

"I know a couple of places down around Dickson and I have friends who live in Smith County and up near Monterrey, TN. The place in Smith County has over a hundred acres of woods. I go there quite a bit. It's convenient, and I know the deer trails."

"Sounds nice. You ever bow hunt?"

Kessler shrugged. "I tried it, but I've got a torn rotator cuff injury from playin' softball and I have some trouble holdin' back the string. I just stick with the gun."

".308?"

"Yeah."

Mike paid particular attention to Kessler's eyes and his body language as he seemed to answer his questions truthfully. After reviewing Franks and Slater's files on the Kemp case, Mike knew the answers to many of the questions he would ask. His attentive focus on Kessler as the man answered questions may have appeared as heightened interest in his responses. In reality, the attentiveness came from Mike's desire to establish a kinesics baseline for Kessler's physical reactions to questions he answered both truthfully and otherwise.

"I still get the fever when it gets good and cold," Mike said. "I don't have the time I used to have for things like that."

Kessler nodded.

"What's your biggest rack?"

"I got a ten-pointer two years ago."

"Nice. Did you hang the trophy?"

"Yeah. It's in my den."

"Impressive." Mike hoped Kessler was beginning to loosen up some.

"Buck, I want to thank you for coming in voluntarily to talk with me today. I really appreciate your help. Did anyone explain to you why we asked you to come in and talk?"

"Not really."

"I'll try to explain then," Mike said. "We're investigating a murder that took place Monday night. One of our veteran Homicide Detectives, Tim Slater, was ambushed and murdered."

Kessler tilted his head as he wrinkled his brow, displaying what Mike saw as counterfeit surprise.

"You haven't heard about it?"

He shook his head slowly. After a few seconds Kessler said, "No. I don't watch the news much any more."

Mike nodded. "We're talking with anyone and everyone who knew Tim or had dealings with him in the past to see if they might have any ideas for us about who could have wanted him dead. You remember Detective Slater, don't you?"

"Yeah. I think so." Kessler acted as if he was straining his memory to recall Tim.

"He was one of the detectives who arrested you for the murder of Vanessa Kemp, wasn't he?"

"Yeah. But, I was acquitted."

"That's right. Can you refresh my memory about the case and why you were arrested?"

Kessler stared at Mike as if to say, 'You've got to be kidding me?' He hesitated, and then sat up straight in his chair.

Mike did not alter his expression in response to Kessler's sigh of disgust.

After blowing out a large breath, he said, "It's been over three years. I was arrested because I had dated her and the detectives couldn't find anybody else to pin it on. So, they picked me."

"Were you two still dating at the time of her death?"

"No. I broke it off. I ended it."

"You ended it?" Mike said, as if he took it to mean Kessler was admitting to killing her.

"I broke up with her." Kessler said with a lowered brow to accent his irritation at Mike's innuendo. "What's this got to do with anything, anyway? I didn't kill her. I was acquitted. I think you know this already."

"You sound a bit perturbed, Buck. Why?"

"Because, for some reason, you people won't let this thing go. I went to court. I defended myself. The jury said I was innocent."

"Not guilty." Mike corrected him. "What do you mean by *you people*? The police?"

"Yeah. I feel like I'm gonna end up gettin' hassled about this the rest of my life."

Mike let Kessler's comment go unaddressed. "So, tell me Buck. Why am I hearing that even after your acquittal, occasionally, you were still in contact with Detective Slater?"

"I don't know who's tellin' you this stuff. I never contacted Slater."

"What do you mean?"

"Slater was stalkin' me."

"He was what? Stalking you?"

"He was huntin' me and harassin' me every chance he got."

"Did you report it to the police?"

"Oh, yeah. Like *that* would have done any good. I ain't stupid."

"It would have confirmed or denied what you're telling me now."

"You guys are all the same." He leaned back in the chair.

"So, you claim he was harassing you, but there is no record of it. How did he harass you? What did he do?"

"Several times he stopped me on the street and acted like an ass askin' me a bunch of stupid questions. He told me I wasn't gonna get away with killin' the girl. I reminded him I didn't do it and I was acquitted, but he didn't stop. Not long ago he started makin' what I consider serious threats."

"Threats? What kind of threats?"

"He said, 'If the courts won't do their job, he would have to do it for them. An eye for an eye and a tooth for a tooth.' That sounds like a damn threat to me. I was gettin' to where I was afraid to walk the streets at night."

"What were you afraid of?"

"Him. I was afraid of him. I was afraid of what he might do. Hell, he was a damn cop. He had a gun and he could get away with usin' it. He could do whatever the hell he wanted to and get away with it."

"Do you honestly believe that? Do you believe as cops we can do whatever we want to?"

"Hell, yeah. You guys get away with all kinds of shit."

"Like?"

"Like beatin' up on folks when they don't want to get arrested. Breakin' in people's doors to search for grass and drugs and stuff."

"Resisting arrest is also a crime."

"Citizens have rights. You guys hassle whoever you want to."

"So tell me, if you were innocent of the girl's murder, why do you think you were arrested in the first place?"

"I have no idea. I dated her back before she was killed. You cops assume whoever had a relationship with a person, killed them. That makes your job easy, don't it?"

"I wish it was that easy. How long did you two date?"

"A few months, I guess."

"What happened?"

"What do you mean?"

"When did you stop seeing each other?"

"I don't know—maybe a couple or three weeks before she died."

"Was that when she stopped seeing you or when you stopped seeing her?"

"What's that supposed to mean?"

"I heard she broke it off and you couldn't deal with it."

"Where did you hear that?"

"I forget."

"That's bullshit, man."

"Okay, why did you stop dating?"

Kessler rubbed his palms on his jeans.

"She was gettin' too clingy, too controllin', always wantin' me to do stuff with her I didn't want to do, like goin' to movies and out to eat, wantin' me to buy her flowers, spendin' my damn money, all the time spendin' money. I had to finally cut her off and just say no. That's it. No more. I'm done."

"Really? What did she say?"

"She got pissed. She was in love." Kessler leaned back in his chair with a half smile. "She started callin' me a cheapskate. She criticized me, said I didn't know how to treat a lady."

"Really?" Mike said, playing along.

"Yeah. I told her if I ever meet one, I'll know how to treat her."

"Uh oh." Mike grinned in an attempt to elicit more information from Kessler.

"Yeah. That pissed her off right there. Her face got red as a rooster's comb. She was hot. She started throwin' things at me."

"You're kidding. Then what happened?"

Kessler stopped talking. His mood changed. He sat back in his chair for a minute and went mute. He looked as though he realized he was getting carried away with his explanation. He crossed his arms over his chest and took a big breath. He settled his emotions down and shut his mouth.

Mike leaned forward close to Kessler. "What's the matter?"

"You're tryin' to set me up, like that damn Slater. I ain't stupid."

He stared down at the floor between them.

"I'm only trying to collect the facts to go along with the evidence. You know, giving you a chance to offer your side of the story."

"You may have evidence, but it ain't on me cause I ain't done nothin'."

"So, tell me Buck, where were you this past Monday night between eight o'clock and ten?"

"At home."

"Who was there with you?"

"I live alone."

Mike nodded. "Who did you talk with on the phone while you were at home that night?"

Kessler acted as if he was pondering the question. "Nobody."

"Did you order a pizza or any other delivery?"

"What? No."

"What did you do at home that night."

"I watched TV and drank a few beers. That's what I do most weeknights."

"How long did you watch TV?"

Kessler rolled his eyes. "I don't remember. I watched it—a while."

"What did you watch?"

"What? I don't remember."

"It's only been five days. Was it a comedy? A drama? Reality show? Ballgame?"

"I think I watched a ballgame Monday."

"Okay. Good. A ballgame."

"Baseball? Basketball? Football?"

Kessler took in a deep breath and rolled his eyes. "Baseball."

"Baseball. Who was playing?"

"Man, what is this shit?"

"They're only questions—Buck. Who was playing baseball on Monday night when you were home alone watching TV?"

Kessler took in another large breath through his mouth and exhaled through his nose. "Uh—Atlanta I guess."

"Atlanta you guess. Okay. Who do you *guess* Atlanta was playing on Monday night when you were at home watching them on TV?"

"I don't remember." He threw his hands up and let them fall to his lap. His facial expression reflected his angst.

"Buck. I'm trying to establish whether or not you have an alibi for the range of time during which Tim Slater was murdered, but

I'm not getting much help from you."

"I told you where I was and what I was doin'. What else am I supposed to do? I told you the truth."

"None of the things you've told me about your whereabouts and actions on Monday night can be corroborated. This causes problems, Buck. It leaves you without an alibi."

Kessler folded his arms in a jerking, angry motion.

Mike heard, and felt, his phone vibrate from atop the stack of files. The signal was notifying him he had an incoming text message. He stopped to read the message.

"Will you excuse me for a few minutes, Buck?"

Mike collected his files and exited the interview room. As the interview room closed behind him, Mike turned to see Wendy waiting.

"Well?"

She held up two sheets of paper and smiled.

Chapter 49

Criminal Justice Center
Downtown Nashville

It had been about twenty-five minutes since Mike left Kessler alone in the interview room. During which time, Wendy gave Mike a report on her visual inspection of Kessler's stretch-cab pickup truck, parked at a meter on Third Avenue outside the CJC.

Mike didn't feel it was necessary to order a search warrant at this time. He could get this accomplished rather quickly whenever he found it was needed. But, he thought it might be helpful for Wendy to check out the truck in case she might spot something helpful.

She found a dark blue hoody laying on the camouflage seat covers in the backseat. Two well-worn deer stands were laying in the topper-covered bed with a long length of paracord, maybe eighty to a hundred feet long. All the deer hunting equipment, gave her reason to believe, should Mike order a warrant, she would have a good chance to match some hair and fibers to those found at the crime scene.

The layer of crushed peanut shells on both sides of the front cabin floor caused Wendy to question her chances for matching any of her soil samples from the scene to specimens taken from his truck.

A black canvas holster, mounted with velcro beneath the truck's dash and to the right of the steering column, was empty.

Since he'd left Kessler, Mike had spent some of the time behind the one way mirror in the adjacent room, watching his suspect as he sat—just him and his thoughts, simmering.

Kessler's frustration was showing as he regularly rubbed his face with his hands and made occasional jerking movements in response to what Mike perceived as his anger boiling over inside him.

Mike reentered the room with a fresh cup of coffee, a bottle of water for Kessler, and a plan.

"You want some water?" Mike thought Kessler looked like he actually needed a shot of whiskey—or two.

"Yeah," he exhaled the word along with an extended breath.

Mike parked his cell phone on the table, off to the side. He sat and rolled his chair about a foot closer to Kessler than he'd been earlier. In response, Kessler leaned back in his chair.

"Okay, Buck. Let's get back to the facts."

Kessler said nothing.

Mike continued. "Based upon what you've told me, Tim Slater seemed to be hassling you about his Goddaughter's death and the fact you were found not guilty. You said he was threatening you, saying he was going to see that you paid for her death."

"Yes, he did, several times. He kept sayin' it, and sayin' it."

"I don't suppose you have any of those alleged threats on a recording?"

"Hell, no."

Mike thought for a minute and then said, "Buck, I'd like to tell you about a shopping trip I made this morning. I went shopping for a nine millimeter semi-automatic pistol. I wasn't sure of the best place to go so I asked a friend who told me Precision Arms was a nice local shop with knowledgeable people who knew how to handle weapons and knew how to shoot."

Mike paused.

"When I got to Precision Arms, I looked around and then asked the fellow who offered to help me if he had any nine millimeter pistols. He told me he had eight different ones in the shop. So, I asked to see them all.

"He laid them out on the counter for me. I asked him if these were all the nine millimeter pistols he had. He said they were.

"I told him I needed to borrow them for a few hours. He said he couldn't do that. That's when I showed him my badge, my gun, my ID and my search warrant allowing me to borrow the pistols. I gave him the warrant and a receipt. He gave me the eight pistols.

"I took them to the crime lab in Madison where I had a crew waiting to analyze casings and lead from bullets fired from each of these weapons. We did the analysis and you know what we found, Buck?"

After a minute, Kessler answered, "What?"

"None of the casings fired from these pistols matched the casings from the murder scene."

Kessler was visibly pleased. His eyes opened wider and a slight smile crossed his face.

"So, I took the pistols back to the shop, showed my ID again and thanked another young man who offered to help me this time. The first guy to help me wasn't there. As I was placing the eight weapons on the counter top, I asked this new guy if these eight pistols were the only nine millimeter pistols in the shop. He said, 'Yes.' Then, his face wrinkled a bit and you know what he said?"

Kessler said nothing.

"He said, 'You know? We do have one other nine in the back, but it's been sold'. I said, Oh? Sold?"

Kessler's face sagged in response to Mike's animation.

"He said, 'Yes. It's being held, waiting for the customer whose buying it to pay the balance and pick it up'. I asked him if I could see the weapon. He hesitated, but realizing I was with the police, he complied.

"I looked at the pistol. It was a Smith & Wesson M&P. I explained if he would check the wording of the search warrant I'd given the first young man, he could see it specified 'all' nine millimeter pistols on the premises. Since this pistol was a nine and is obviously on the premises, I needed to borrow it for a while under the same warrant as the others. He said he understood."

"As I was leaving, I turned back and asked him who the buyer was for the M&P. He said he didn't know. He said, 'All I know is Buck Kessler sold the gun and had it marked On Hold, so you'll have to ask him'."

"So, I'm asking him." Mike moved his head until he grabbed Kessler's attention. "Who bought the gun?"

"I—I don't remember his name."

"Really? You don't remember? How convenient."

"No. I wrote it down on the invoice. It's there in the back of the store."

"I'm sure it is." Mike paused. "Okay. In case you're interested, the brass casings from the test firing of this *sold* pistol showed the same extractor and ejector markings as both casings from the crime scene outside Tony's Cafe. This pistol you sold to whomever it is you can't remember, is the murder weapon used to kill Tim Slater. It doesn't look like your customer will be buying it after all. Buck, do you have any idea how this new weapon could be a match for the one that killed Detective Slater?"

"I have no idea. That's not the gun I sold."

"According to the guy at the shop, it is."

"He'll never testify to it. You won't have anything—no proof."

"You know, I can understand how you might think this. I'm sure you guys are friends, but after I explained to him the ramifications from withholding evidence and the consequences to a charge of conspiracy after the fact to first degree murder, he seemed to feel differently about it. He was actually helpful and assured me he would cooperate with our investigation, including testimony in court, if necessary. He was truly quite helpful."

Kessler was shifting in his seat. He looked to be searching for a more comfortable position.

"And, as if that wasn't enough, I have this." Mike pulled Tim Slater's digital recorder from his pocket and placed it on the table between them. He said nothing. He waited and watched Kessler.

"What? So you've got a recorder. So what." He said, feigning confidence. His head was still. His eyes were darting from Mike to the recorder and back.

"Everything you and I have said in here today was recorded." Mike pointed to the small signs on the wall by the door that read: *Conversations in this room are recorded.*

"It's standard procedure. So, therefore, we have your voice print. Since we have a recording of our conversation today, we'll be able to match it up and confirm it's you threatening Detective Slater on his recorder."

"I ain't threatened nobody. You can't prove shit."

"Oh, I'm afraid that's not true, Buck. You see, voiceprints are much like fingerprints. They are distinctive and unusual, particular to the owner. And the best part is, they are accepted as valid evidence in court."

Mike watched Kessler's indignant response to the unexpected education about voice prints.

"Would you like to hear what's on Tim Slater's recorder? By the way, in case you were wondering, this isn't the only copy of Detective Slater's recording."

Mike pushed the Play button and placed the recorder on the table between them.

Chapter 50

Criminal Justice Center
Downtown Nashville

> *"You confessed. Damn it. You admitted you killed Vanessa Kemp. You need to man up and turn yourself in."*

> *"I only admitted it to you, asshole and only after I was acquitted by the court. In case they don't teach you knuckleheads the law, you can't indict me twice for the same crime."*

Kessler allowed himself to slide down in the chair. His chin dropped slowly to his chest. His eyes closed as his expression seemed to brace him for the rest of what his memory reminded him was coming.

> *"A flaw in our system; I assure you."*
> *"Just because you and the DA screwed up on this one, don't mean you get a second chance at me. And,*

if you don't stop harassin' me, I'm gonna take care of your irritatin' ass like I took care of hers. And, like her, nobody will know who did it."

Kessler crossed his arms over his chest as if to block out anything else he'd said to Slater.

"Listen. I know you pukes ain't that sharp. Hell, if you were, I'd be in jail right now. You ain't got nothin' on me. So, leave—me—the hell—alone. I ain't warnin' you again, Slater. You got it?"

"Oh, I got it. I definitely got it."

Mike stopped the recording and sat looking at Kessler, who was staring at the floor.

Mike raised his eyebrows and said, "You know, with all this evidence, the DA is going to be a pretty happy fellow with a slam dunk package like this."

Mike picked up the recorder, turned it off, and returned it to his pocket.

Kessler gazed up at him briefly with an empty-eyed look, appearing unsure of what he could or should say at this point that could possibly help his cause.

"We spotted an empty canvas holster mounted beneath the dash in your truck. I'm told it's the right size to hold a large frame semi-automatic pistol. One similar to the 9mm that killed Tim Slater. Where is the pistol that goes in your holster?"

"I sold it."

"To who?"

"I don't know his name. I sold it at a gun show," Kessler said with a tone of sarcasm.

Mike nodded. "You know Buck, you're not helping yourself at all."

"What do you want from me? I've answered your questions."

Mike sat, staring at his suspect. He was ready to sum it up and go for the gold.

"Buck, I have video of you following Detectives Slater and Thurman when they pulled into the parking lot at Tony's Cafe the night Tim Slater was murdered. You were driving a stolen dark red Camry that was missing the rear bumper."

"Bullshit."

"No bullshit, Buck. Video. Pictures don't lie. Think about it. How else would I know?"

"I have Crime Lab analysis on hair and fiber samples found on the tree you hid behind prior to firing the shots that killed Tim Slater. I'm confident these samples will match hair and fiber taken from the hoody our crime scene investigator spotted earlier in the backseat of your truck, parked out here on Third Avenue.

"I have signed written testimony from two eye witnesses—two." Mike held up two fingers. "One saw you more than once arguing with Tim Slater on the street. The other one saw you the night you shot Tim Slater when you walked through her front lawn and across her sidewalk prior to crossing the street and driving the red Camry you stole and later torched in Joelton.

"I know you realize this is a lot of evidence. The gun and the recording sort of wrap it all up in a package for the District Attorney.

"I'll tell you what. You sit back and relax. Give some thought to the recording I played for you and to what I've told you about the match of the brass casings and all the other evidence. I'll be back in a few minutes."

Mike closed the door behind him and walked to the adjacent room and stood watching Kessler through the one-way mirror. His elbows were on the table and his hands were supporting his head as it moved from side to side. His lips were moving, but Mike couldn't hear anything.

Mike walked five doors down the hall to check on the plans for the lineup.

"Good afternoon, Mrs. Jackson." Mike smiled at her and then nodded to the officer who'd been assigned as her chauffeur for the day.

"Hello, Sergeant."

"Thank you for coming in to help us. This shouldn't take long and then we'll take you back home. Is Mr. Jackson doing okay?"

"He's—. Well, he's Jackson." She gave Mike a snaggletoothed smile.

"Stick with the officer here. I'll be back shortly and we'll get started."

Mike looked at his wristwatch as he retraced his steps to the interview room. It had been three and a half hours since he'd started with Kessler. On average, he felt he was on schedule. He pushed the door open and held it.

"Let's go."

"Where?" Kessler made no effort to get up.

"We have some folks who would like to get a second look at you."

"What are you talkin' about?"

"Come on. Let's go. They won't wait all day."

As they left the interview room, Mike reached into his pocket and turned on his digital recorder. If Kessler was to say anything revealing while outside the room, he wanted to be sure he had it recorded.

"What is this?" Kessler asked as Mike pulled on his arm, escorting him down the hallway.

"In here." Mike gestured at a door. He handed Kessler a dark blue hoody. "Put this on."

"Why?"

"Just put the thing on. You're going to be a part of a line up. I told you we had two people who've seen you. They need to see you again to identify you."

"This is bullshit."

"Call it what you like, Buck. This is the real world."

"I'm not sure you have the right to do this."

Mike ignored his comment and pulled the hoody up so it was in a position similar to what Mrs. Jackson said she saw the night of Tim's murder.

"Listen. There will be five other men in the lineup similar in stature to you. The witnesses will be behind an opaque screen. The lights will be bright. You won't be able to see them, but they can see you."

"Wait a minute. This don't seem fair."

"Buck. You said you didn't do it. Why are you worried about it being fair?"

"I don't want to be picked out of a lineup even though I'm innocent—or not guilty."

"The person we're convinced killed Tim Slater is in this lineup. If that person isn't you, I'd say you have nothing to worry about. If it is you, I'd recommend now as the time to seize the opportunity to minimize the length of your stay as a guest of the state of Tennessee. You will not get a better chance than this one, right now."

"I think I want to—."

"Hang on." Mike was ready. He'd been ready for a while in case Kessler started to ask for his counsel. Mike made the sign of a football player's 'Timeout'. "Before you say what I'm sure you're about to say. Let me make sure you're clear on what happens once you call in the cavalry."

Mike took Kessler's arm and moved him back into the hallway, away from the other officers. "If you choose to start working through your lawyer, the DA's willingness to accept a deal and limit the length of your punishment goes away. You need to be sure you understand, since there will be no turning back."

Kessler listened intently with a look of desperation on his face.

"Pay attention, because this will be the best advice you'll ever get. I think you have come to realize during our discussion today, we have a large amount of hard evidence against you in this case. If we add two eye witnesses, one who saw you fighting with the victim at least twice, and one who saw you leaving the scene of his murder, you're going to spend the rest of your long life in prison, or—you're going to die there in the electric chair. You don't want to do that, Buck. I know you don't. So, you have to make a decision and you have to make it now. Do you want to confess to what we know you did and minimize your punishment? Or, do you want to stand your ground, take your chances against all this evidence and these two witnesses and gamble twelve citizens of Nashville, Tennessee will let a cop killer go free. Which is it?"

"He was threatenin' me. It was him or me. I didn't have a choice."

Mike looked at Kessler, eye to eye. "Based upon my experience, and I've been doing this a while, it sounds to me like you were trying to see to it he didn't get the chance to pop you when you weren't looking. Instead, you shot him." Mike hesitated. "Right?"

Kessler said nothing, but his facial expression said 'Yes'.

"So, are you ready to end this and try to minimize the consequences of your actions by confessing to the killing of Tim Slater?"

Kessler's face wrinkled and he began to cry.

Mike put his hand on his shoulder. "You want to go back to the interview room now and write out your confession?"

Kessler stared at Mike for a moment, wiped his eyes and nodded.

"I need you to say yes or no, Buck."

"Yes, I'm ready." He looked at the floor.

"Okay."

As they started down the hallway, Mike looked back and caught the attention of Dave Thurman. As he walked away holding Kessler's upper arm in his left hand, he held up his right hand, out of Kessler's line of sight. His thumb extended upward, signifying he was about to get what he'd been working for. The line-up would not be necessary.

Mike turned to Kessler. "Buck, you have the right to remain silent ... ."

Chapter 51

Woodlawn Memorial Park
Nashville

Mike was confident his investigation into Tim's murder had run its course. He was ready to discuss his findings with Lieutenant Burris, and make some final decisions on how to proceed in order to provide the DA what he needed. But first, there was something he felt he had to do.

As he exited Interstate 24 at Briley Parkway and drove Thompson Lane past Saint Edward Church, he recalled the emotions from Tim's amazing tribute and the procession of the law enforcement vehicles to the cemetery. The commitment he'd made as he looked down on Tim in the casket, now fulfilled, the faces of Megan, little Sophia, and Tim's family were all still fresh in his mind. The throng of uniformed law enforcement professionals showing their respect was inspiring.

Mike drove his car up the access lane to within sixty feet of Tim's grave. The dirt, once piled above his grave, had begun to settle. Mike parked and sat for a few minutes focusing on where he was, both physically and in his life. Before leaving his car, he collected his thoughts surrounding Tim's complicated ordeal.

The colorful flowers still on Tim's grave had begun to wither and would likely be taken away today or tomorrow, though the love and respect they represented would never leave. Mike approached the grave and stood at the foot of the dirt, looking toward the headstone marker and the wilting arrangement that read 'I Love You, Daddy'.

"Well—I'm back." Mike gave his words as much thought as if he was speaking with Tim face to face. "It feels a little strange to be here, talking to you like this. I've only done this with one other person. That's my little sister, Connie. I've been visiting her grave regularly for over twenty years now." Mike smiled. "We've visited a lot in those years. I miss her."

He stood with his hands in his pockets. "I guess I needed to do this before going to see the Lieutenant." Mike took in a large breath and paused. "If I hadn't finally opened the autopsy report, I'm not sure where I'd be at this point. I feel certain, if you were the one working this case, you would have read the autopsy report long before I did and would have put all the pieces together much sooner.

"I think I know what you did and how you did it. I even feel like now I understand why you did what you did. With Kessler getting away with Vanessa's murder, you had to be absolutely furious with yourself as well as with him. His insistence on rubbing it in your face only made it worse. Your decision to taunt him until he felt he had no choice but to take you out, not to mention your recording his threats as evidence, was frankly pure genius. Your selfless willingness to sacrifice the balance of your life in order to bring Vanessa Kemp her justice, and put this worthless bastard away, was a brand of courage I have never seen, or heard of.

"You are a hero, my friend. You are every bit the detective and the man I thought you were. As I stand here today, I promise you; I will make it my mission to see Sophia Slater grows up knowing who, and what kind of man, her daddy was. She will know without a doubt, her father loved her more than life itself."

He paused a moment.

"I guess the thing that still puzzles me a little is why you wouldn't want to share your last months, days, your last minutes, with Megan and Sophia. Wait, I think I said it wrong. I know you *wanted* to tell them about the cancer and spend every minute with them both, but doing so somehow would have jeopardized your plan. I think, rather than satisfying your desire to be with them as much as time allowed, you were thinking of them long term, going for the larger benefit, not just more time with you, as you lay dying —like your dad.

"You opted to go for what would provide for them best when you couldn't. You sacrificed possibly months of your life for them, to help Megan be able to provide for Sophia as she grows up, for her health issues, and later for her education. The line of duty benefits will help do that. Forgive my rant.

"All this being said, I think you know me well enough to know while I try to be a compassionate person, I am also a detective, like you, who works by the book.

"Sometimes it's good, and sometimes it can make things painful. Your decisions are understandable and ones I myself likely would have made if I'd been in your position. However, we have rules, rules established for the greater good. I cannot be honorable and ignore them, so I'll be visiting with Lieutenant Burris when I leave here in order to present my findings, get his input and attempt to reach a decision that accomplishes this."

Mike tried to think if he'd said all he wanted to say.

"Oh. I almost forgot. I promised Donny Knox the next time I spoke to you I would let you know, he's finally going to get some help with his disorder. Judy still doesn't feel he's ill and doesn't want to pay for him to receive treatment. I was able to get a psychologist I know at Vanderbilt to agree to see him and try to find some financial assistance. Donny thought you'd want to know."

Mike was quiet again.

"I've heard about people turning negatives into positives all my life, but I don't think I've seen an example quite like yours. I admired you in life, and now, I admire you even more. If you don't mind, I think I'd like to come back and talk with you again."

After a moment, Mike put his heels together and snapped to attention. He saluted Nashville Homicide Detective Tim Slater once more and thanked him for his service.

Mike turned back toward his car and pulled his cell phone from his jacket pocket. He made a call.

"Hello."

"Lieutenant, it's me.

"Hey, Mike."

"Are you at home?"

"Actually, I'm in my office at the CJC."

"I hate to bother you. But, I have something we need to discuss. I'd rather it didn't wait until Monday."

"Not a problem. I'll start a fresh pot of coffee."

"Thanks, Lieutenant. See you in about ten."

Chapter 52

Criminal Justice Center
Downtown Nashville

"Come in."

"I appreciate you finding time for me today. It's been quite a hectic day so far."

"Mike, you always have my ear."

"Thanks."

Burris stood. "Let's grab some coffee."

They brought their coffee back from the break room, and sat facing each other in front of the lieutenant's desk.

Burris already knew the facts involved in the Victor Ross case. He also knew about the murders of Lian Xiong and Dwayne Puckett, both cases now with the District Attorney. With Puckett dead, the Davidson County DA was expected to pursue charges of conspiracy to conceal evidence in a murder case against Victor Ross and then close the Lian Xiong murder case against Puckett.

The DA planned to prosecute Ross for the murder of Dwayne Puckett and as soon as the evidence was processed from the Coyne Court crime scene, Ross would likely be charged in the murder of Dawn Morris, whose decayed corpse was found this morning near the rear of her property by the cadaver dogs.

When the Davidson County DA was finished with Ross, the U.S. Attorney would indict him for international gun smuggling and numerous other federal gun charges. It's almost certain he'll never see freedom again.

"So, what's on your mind?"

"It's Tim's case. A lot of information has surfaced since this morning and I wanted to be sure I brought you up to speed on all the facts."

"Shoot."

"First off, Buck Kessler confessed to killing Tim."

"Outstanding, Mike. That's good news. How was he involved with Tim?"

Mike explained his discussion with Robert Franks, the Vanessa Kemp case and its relationship to Tim Slater and Kessler.

"The thing that did him in, was the threat of two eye witnesses picking him from a lineup. For some reason, he seemed to fear this more than all the other evidence combined. Honestly, with the physical evidence we had, I believe we could have obtained a conviction without the lineups. But, I'm glad we planned them. They're what closed the case."

"That's great news."

"He was so confident, he didn't start to lawyer-up until he put on the blue hoody and we were about to enter the lineup for Mrs. Jackson. That's when he started to get nervous. I stopped his request for a lawyer before he could say it and laid out all the facts for him. He decided to get smart and for once make a wise decision. It may mean the difference between life without the possibility of parole and the death penalty."

"I'm sure the DA will appreciate all your hard work. Sounds like you've had an especially productive Saturday."

"That's for sure. Starting about 08:00, I met with five different people this morning before even getting around to Kessler. Today's discovery was ... not anything I could have predicted. I'd like to run through it with you and get your feedback."

"I'm listening."

Mike spent over an hour going through his efforts and discovery of all that was involved in Tim's case, including Tim's recording of Kessler's threat and portions of Mike's interview with Kessler.

As Mike finished up with his determinations on Tim's actions and motives at the end of his life, Burris leaned back and exhaled.

"Wow. All I can say is, I'm amazed."

"Yes sir. Me too. The thing I most wanted to run by you was the fact Tim seemed to more or less solicit his own murder in order to send Kessler to prison with the sentence he deserved for killing Tim's Goddaughter, Vanessa. I'm not sure how the DA would look at this.

"And, while from our perspective the sacrifice seems admirable on Tim's part, trading his own life for her justice, we then have to consider the gain for Tim's family resulting from his dying in the line of duty. Had he not provoked Kessler's actions, a conscious act, there would have been no line of duty death. Tim likely would have died from his cancer in the coming months. And if so, the benefits paid out at his death would have been minimal compared to what Megan and Sophia will receive now."

"Hmm." Burris nodded as he contemplated Mike's conclusions.

"So, you see why I'm concerned about my discovery and what it could mean to Tim's family?"

"Yes. I see." Burris sat for a moment, the fingers of both hands interlaced. He was tapping his index fingers together as he considered Mike's concern. "Tell me. Does this file you've been going through have everything in it on Tim's efforts related to his interactions with Kessler following his Goddaughter's death?"

"Yes, sir. Everything is in this file."

"Good. I need to review all this again before I discuss it with Captain Moretti. I needed to be sure all the data is here. You know how particular he is."

"Yes sir."

Burris reached for the file and then placed it on the corner of his desk.

"Okay. I'll review this and get back to you with a plan of action as soon as I can get with the Captain. Meanwhile, you get with Sergeant Smith. Help him find a new partner for Thurman and get the man back to productivity. I'm told he's still not functioning at a hundred percent. I know you'll be able to help him, now that you two have a relationship."

"I'll do that, but I'm not sure how much of a relationship we have after the ass chewing I gave him this morning when I thought he was holding back information on Tim and Kessler. Anything else?"

"Mike, as always, you do good work. I appreciate your extra efforts and I'm certain Megan Slater feels the same way. In fact, she told me so."

"That's good to hear. I can't help but worry a bit about her and Sophia." Mike stood with Burris. "Thanks again for seeing me."

"No problem."

As Mike cleared the Lieutenant's doorway and started toward his own desk, he heard a loud metallic sound. He stopped and turned a one eighty. He could see the manila file he'd given Burris was no longer on the corner of his desk. It was now in the metal trash can at the end of his desk.

"Something else?" Burris asked, with a solemn face.

"Uh, no sir. Nothing."

"Enjoy your Saturday, Sergeant Neal." His eyes went back to his work.

"Yes, sir. I will, and thanks again." Mike smiled as he walked away. Tim Slater's strategy wasn't the only one that had worked as planned.

Chapter 53

Mike Neal's Home
Green HIlls Area

With their need to not be seen together outside of work, Mike and Carol spent many evenings cooking for each other and enjoying a streaming movie on Mike's large screen television. When they felt especially adventurous, they would go to a late movie at the theater, walk in incognito at different times, and then hook up at the same upper level seating area.

Tonight, neither of them were near the top of their respective on-call lists at work. So, assuming the citizens of Nashville cooperated and refrained from killing each other in large numbers, they had a good chance of being able to savor the entire night without interruption.

It was Mike's night to cook and Carol's night to clean up. In order to have some time to talk and enjoy each other, Mike planned to cook steaks on the grill and bake potatoes in the oven. With the salad coming from a bag, there was virtually nothing to clean up but their plates, salad bowls and silverware.

Carol was loading their dishes into the dishwasher when she heard a pop. She turned to see Mike rotating a wine cork from his sommelier tool after opening their second bottle of Cabernet

Sauvignon.

He poured each of them a half glass and said, "Meet you in the living room."

Carol finished her kitchen chores and found Mike on the sofa swirling his glass of Cab and taking in the wine's nose of berries, pepper and smoke they'd discussed at dinner. She sat on the sofa, tossed her long brunette mane behind her shoulders and reached for her glass as Mike's cell phone started to ring. She chuckled at the timing of the call.

"Mike Neal."

"Mike, I knew you'd want the update as soon as I heard."

"Hey, Lieutenant. You bet I do." Mike held the phone angled away from his head so Carol could hear. He smiled at her and winked.

"The ATF, along with the Louisiana and Texas State Police closed in and arrested everyone at the two third-party logistics warehouses in New Orleans and Houston. They said every casket on the two trucks was full of AK-47s, M-4s, SAWs, RPGs and various other light weaponry along with lots of ammo. They were indeed about to be loaded for South America."

"That's great. Have you heard anything about the Lieutenant Colonel who was calling the shots from Bagram?"

"Yes. I received an email today from Ft. Campbell. He's been placed under arrest and is awaiting transport to the U.S. and arraignment on multiple charges. Also, my friend at ICE is planning a group visit to the factory on Monday. Keep this under your hat."

"That's good to hear. Thanks for letting me know."

"I appreciate your hard work in uncovering this smuggling operation and all the additional crime riding with it. Thank you again for clearing Tim's case."

"You're welcome. I figure he's looking down on us and smiling about now."

Carol smiled at Mike's words.

"I hope so. Have a good evening, Mike."

"You too, sir."

Mike disconnected the call and put his phone on vibrate. "It sounds like today was quite productive for you."

"Very much so."

"Good. Since your suspect in Tim's case confessed, what does that leave undone on the case?"

"I have to turn over everything to the DA's office on Monday and set a date and time to meet with the Assistant DA to discuss the facts of the case. They're pleased with everything, especially his written confession."

"I'd say. Have you talked with Meagan since he confessed?"

"I called her on my way home today. Needless to say, she was pleased and grateful. She asked a few questions about Kessler and talked about the things she remembered Tim telling her about his Goddaughter's death.

"I feel sorry for Meagan and Sophia," Mike said. "It won't be easy for them, but at least the line of duty benefits will mitigate some of the financial stress. Sophia will get her education paid for through four years of college."

"That's good. I'm sure Meagan will go back to work in the court before too much longer. Stenographers are in demand. And, Sophia should start pre-school in the fall."

"Yes. She'll be five on her birthday." Mike took a sip of his wine. "Meagan is a strong girl. I think she'll be okay. I plan to keep an eye on her, and be there when she needs me."

"She's been through so much. I don't know if I could handle all of it as well as she has. If anything happened to you, I think I would be beside myself."

"Early in the week, when I was investigating Tim's murder, I interviewed Meagan at the CJC. We talked for quite a while about a lot of things, about life and about family. She and Tim weren't together a long time, but they had a strong bond.

"I told her about the day of her fortieth birthday party at their home when Tim and I went back in the house to get our drinks and Tim started talking about her. He told me how grateful he was to have found her and how she completed his life. He said she was exactly what he needed.

"Then she started grilling me about why I'd never found someone and settled down."

Carol smiled. She'd shared this current relationship with Mike for so long, it had become somewhat normal. "What did you say?"

Mike sipped his wine, buying time. He held the glass in front of him and said, "You know, this is really an excellent Cabernet."

Carol leaned over and slapped him on his thigh.

Mike laughed as he worked to avoid spilling his wine. "Don't do that. This stuff was thirty-five dollars a bottle. I'd hate to see you spend the rest of the night trying to get it out of the sofa."

"I'm waiting."

"At the risk of sounding like a politician, let me say this. What I said to her, and what I was thinking at the time and wanted to say to her, were quite different.

"I told her about all the loved ones I'd lost in the last few years and how it had made me gun shy about relationships. She said she understood, but she knew there was someone out there for me who wanted to love me and build a family and a life with me.

"She said although she and Tim were only together for a few short years, she didn't regret a single moment of their time. She talked about the tough times, such as when Tim's daughter Becky was killed in a car wreck and when they found out recently that Sophia had Type 1 Diabetes and would have to live with it the rest of her life."

Mike could see the glassy sparkle at the bottoms of Carol's eyes. He knew it wasn't the wine.

"Her description of their life together was ... touching. I'm glad they found each other and had the time they shared. Tim was a truly special person. I believe it even more today than before."

Mike finished his wine and sat the glass on the end table. He looked at Carol and smiled, causing her to respond in kind.

"I wanted to tell her all about us. I wanted to tell her I had someone who I loved dearly and who loved me. I wanted to tell her I was growing tired of sneaking around and worrying about Captain Moretti's stupid fraternization law.

"I wanted to tell her she was right. I wanted to tell her how my fear of losing love had prevented me from experiencing it fully. I wanted to explain how I planned to cook you a nice meal, serve you a great wine and then make love to you like you were the only lady in the world."

Carol's smile grew larger.

"I wanted to tell her I had realized I'd been a foolish and selfish man for much too long."

Mike shifted closer to her. He took Carol's glass and sat it next to his.

Her facial changes asked him what he was doing.

He slowly slipped off the sofa and lowered himself to the floor on one knee. He pulled a small black velvet-covered box from his pocket.

"Oh, my God!" Carol shouted.

Mike laughed.

"Oh, my God."

"Uh. Your attention, please. I'm not finished here," Mike said as if talking to a crowded theater. "Quiet, please in the audience. I need your undivided attention."

She covered her mouth with both her hands, laughed, grunted and began to cry.

"Ms. Carol Spencer—I have a question." He paused, smiling. He was enjoying watching her emotions flow. "Will you do me the honor—of becoming my wife?"

Carol screamed, "Yes!" She began to sob as Mike took her left hand and pushed the 1.5 carat diamond engagement ring onto her finger. She pulled it up to her eyes to get a closer look. She tried to blink away the tears in order to see it.

"Oh, Mike." She tackled him and they both fell to the floor. She was laughing and crying at the same time.

Mike rolled onto his back and pulled Carol down on top of him. He laughed out loud and shouted. "I love you, Mrs. Carol Neal."

She burst out laughing at the sound of her new name. She pulled away, forced his shoulders to the floor and held her face two inches from his.

"I love you too, Michael Neal."

They kissed and laughed for several minutes. Mike pulled her head back from his and tucked thick brunette strands behind her ears.

"So, when do you want to do this thing, tomorrow or next week?"

Carol laughed. "After all this time, and now you want to rush things?"

Mike became quiet. He grabbed her, rolled them both onto their sides and they shared a smile. He caressed her cheek in his hand. Mike took a deep breath and sighed.

"Tim's death and my talk with Megan cleared away much of the fog I've been looking through for several years. It's helped me to put some things into perspective."

"Oh?"

Mike was quiet for another minute.

"When I looked at Megan and little Sophia at the funeral, I focused on what Tim had risked each day when he went to work at the unpredictable and sometimes dangerous job we feel compelled to do. I saw his life and his loss there before me. I used to see this as justification for my hesitation to make a commitment and build a normal life, at least a somewhat normal life. I saw what he indeed gave up as well as what Megan and Sophia were forced to give up in the end.

"At the gravesite, I saw Megan's unbearable pain. I saw Sophia's four-year-old confusion when she asked her daddy to come out of the casket, to come back to her—and he didn't. Her heart was broken. Frankly, mine was too."

Carol nodded.

Mike took a large breath and let it out. "These are examples of why I've believed for years I had to guard myself from wanting all this. As you already know, I've lost a lot of great people in my life. People who were very close to me. I've not been too anxious to risk additions to that pain."

"I know. I understand."

"I guess what I've realized since the funeral and since the unbelievable sacrifice Tim made for his family, is that all these years," he paused, "I've been looking at the wrong side of this. I've let my fear of possible future pain create a loss in the present. It has forced me to live with the real loss today rather than a potential loss in the future. I've let emotional fear drive my choices. It has prevented me from embracing the love and the life I've had available right before my eyes all along."

He stroked her dark hair and caressed her neck. Mike wiped tears from both his eyes. "I'm so sorry. My fear caused me to be so selfish."

"Oh Mike, you've not been selfish. You've only been trying to protect us both. I know that. After twelve years, I know *you*. You're a good man and you have nothing to be sorry for. So you'll know and never doubt it. I would have waited for you forever. If all we ever had together was what we had prior to today, I was prepared to continue to thank God for it and enjoy the blessing."

"You are so special," Mike said.

"Thank you." She pulled him close, hugged him hard and kissed him. "I love you so much."

"I love you, too. So, seriously. What do you want in the way of a wedding? A big one? A little one? What about a quickie in Judge Hartnett's office?"

She laughed. "I had a big wedding once. It didn't lead me to a long and secure relationship like I'd hoped. Why don't we have a small wedding with maybe a dozen of our close friends? That way we don't have to spend months waiting and working on it?"

"You have my vote."

"When is your next vacation?"

"I don't know. I'll have to check with Burris. I don't keep up with those things. He usually comes to me when he sees I'm getting stressed and says, "You need to take some time off.""

"We are supposed to have a honeymoon you know."

"We just got back from Cancun last week. What if we call that our honeymoon?" Mike tried his best to hold back his laughter and look serious.

"Do what?" Carol stood and put her fists on her hips. Mike stood as well.

"You went to Rome last year with Cris Vega and now you want to consider a five-day covert trip to Mexico, we've already taken, as our honeymoon? You have to be kidding me."

"Yep." Mike smiled. "What say we tour Italy for two weeks?"

"Don't joke around, Michael." She pointed her index finger at him.

"I'll have to clear it with the lieutenant and it may be a couple of months from now before we could go. The brochure is on my desk." He smiled again.

Carol took two steps and leaped into Mike's arms.

"Oh, Michael, *mi amore.*" She kissed him long and hard.

He pulled away from her lips just long enough to look into her eyes and say,

"Cara mia."

Acknowledgements

For their unending support, contributions, encouragement and critique. I must thank Dew Wayne Burris, Pat Postiglione, Steve Teer, Beth Teer, Ken Howell and Glenn Akridge.

To the members of The Sisters (and Misters) in Crime, where I found a welcoming family of authors and genre enthusiasts, encouragement and lots of fun. Thank you.

To my wife Sandra, for thirty-eight happy years, for your undying support and your exceptional graphic design skills. But most especially, for patiently believing in me. Thank you, always.

Author Bio

Ken Vanderpool is a life-long fan of Crime Suspense and Thriller fiction who began writing his own in 2006 following an eye-opening medical procedure and an intimate encounter with his mortality.

Ken is a graduate of Middle Tennessee State University with his degree in Psychology and Sociology with a concentration on Criminology. He has also graduated from the Metropolitan Nashville Citizen Police Academy and three times graduated from the Writer's Police Academy.

His first novel in the Music City Murders series, **When the Music Dies**, was published in 2012. Second in the series, **Face the Music**, was published in the summer of 2014. Number four, **Kill the Music**, is due out in the fall of 2016.

Ken has spent his entire life in Middle Tennessee and proudly professes, "There is no better place on earth." Ken currently lives near Nashville in Murfreesboro, Tennessee with his wife Sandra and their Cairn Terrier-ist, Molly.

www.kenvanderpool.com

Made in the USA
Charleston, SC
03 January 2016